For my _____ ew

Love

Robi

How the

Light Shines

How the Light Shines

Published by The Conrad Press Ltd. in the United Kingdom 2022

Tel: +44(0)1227 472 874
www.theconradpress.com
info@theconradpress.com

ISBN 978-1-915494-19-1

Printed and bound in Great Britain by Clays Ltd, Elcograf S.p.A

Typesetting and cover design by The Book Typesetters
www.thebooktypesetters.com

The Conrad Press logo was designed by Maria Priestley.

How the Light Shines

ROBIN VICARY

This story is dedicated to Louis Leopoldt, paediatrician, poet, writer, creator of a school for poor orphans, and general polymath.

The Worst Horror

This is the bitterest thing of all my days,
That which I have loved so well, that now is dead
And in a coffin laid away, of lead
And cedarwood, immortal somewhere stays,
Or as a ghost-cloud goes its lonely ways
By strange and boundless forces urged ahead,
Perhaps, like me, forlorn, uncomforted,
But out of reach, howe'er one pleads or prays,
Day after day with unending lament.
This is the bitterest thing, that I no hand
Can reach to help, or comfort to impart,
No aid can give, and no encouragement;
And that there wanders in that ghostly land
Forlorn, that which I loved with all my heart!

(The start of a poem by Louis Leopoldt, translated from the original Afrikaans.)

Characters in order of appearance

1. Peter Gerhard Shroeder – Officer in the Abwehr (German secret service)

2. Amit Jaipur – Chemistry student University of Leipzig; chef at the Royal Livingstone Hotel

3. Carl Hans von Wasserburg – German diplomat

4. Morris Shuttleworth – Captain, Special intelligence Service

5. Alan Drayson – Lieutenant, S.I.S.

6. Sarah Grandison – Lieutenant, S.I.S.

7. James Pringle – Military Attache to the British High Commission in Cape Town. Also Lieutenant in S.I.S.

8. Gloria Simpson – Personnel clerk at the British High Commission and Head of S.I.S. in southern Africa

9. Hermann von Bauer – German Ambassador to the British Dominion of South Africa

10. Sir Robert Lancaster – British High Commissioner to South Africa

11. Judit Helmholtz – Cultural Attache to the German embassy

12. Louis du Plessis – Writer, doctor and food expert

13. Roderick Patterson – Deputy Head of Contracts at De Beers

14. Cornelius van der Linde – Manager of Cape Connections Ltd

15. Sir John Simon – Foreign Secretary

16. Dieter Furtwangler – Manager at an ostrich farm

17. Vladimir Bukovsky – Jeweller and poet

18. Michel Udenay – French agent of S.I.S.

19. Roland Barre – French agent of S.I.S.

Preface

In the early 1930s, the great nations of Europe are slowly recovering from the effects of the Great Depression. By a series of manoeuvres, a small, moustachioed corporal has seized power in Germany and is determined to re-build the Reich into the great power that it had been.

Central to all of the Nazi planning is the re-constitution and re-arming of the nation's forces. However these two pillars of strength are strictly forbidden under the Versailles Treaties, forced upon Germany at the end of the Great War. In Berlin, plans are being hatched to circumvent these impositions.

Many years later Winston Churchill will note –

'The English-speaking peoples through their unwisdom, carelessness and good nature allowed the wicked to re-arm'.

But maybe not all of those peoples were so allowing…

– Robin Vicary, September 2022

Chapter One

The meeting

He first noticed the exquisite taste of kedgeree while seated on the wide wood-boarded terrace of the Royal Livingstone Hotel, within a few metres of the banks of the mighty Zambezi River. It was the morning of March 18th in the year 1933, and the Victoria Falls, named by Dr. David Livingstone after his beloved queen, were tumbling in fine form following plentiful spring monsoon rains. The local people had called them the Mosi-oa-Tunya, 'the smoke that roars', long before Livingstone was even born. Peter felt that this was a far better name as the water was making a magnificent racket, creating a vast cloud, pressing ever upwards into the blue sky and remaining visible from miles away. Gusts of air blew at the droplets, sending waves of the mist over the hotel lawns.

He, Peter Gerhard Schroeder, had a firm understanding that he should really start his story at the beginning in time-honoured fashion; although apparently, in these modern days, eminent chairs of literature the world over were encouraging story-tellers to start anywhere in their tales. But, to the ordered and carefully-raised Schroeder mind, the more he delved into the subject the more he appreciated the need for some care.

In his world of Teutonic rectitude he had come to understand that there were people out there who had devoted a life to the fishy melange steaming before him. But if he was really being honest, he needed to admit that the story had started for him a while earlier.

Despite the vague rigidity of his upbringing, Peter's early childhood had been for him a time of unalloyed pleasure. The home was happy and although Peter was an only child, the house had bustled with activity. His father was a man of substance in the town, being both a well-respected wine merchant and a local councillor for many years. The family had lived quite close to the centre of Colmar and he had gone to the neighbourhood school. At first, his beloved mother had walked him along the cobbles and canals of La Petite Venise to school and collected him at the end of his school-day. They had often walked with Carl's mother, as the two women lived close by each other and were friends, and his friendship with Carl had grown alongside. The cobbles had hurt his feet as his mother had insisted that sandals were the best shoes for a child of his age and only relented and bought him proper shoes when he fell and sprained his ankle. Their doctor Schmidt had berated his mother, and Peter was secretly grateful to the old man. So when he was young he was determined to be either a doctor or a mathematician but, notwithstanding his ability at chess and his reaching the top Board of his school's chess team, he found higher mathematics and, in particular the complexities of calculus, incomprehensible. His friend Carl was the number two Board and their friendship became all-encompassing.

He graduated with ease to his secondary school in Colmar and he and Carl took the bus to the large rambling College on the outskirts of town. The school had stopped being a religious establishment but nevertheless, many of his teachers were from religious orders and they enforced discipline with ferocity. Peter had chosen the path of rebellion and was frequently in trouble with the authorities, whereas Carl was the more peaceable. But, being fast on their feet, they both excelled at playing the new English import of 'le rugby.' Peter played on the wing and his bursts of speed caused serious problems for opposing backs from rival schools. As long as he could play the game over the winter there was an outlet for his anger, but in the summer he fumed and raged in teenage angst. His mother bore it calmly but his father was outraged. At last, the final year was there and Peter held onto himself enough to enable superior grades in his Abitur, and his onward progression to University.

Peter was a man who had grown into his handsomeness. As he had passed through his twenties, his angular features had softened and his dark symmetric face had proven attractive to others. Normally he was good at socialising and enjoyed the company of others – the to and fro of dialogue, a little repartee to enliven the mind. This morning he was grateful that he was eating alone and the thought that he might have had to entertain over breakfast, following the catastrophe of the preceding evening caused a little shudder to trickle downwards from his shoulders.

These shoulders were a part of his body that, in his younger days, had caused him some alarm due to their unusual and profligate hair growth. He had observed other men at the baths in his home town and appreciated that the hairiness of his shoulders was quite outstandingly abnormal. Later, when he had taken lovers, the braver ones had often commented on those shoulders, but not always in a tone of disgust. He had discovered that there was a certain type of woman who rather liked exotic physical features in a man. He had wondered whether he might be able to notice certain personal characteristic features in those women who appreciated the hairiness of his shoulders. Perhaps then he could focus his attention on the seduction of those women, and not waste his time lavishing his attentions on the unappreciative. So, in accordance with the genetic fashions of the age, he had looked to see whether they all had small chins, moles in their axillae and so on. His studies were in vain. He could detect no physical features, nor indeed emotional characteristics, that were associated.

His solution was to ensure that the initial copulation was performed either in as much darkness as possible or with his shirt partly buttoned, with his shoulders covered, thus ensuring no need for shocked intimate personal discussions, which he found put him off his coital stride.

He had of course considered the possible shaving of his shoulders, but was put off by a friend's news that shaving a part of his skin might only cause the hair on that area of skin to grow faster than normal. This friend confided in him during one long heavy-drinking evening in a bier-keller, that on the strength of this rather dubious rumour, he himself was attempting to grow a beard just below his left knee, by shaving the area regularly. The next day Peter was uncertain whether this was a drunken joke, but did not have the courage to ask.

He had checked into this charming incongruously Indian-themed hotel on the previous afternoon and had spent the hot and humid evening drinking unwise quantities of the cooling local beer. In the evening, he had apparently behaved in a marginally unsatisfactory way, dancing too close to an attractive and charming English woman, until her husband had decided that the Great War had not ended fifteen years previously and that Peter's closeness to his pretty wife was about to be a cause for violence. The Englishman was not as tall nor, Peter suspected, as well able to handle himself as he was, but nevertheless, Peter could see the wisdom of avoiding an international incident preceding his somewhat 'delicate' mission.

This morning he had been awakened by a crashing noise and had crept bleary-eyed from his bed on the first floor peering from the balcony into the early morning mists. To his amazement he spied a hippopotamus strolling past on its way to the water. Suddenly wide awake, he hurried to dress and walked the few metres down to the edge of the water, passing the small rondavels with straw roofs, occupied mainly by honeymooning English couples. Two of the enormous beasts were entering the water when he arrived so, not wishing to disturb their early morning frolics and having observed their antics, he walked slowly and carefully up river watching a wealth of other animals drinking and washing in the warm early morning sunshine, their coats glistening in reflected light.

He had returned to find the dining room apparently open for nourishment but deserted of any other guests. Two waiters stood as a welcoming committee on the wooden steps, which were rotting slightly at their edges, and which themselves formed an entrance-way to the large covered terrace. The waiters were rather tall men, impressively dressed in traditional Indian servant dress with red jackets, white trousers, spats and shoes.

'Would Sahib like breakfast?' the taller one asked with a small welcoming bow.

Sahib would.

'On the side here are a wealth of delicious eatables, Sahib.' The other waiter informed him, pointing to half a dozen ornate silver salvers.

He peeked nervously under, and to his delight there were indeed a 'wealth of delicious eatables'. The scrambled eggs looked splendid, but as he descended the row and lifted the fifth lid, he was surprised by a dish that he had never seen before. It had a fishy smell.

'What is this?' he asked, not ashamed to appear ignorant.

'Sir, this is a most delicious Indian dish named Kedgeree. It is made of fish and rice and many spices. May I bring you some?'

He may. Peter seated himself at an outside table on the edge of the veranda looking towards the water and the cloud of spray rising high into the blue, blue sky. As the waiter delicately placed the plate before him, a small man in white overalls wandered over, a chef's toque balanced precariously over his smiling face,

'Good morning, Sahib. My name is Amit and I am the chef. My colleague tells me that this is your first eating of our Indian breakfast. May I tell you of it?'

'You may indeed, Amit,' he replied, hoping that it would not be too long. His mouth watered even as he spoke. Despite his previous reservations about breakfast company, he knew that he would not be alone soon,

'But as I tell you the story,' Amit said, 'I would wish that you eat, as the meal is best consumed in a warm condition.'

'If this is to be a long story, please join me,' and Peter gestured to the vacant seat opposite, which hopefully would be filled with a lugubrious German colleague and old friend at some point after the chef's story had ended. His colleague's punctuality was never a matter to be taken for granted at the best of times, and on this occasion there was also the flight from Cape Town to take into account. The early morning rains had ended but dark clouds would arrive as the land warmed later in the day.

Amit bowed his head, seemingly in prayer, as he begun to speak,

'The story of kedgeree commences in India around the time that Sandro Botticelli was in his studio in Italy completing his masterpiece of the Primavera.'

The German fork with some of the tasty food slowly descended from its original target. Peter Gerhard Shroeder looked carefully at the little man sitting opposite and decided that a moment of reflective re-appraisal was in order. Here he was, in the middle of the African bush, and a small Indian chef was regaling his brain with a brief historical tale about an Italian Renaissance painting. His brain focussed carefully on the chef's next words.

'To my mind it is a sadness that we have no earlier documentation, but recipe books were not so fashionable in ancient Indian writing at that time.'

'Indeed,' Peter muttered, not at all certain in his own mind that there were writers of cookery recipes in his own land at that time either.

'Before the British arrived and took over our customs, we understand that it was a common dish. Usually in the poor benighted country that was pre-colonial India, we know that the recipe for kedgeree called simply, Sahib, for a mixture of rice and vegetables. But even early on, the spices were of most great importance, yes most great importance'. He paused and a smile twinkled across his deep brown eyes.

'But somewhere the fish was added. Perhaps it started in coastal regions where fish is plentiful, maybe in a similar way that fish was added to the recipe for paella in the country of Spain, whereas it commenced there of course as a meal from the interior of the land with chicken or rabbit as the prime ingredient.'

'Of course it did,' the German muttered silently to himself. 'This is fast becoming a culinary master-class.' He was in truth having a little difficulty absorbing all the chef's words of wisdom, while tasting the delicate flavours and savouring the smells of the dish before him.

'But I digress into my subordinate clauses like Proust.'

The chef was metamorphosing into an intellectual giant before Peter's eyes.

'Perhaps all that you wanted to know were the ingredients. So, let me tell you what I use myself and then, if the cat permits, I will bore you with more detail.'

'The cat?' The German was dizzy attempting to keep all the threads of this diverse conversation together in his head.

'Yawohl, mein herr. Die Katze. Forgive me but my German is so rusty these days.'

'German too?' Peter was losing his grip on reality.

'And how, my friend, do you speak faultless German?'

'I was fortunate to spend three years at your Leipzig University studying Chemistry around 1925. My father was very rich, you understand. We owned a few mines in Jaipur state.'

He looked at Peter, anticipating the question. 'Diamonds, mostly.' Of the two words, Peter realised that it was the word *mostly* that unnerved him the more.

'Chemistry is so like cooking, following the recipe or formula, I am sure that understanding you are,' he continued.

'Of course it is,' Peter told himself, noticing out of the corner of his left eye some movement. Turning slowly, he saw an extraordinary animal. It must have been the largest cat that had ever crossed his path; a lordly orange and white exotic creature, eyeing him as it approached. He suspected that it might be eyeing his plate with greater fervour.

'Bronwen,' called one of the attired waiters. The cat

stopped, balancing a wish for obedience with its lust for the delicacy of the fishy odours. Obedience, as it often does, won. Reluctantly she turned away and collapsed herself on top of the steps of the terrace, the better to bask in the warmth of the morning sun.

'She is Welsh.' The waiter apparently thought that this was sufficient explanation. 'Cosmopolitan Livingstone has a Welsh cat,' Peter mused with some internalised laughter.

'But I was interesting you in the spices, I had hoped,' the chef continued. 'I cannot over-emphasise the importance of the delicacy of the balance between the curry powder and the turmeric. As I mentioned earlier, the British have no style in these matters. Perhaps you will not believe me, sir, that in the 1885 edition of Culinary Jottings for Madras one of our own Indian army colonels points out that the 'English type' of kedgeree has no spices – 'Boiled rice; cold minced fish; chopped hard-boiled egg and a lump of butter' are his words. A disgrace. Not a spice in sight.'

Peter understood that the lesson was approaching its climax, and indeed the chef's voice had risen in excitement.

'But for me the moment of ecstasy is reached when I add the turmeric and green chili to the curry. At that moment plenty of ghee is included and your breakfast dish is perfected. Not only deeply nutritious but a guaranteed cure should too much excellent German, or less excellent African beer, have passed the lips the night before.'

Peter acknowledged the triumph of the food as the small, unusual man seemed to disappear, in a manner somehow remarkably similar to his childhood memory of Lewis Carroll's cat.

Smells wafted up from his plate and the extraordinary combinations of the spice and the curry surrounded him in vivid colourful delights. The distant thunder of the water filled the air but, within the room, nothing stirred. The waiters were immobile, while the cat lay stretched out asleep, almost obstructing the entrance, so vast a creature was it. Tranquillity spread over the room in a tidal wave.

This calm was somewhat disturbed momentarily by Peter's thoughts. He wondered 'when would Carl get here? Would he come today?' In this age of modernity the aeroplane was starting to dominate across the blue skies of the world. Even now… and his thoughts were interrupted by a very mild distant buzz apparently emanating from the sky in a southerly direction. Perhaps he had somehow wished the plane into existence, and he laughed at the absurdity of his mind. 'All those tricks that one can play on oneself. The important thing is to keep the mind under control at all times. Purity of thought is simply a matter of control. And control is the engine for the production of power. And order of the thoughts produces control. It is simply a circle of purity.'

The buzz grew louder and there could be little doubt that an aeroplane was approaching the recently-enlarged Livingstone airport, built a few miles east of the city. Suddenly it was almost overhead, and Peter marvelled at the sleek biplane roaring across the sky, with its triple tail fin and the words 'Imperial Airways' emblazoned along its fuselage. Most of the animals ran terrified for cover but the hippos just glanced upwards and then continued their drinking. Peter did not move, mulling over in his mind the meeting that had been prepared. His friend Carl Hans von Wasserburg would be with him in an hour, or however long it took to emerge from Customs' formalities – and he wanted to savour the pleasure of greeting his friend, precious to him for so long, and so close to his heart.

They had been to the same school in Colmar and although Alsace was at that time nominally French, both of the boys' families were of German origin. After their schooling, they had both entered the Humboldt University in Berlin on scholarships, he at the School of Philosophy and Carl studying Diplomacy. Shortly after graduating, Carl had joined the German civil service and had talked of the work of international relationships with delight. Carl had known that Peter had joined the Abwehr and understood that talking of his work was not possible, but it had hardly affected their relationship as they were at the time both obsessed with chess. Sometimes their relationship consisted of little more than pawn-pushing. They would sit at lunch times in a park near the Unter den Linden and discuss modern chess theory over a beer and a sandwich.

Two years previously, Carl had been posted to the South African embassy in Cape Town, and their correspondence had become desultory. Carl did mention the possibility of a marriage in one of his sporadic letters but little else of substance, except that he was enjoying the climate and had made a few friends.

Peter meanwhile was climbing steadily in the Abwehr and had entered a section responsible for Africa. The apparent aim of his section of the organisation was to gain as much knowledge and access to Africa as possible so as to ensure the success of German diplomatic policies. Initially Peter had had difficulty at times with understanding this concept as no-one had been able to explain to his satisfaction as to exactly what was the aim of German diplomatic policy across Africa. But eventually one day his boss had sat him down and explained that the basic aim of their section was to ensure that, should there be further war, Africa was favourably disposed towards the Reich.

After a few months he had been sent to Morocco, ostensibly to discuss the purchase of iron ore but in reality to set up a chain of agents to report on all matters of interest. Three months later he performed the same role in Algeria leaving a member of the Consulate in charge on both occasions. He understood after a while that he had become a secret agent himself, although no-one had used those words. He had few qualms about his job, and although he understood that this work had possible dangers, for the most part he was not unduly bothered. He had never quite acquired a wife in the way that most of his friends had, although there were a steady stream of girl-friends. His father had died and his mother was getting old, living in a vast farm-house with his sister Greta, who had married an East Prussian farmer and produced the requisite pair of blond Aryan children.

And then one fine Berlin Spring day, he was seated in his office when his boss, Rudolf Schmidt, had entered and sat down in the chair opposite Peter's desk.

'Peter, we have a little task for you which follows on

from your work in northern Africa.' Although Peter was focussing carefully on the older man and his words, his eyes could not help but to wander to the small patch of discolouration on the collar of the otherwise immaculate uniform. His boss continued.

'You will know of course that we have a Diplomatic mission in South Africa. South Africa is a land that may be of some interest to our nation. Why do you think that that might be, Peter?' Peter dragged his thoughts away from the collar, realising as he did that a question had been thrown into the room.

'It belongs to England?' Peter's spinal response caused a smile to appear on the face of his colleague.

'Undeniable, undeniable. As regrettably now does German West and East Africa, that the British call Tanganyika.'

'And diamonds, sir.'

'Yes that is rather important I think. Not only for the wealth that they inevitably bring but also for their use in machinery. And finally of course the British, by controlling the Cape, also control shipping around the tip of Africa. So we have work to do in South Africa and we need you to be involved. For various reasons, we wish you to travel to Rhodesia and deliver a number of requirements to one of our diplomatic service there. We believe that he is an old friend of yours – one Carl von Wasserburg.'

Peter had been delighted. He had asked the obvious question about why they had to meet in Rhodesia but was rebuffed with some muttering about not disturbing the British by his visit. He had wanted to ask as to 'why the

24

British would be less disturbed in what was, after all, their colony of Rhodesia,' but in the end had thought better of it.

And indeed Carl was now here. Peter watched from the terrace at the front of the hotel as Carl unwrapped his long frame out of the rear seat of the taxi, paid the driver and paused as he was surrounded by a flurry of young boys eager to carry his lone bag up the hotel steps. When the mob had disappeared inside, carrying its prize between them, Carl had scanned the impressive old colonial raj-style front of the hotel. The white-painted boarding gleamed in the new day's sunshine. Eventually he spotted his friend lolling in a wooden armchair on the terrace. Peter rose to greet him, shook his hand with enthusiasm and asked

'Breakfast, shower, or sleep? Remarkably I can recommend all three, here in this outpost of England.'

'My friend, it is wonderful to see you again after all this while. The journey has been a little trying, but let us eat first and then maybe I will lie down for a while.'

'Over breakfast I will tell you of this remarkable hotel, its unusual chef, and of course the business that brings me from Berlin.'

Chapter Two

A job opportunity is presented

The two men between them were about to stir up the British in southern Africa. There was already little love lost between the dominant peoples, the British, and the less well-off and consequentially less influential Boers, a polyglot mob, descendants mostly of Dutch ancestors. There were also of course the native peoples, discounted and mostly ignored where possible by the sparring white tribes.

'Now my colleague, before you sit down, come and peek at the delicacies under these silver lids,' and he led his friend gently to the array and lifted the first lid. The scrambled eggs continued to shine out their wondrous eggy yellow, like a steaming early morning African sun. And when they came to the kedgeree, Peter was mildly irritated to hear

'I wonder how much turmeric the chef uses?' from his friend's lips.

'You can ask him, if you must. He will doubtless appear at some point.'

'I shall, I shall,' enthused Carl, heaping some of the white steaming mass onto his plate. They sat, drank hot tea, and noted the waiters standing alert to their every needs on the edge of the terrace while Bronwen, the vast Welsh monster, was succeeding in her apparent aim of doing as little as possible. As predicted, Amit magicked himself to the side of their table without apparent muscular effort.

'Sahib is enjoying the fishy Indian mess?' he enquired of Carl.

'Perfectly cooked – and just the right balance of the turmeric.' Amit looked as if a small dust devil had arisen from an arid central Indian desert.

'Sahib is an expert in Indian food?'

'Not at all. Kedgeree was the favourite dish of my mother. She had learned to cook it from my grandmother who had accompanied my grandfather to Goa in the mid-nineteenth century. She had always insisted on the importance of the turmeric.'

'Sahib, if I may presume our grandmothers were clearly both fine personages. My own grandmother had many servants but always insisted on cooking the kedgeree herself, and of course she taught me. For myself I was always enjoying the cooking. And so I forsook the ways of Chemistry for a more enlightening life.' Peter could see that Carl was as intrigued as he had been.

'Your family was rich, then,' he asked, rather unsubtly to Peter's mind.

'Oh, yes indeed. We owned palaces and gems and so forth.'

'But you have chosen to be a chef. What did your family say?'

'Not saying was the way of life for my parents. Both of them were most tolerant, most tolerant. And for myself, I have few needs. I will leave the Sahibs to their friendship,' and he did his vanishing act.

'I wonder,' said Carl.

'You wonder…' and he left it hanging.

'In our embassy we have appalling food. Mainly because we have appalling chefs. All are locals and they have not a clue how to prepare anything of any subtlety. I was wondering whether I could entice him to Cape Town.'

'But you know nothing about him.'

'He can cook a fine kedgeree. Do I need other references?'

'Well, how about understanding the German mind if you are thinking that he would work with a collection of Germans?' Carl looked pensive.

'You may have a point.'

Peter looked his friend in the eye and laughed.

'What is so funny?' Carl looked affronted at the laughter.

'I have yet to tell you the part of his story that you may find helps your decision-making.'

'Out with it.'

'He has spent three years in the Reich, at the University of Leipzig no less.'

'Mein Gott. And what was he doing there?'

'Chemistry, of course,' and they both laughed.

'Hence the reference…'

'Indeed.' They sat in contemplation of these matters, allowing the warmth of the country to seep into their hardened North European skins. For Peter, accustomed as he was to the coolness of an Alsace spring, this was a true luxury; to loll back in comfortable chairs, eating well, his longstanding comrade exuding his customary warmth and charm, all somehow completed his scenario of personal bliss. A contentment of the soul, one might say.

'And how was the flight here?'

'Long and exhausting, but intermittently exciting. Flying along the Nile was exhilarating. The beauty of the green strip winding its way through the desert is like those school geography lessons come alive. Our pilot took us down so that we were a few hundred feet above the temples of Abu Simbel and we saw such detail. It was a better view, I suspect, than if we had been on the ground.'

'After a few days and nights, we landed at Mpika, just north of here. Just before we landed the pilot warned us about lions being in the locality. A couple of the lady passengers were terrified. Apparently the landing-strip is mown by a grass cutter, dragged along by a team of oxen. The smell of the oxen attracts the lions. The engineer-in-charge at Mpika, who met us on landing, carried a pistol that apparently he used to frighten the lions away. Interestingly the ladies were even more terrified by his brandishing of the pistol, which he had apparently hoped would be reassuring.' They both chuckled, but Peter knew that it was time for serious discussion. The place was ideal; there were no prying ears to hear the words of the strategy that he was to discuss.

'I would like now to discuss with you the reason that we are both enjoying this African idyll,' and for some reason he gave a slight, nervous laugh. Later when Peter looked back, he understood that he was about to make a proposition to this good-natured man that would put him personally at some risk. That he would be the bringer of this possible catastrophe upon his friend might in later times cause him some inner turmoil. But he had a clear understanding of where his duty lay; nevertheless his core was not at peace. Maybe Carl had some premonition also of what was to come, as a tiny crease appeared, ruffling his normally smooth forehead.

There was a short pause as Peter chose his words with care and Carl waited, understanding that he would be required to listen with inordinate attention. The tension crackled unseen around them.

'I am here from the highest level of the Reich. Until now, you and your mission have been required to foster amicable relations with the British authorities of South Africa. You will be aware however that, although the country is ruled and controlled by the British, the ruling political organisation is the National Party, an Afrikaner organisation with sympathies to Holland, and possibly to our land.'

'Our country,' Peter continued, 'does not like the prospect of the sea routes around Africa being controlled by a well-armed nation and dominated by the British. So the first part of your mission is to cause trouble for the British. We suggest that you stir up the Blacks and the Afrikaaners. You may use any means that you wish, and we will be providing you with extremely large sums of money via a new bank account that you alone will have access to.' He watched Carl as he was speaking. Carl reacted as Peter would have wanted – with little hesitation, simply a boyish eagerness and in fact exactly as he would have predicted.

'And the second part is a rather more sophisticated task. The Reich requires diamonds; many, many diamonds for its machine-tools. In fact we will be using the diamonds on the machine-tools for the manufacture of weapons, both rifles and larger calibre weapons. But we do not want to raise the price on the international markets by being seen to be a buyer. And in particular, we do not wish for the British or French to know that we are buying large quantities of diamonds, as we do not wish them to guess what we are manufacturing. It would be contrary to the Treaties signed at Versailles after the last war.' Carl stared at him in amazement.

'There will be a second bank account for you to buy industrial diamonds. You will need to smuggle the diamonds out of the country in whatever manner you wish, even in our embassy's Diplomatic Bag if absolutely necessary. But it would be much better if you could think up a means of smuggling them through unofficial channels into the Reich.' At that point one of the waiters approached, asking about their needs, and Carl collected his thoughts. He was more pensive after this interruption.

'I am excited by both parts of this mission but I am going to have more trouble with the second section. I know little of diamonds or the market. May I recruit assistants?'

'Absolutely. If necessary a team of assistants. We will

need the diamonds to flow into the Reich for the supply of the factories at regular intervals.' Carl gave that short laugh of his, so familiar to him from their school days in Alsace.

Peter remembered Carl's family so well. Carl's father had been slightly strange; a rather detached man and truly vague at all times. 'Short and treacly' was his view of the man. He could never quite latch onto the words and the person; the old man had slipped through the fingers of his mind. The mother was quite the opposite; large and buxom and charming and more laughs per minute in her conversation than the whole of his own family put together. Carl's mother was French by origin – 'but of course all of us Germans and French were rather mixed up in Alsace,' he mused. There were times when he had wished that he was the son of this marvellously cheerful woman in the way that small boys do sometimes wish to cling on to bits of other people's families. But he suspected that the ambiguity of Carl's father would have distressed him.

Carl was completely his mother's son. A man totally at ease with all types of people, he was clearly a great asset for the diplomatic service and that very familiarity of his laugh re-awoke in Peter the reasoning behind his anticipated pleasure in the few hours that they would have together.

After breakfast, they strolled down towards the Zambezi and there was Amit, sitting in the garden on a native three-legged stool, smoking a cigarette. He waved at them in a rather melancholic way and they stopped.

'You seem to have the cares of the kitchen on your shoulders,' Carl told him. Amit looked carefully at Carl.

'Sahib, you have the magical ability to see into this skull

of mine and be enlightened by my recurring trouble – my colleagues. Sometimes we Indian fellows expect too much of others and then we launch ourselves into a veritable stew of meat and vegetables.' Both Germans smiled.

'Well, leave these troubles behind you.'

'If I could, I most surely would. There is an English marching song calling on a man like your humble chef before you to 'pack up his troubles in his old kit bag.' For myself, my kit bag is ready to march from these people who cause me such sadness and pain in my heart.'

Carl had developed that look in his eye that Peter recognised – the look which told him that a charm offensive was being prepared. And he watched the preparation with amusement knowing precisely what was about to happen. Amit of course was totally unprepared, which made the game all the better. There was another seat and Carl lowered himself onto it.

'Amit, look at yourself. Not only are you a man who can cook a delicious melange, but my friend here tells me that you also know the world of chemistry and have many other skills. You're being undervalued. The brain within the cranium is dormant.'

'The brain within the cranium is dormant,' Amit repeated in a trance-like state. 'Such truth, wise Sahib. But perhaps the fault is mine. I have made the choice to be a cook, and I drifted here. I did not appreciate that there would be no opportunity in this backwater of civilisation for culture, thinking of the profound matters and the other subjects that used to happen all of the time in my house and then at my University. Here I am 'crying in the wilderness,' as they say in the book of the Christians.' He looked at Carl.

'My father, you know, was a well-educated man. He had been sent to an English public school where he learned to speak the language of the ancient Romans. When anything went wrong in our house, he would blame himself saying 'Mea culpa, mea maxima culpa."

'All my own fault,' Peter muttered.

'Aha, sahib, another master of the Latin language.'

'Yes he is,' Carl interjected and they smiled in a shared recalling of their fierce old Latin teacher who would hit them on the wrist with a ruler if they declined their verbs incorrectly.

'But if you are not happy here, Amit, let me share a thought with you. I would like to employ you in our Embassy in Cape Town. We have no proper chef at the Embassy. We employ three scoundrels in the kitchen who have no understanding of the value and importance of food, and certainly no appreciation of international cooking. At present, if we have a visitor at the Embassy, the Ambassador and I have to take the guest out to a restaurant. This is simply because we are ashamed – yes, ashamed – of our food. And you will understand that there are often times when we need to talk of confidential matters and would want to eat in the security of the Embassy. We have been searching for a cook for many months. And now perhaps I have found him here on the banks of the mighty Zambezi River.'

'And you will also know, no doubt, that Cape Town is a city of international culture. We have musicians, poets, writers and of course an excellent university, founded ten years ago. I think that it may even have a Chemistry department.' They all chuckled lightly.

'And of course we will pay you and provide you with accommodation. Now, I and my friend are going to have a beautiful walk up the banks of this charming river, take a look at the animals and appreciate the wonders of nature. And when we return, in maybe an hour, I will ask you for an answer.' Carl laughed and turned away, but then clearly had a final thought.

'Oh, and should your answer be in the affirmative, the next Imperial flight for the Cape will be leaving tomorrow morning, and I would expect you to be travelling with me.'

Peter and Carl strode off towards the thundering water, leaving one shocked chef staring after them. The Zambezi seemed so tranquil from the bank at the point where they stood just before its downward plunge. They were rowed by a native from the bank of the river in a small boat to one of the islands where the water cascaded down. They disembarked and walked on the land of the island. Reaching the edge, Peter leant over and watched the torrent plunging below. He told Carl that it was said that Livingstone himself carved his initials on a tree on this island, but they could find no trace of it. The constant downward plunge of the water and the upward movement of the mist mesmerised them. Eventually they returned to the bank and strolled along watching the wildlife and occasionally sitting on the wooden benches provided for tourists.

When they returned to their hotel an hour later Amit was nowhere to be seen, but he suddenly appeared on the terrace, carrying a small valise.

'Goodbye, Bronwen. I shall miss you,' and he turned mournfully to give the cat one final stroke. The cat gave a token purr but failed to stir from its sunbathing.

'You are coming then?' Carl asked.

'Most definitely.'

'Carpe diem then, Amit.'

'Oh yes and maybe more than diem, I am thinking Sahib,' responded one well-educated chef as he left the hotel for his quarters, casting not a glance backwards.

Chapter Three

A cook's flight

A mit failed to find excitement in being at a great height above the ground. His father, the Maharajah, had been a great enthusiast for the aeroplane and had taken him, when a young man and before leaving for his German University, up in his Sopworth Snipe biplane. Amit had been terrified.

He had found the journey to Cape Town frankly appalling. In the few rare moments when his terror had temporarily diminished, he was able to appreciate the fascination of seeing the vast continent passing by underneath him. The aircraft was never at a great enough height to be above the clouds, so that occasionally he would see herds of the larger animals charging across the plains, clearly terrified by the hurtling metal above them. Villages arranged in clusters around a central corale could be seen and occasionally a native would appear brandishing a spear at the large noisy bird above him. As they crossed some of the mountain ranges, they would be so low that he was certain that they would be unable to rise above the peaks, and end up impaled on the rocky surfaces.

They stopped at many places; Salisbury, Pretoria, and Johannesburg the most memorable. They were allowed to alight and walk around a little and he was able to regain his sense of humanity. But then they would be off again tossing around, rising and dropping through the blue inhospitable sky until eventually they came to a halt. He saw the sign saying 'Cape Town' and they walked out of the plane into the warm breeze blowing its moist air off the Southern Ocean. The sky was as clear in its azure blue colouring as the blue of Mary's gown on the picture of the Madonna of the Rocks, which used to hang in his student's room in Leipzig. The breeze seemed to dissipate any haze and the clarity of colour enlivened the views of the town and harbour.

He noted the unwelcoming stance of the surly white immigration officer in the Arrivals Building, but with the German providing official Diplomatic assurances, the officer had had little choice but to provide him with a two-year visa and a welcome to the Dominion. The Embassy car had met them at the airport and the chauffeur loaded their bags.

'And I may travel with you?' he asked in some wonderment, having heard tales of the treatment of Non-whites in South Africa.

'Here in the Cape you will find that you are not discriminated against much,' he was assured by Carl. 'We whites and you Indians all mix in pretty well. It's only the Blacks that are kept out of some things.' Amit understood that Carl's politics might be well aligned with the new regime in Berlin.

Amit settled into his life at the Embassy, and it was true what he had been told about the rest of the cooking staff. They had little concept of culinary skills. He had two of them fired after a couple of days and hired two replacements, one of them a fellow Hindu from Bombay. After a few days, Amit got to know the twenty-odd staff, most of whom stopped treating him badly after they had eaten some of his food. In short he was welcomed. He had overheard Carl, while boasting of his skill in finding the new chef, telling his colleagues of Amit's background at university. And after that, he was treated as a full member of staff by everyone and even occasionally consulted on matters pertaining to chemistry.

A few days after arrival, he was summoned to the Ambassador's office. He knocked timidly.

'Kome herein.'

He pushed at the door and entered to find the ambassador sitting on one side of a large dark wood desk and Carl on the other. There was a third chair and the ambassador pointed to it.

The ambassador, Hermann von Bauer, was a large, cheerful man exuding his bonhomie over all that surrounded him and Amit was buoyed up by the waves of good humour from the man. Von Bauer's marvellous personal skills, added to his fortunate accident of birth into an old Prussian family, had assured that his career in the Diplomatic service had flourished and he was clearly headed for stardom when there was the unfortunate incident in Rome. All had agreed that the misfortune was hardly the fault of ambassador von Bauer but Mussolini and the Italian press had been outraged, so the ambassador had been shunted down south. But being the man that he was, Von Bauer had determined to make the most of it. His love of culture meant that he had immediately joined both the Cape's literary and musical circles. He was a patron of the Cape's Symphony Orchestra and was always seen in a box at the opening of the new concert season. He attended the poetry group and on one occasion he had even read one of his own poems, in English to the amazement of the small group.

He had decided to tell no-one, and particularly not his staff, that his parents had been great Anglophiles. Friday nights had been English nights. His father used to read Shakespeare out loud at the family dinner table, and as the children got older they were encouraged to write and read a piece of composition in English before the dessert was served. Hermann had picked up the language with ease and soon his father had been amazed and delighted at the quality of the poems that the boy had read. Each year the family had visited and holidayed with English relatives. One of their cousins occupied a prestigious chair at Oxford University and the family had enjoyed wandering the streets, shopping and picnicking in the fields on the banks of the Thames. Everyone, and especially his father, had been horrified when in 1914 war had broken out. Hermann evaded active military service due to his asthma, but became an important strategist in the mapping team at military headquarters. After the war, relationships with the Oxford cousins had resumed and although the visits were less frequent, the warmth between the families remained strong.

Hermann was tall and had been a sportsman when younger, representing Dresden University at both rowing and discus throwing. He studied economics at the university but had showed little aptitude for the subject. His forte in communication, his fluency in English and his prominence in the upper echelons of German society ensured that his entry to the Diplomatic service was smooth and, until the misfortune, progress had been smooth.

'Carl has told me that you speak excellent German, but we will speak English as this is English land… at present.' Both Germans appeared to find this enormously amusing. Amit felt that he must do something, so tried to grin.

Over the ambassador's head was an enormous picture of the new leader of Germany, Adolf Hitler. The ambassador saw him looking.

'Our new leader. Carl and I are trying to decide whether we approve. Do you have a view?'

'If I may speak frankly sir, when I was in Germany we students were divided into two camps. There were the communists and there were the non-communists, most of whom worshipped this man. 'Germany's saviour,' they would call him. I was not exactly kneeling at his altar.'

'Indeed?'

'Well his followers were not overly keen on you unless you had blue eyes and fair hair sir. I regret that I do not possess either of those attributes.'

The ambassador laughed. Carl scowled.

'I had noticed, Amit, I had noticed. Now, let us leave

41

matters of politics. First of all – a welcome to our small German colony. My name is Hermann von Bauer and I am the Ambassador. I have already been enormously cheered by the meals that you have cooked. You are a marvellous addition. My colleague Carl has done us all a great service by extricating you from the middle of this enormous continent. Did you enjoy your stay in Livingstone?'

'Sahib, I enjoyed the beauty of the river and I marvelled at the joy of nature, the animals, the birds, the plants, and of course the roaring place where the river falls. Perhaps I failed to enjoy the dreariness of a small town, the remoteness.' There is a pause, broken only by the street sounds through the window, and then the ambassador says,

'Of course, and I suspect that we would find the isolation tedious too.' Carl nods his agreement. 'So for you the joy was the living by the Zambezi. If you have lived by this great river of Africa, maybe you have read a book by the Polish man, Joseph Conrad, called *Heart of Darkness*, also about one of the great rivers?'

'Yes, Sahib, but in English.'

'Me too, and are you Kurtz or are you Marlowe, Amit? Are you in favour of the *civilising influences of colonisation*?' Amit looks at him. The conversation has taken an unexpected turn and although Amit is fascinated, he is circumspect in his reply.

'I cannot give a simple response. For myself, I would need to know what the word 'civilisation' means. My upbringing, my family was of the highest order. Everything that was done was achieved at the highest level. When I came to Europe, I was told that I had arrived at the heart of civilisation now that I had arrived in the centre of Germany. And indeed many things were wondrous to behold, but some things were not.'

'So, may I in my turn,' Amit responded, 'ask you gentlemen of the Third Reich a question? Is the concept of the Reich to produce the most civilised society in the world, a society without parallel in its morals and ethics?' Both men observed the small chef with the greatest of interest. They had been trained in the world of diplomacy and tact but being men of learning and training in German philosophy, they understood the deviations that were occurring from some of the standard greats – from Hegel and Goethe, from Wittgenstein and even Marx. At last the ambassador observed –

'In *Heart of Darkness*, Conrad makes us consider the nature of greatness in our European society. For me personally our twentieth century world, whether it be European or African, fails but in differing ways.' And he paused. 'But maybe I am not a good German to speak so. We Germans have lost our colonies, and for me the moral prerogative of one people to colonise another with the hope of bringing them wealth and religion cannot be justified. And who is to judge 'wealth'?

'As for our new leader, I think that it would be fair to say that Carl and I may not see totally eye to eye on the matter. Perhaps I should simply reply for myself. Whilst I agree with Herr Hitler that Germany must rise and be strong again after the idiocy and tragedy of the last war, nevertheless I believe that the undercurrents associated with his movement are abhorrent to me. The attacks on other races, and other nationalities represent an aspect that I cannot accept. And the thuggish behaviour of his so-called Brown shirts is a disgrace to our nation. We are a people of culture and tolerance. We produced Beethoven and Mahler, Goethe and Kierkegaard, even Marx if you like. Our writers like Thomas Mann and Heine enhance the world of literature. We are not barbarians who need to have the streets roamed by gangs of stupid bullies.'

There is a period of silence. The room is at rest with itself while the three men consider these issues of great standing. The room itself is a testament to High German cultural values with its ornate furniture, lofty ceilings and the vast poster of a leader far away. Amit's background of Hindu and Indian cultural values places him apart somewhat, but nevertheless he feels kindred spirits with what he perceives to be the high moral standing of at least one of the two Europeans. At last he responds.

'For myself, returning to Conrad, my belief is that he did not intend for his book to be a vast question in morality. I am aware that the book has been much discussed and agree that he raises enormous issues which need to be valued in academic circles. Maybe his intent was to use that journey that he made up the Congo River simply to write a good story? But if not, then what he is saying is that the power in the hands of the colonialists results in their behaving in a more heathen way than any 'savage'. The power in Kurtz' hands has resulted in his barbarism; his inhuman unhinging.' And Amit ends with his eyes focussed on the floor and with the power of his speech resonating from the walls of the room of culture and civilisation. He hopes that

44

he has not spoken out of turn. A noise from the street outside wakes the men from their reverie. The ambassador rises to his feet.

'The embassy has gained not only a fine cook but a man of learning and thought. We will continue this conversation at a later time, I hope.' And to Amit's amazement, the representative of German power in Africa stands and performs Namaste to him. Amit responds, rises from his chair and leaves the room in silence.

'Now, Mr. Ambassador,' began Carl,' I must talk to you of my conversations in Livingstone with my friend Peter Shroeder, the representative of the Abwehr. Also I bring you a letter of instruction from Commandant Rudolf Schmidt.' The two men settle into a prolonged discussion of their new mission, and in particular their means of achieving the separate aspects.

Amit wanders back to his small room overlooking the courtyard of the Embassy. He is grateful for the room, as it has saved him from trying to ascertain where he is allowed to live. The South African laws seem a little vague. He understands that he is classified as Non-white but is unsure how it would have been as regards renting a room. The room that he has is, in its' own way, charming. Germans having arrived quite early on in the town's history, they acquired as their Embassy a large old timber-framed boarded three story building situated not far from the harbour. Originally a large family house fronting onto the street, it was enlarged with wings extending rearwards. Then the final side was added more recently, forming a pleasant central courtyard now dotted with flower-beds and possessing a number of benches on which to sit and relax. His room, high up on the third floor is not large but pleasingly irregular in shape. A large window looks almost due north towards the Atlantic Ocean and permits him thoughts of his childhood home, just a boat trip away. The room is comfortably furnished with a bed, chair and desk for writing, and a soft armchair for relaxing. There are two prints on the wall, one of which is of two girls playing the piano. He likes the focus of the girls on the keys of the piano. It reminds him of the musicality in his home. Down the corridor is a washroom that he shares with a couple of others. He feels fortunate to have acquired a pleasant new home in a place where there are men of learning and erudition.

And he knows that it is now time to write a letter.

Chapter Four

A touch of concern at S.I.S.

'I have received a rather remarkable letter, Captain.' Morris Shuttleworth looks up disagreeably at the interruption. He was already irritated at being unable to solve Eight Across of the morning's Times' crossword and has no desire to see the fresh smiling face of Lieutenant Alan Drayson, his junior colleague.

The Captain's room is as plain as a room can be. There are no photographs on the standard civil service procurement desk. There are four upright chairs. There is one lone picture on the wall opposite the desk, which he sees whenever he surfaces from reading papers, or for example, when trying to solve Eight Across. This solitary acknowledgement of humanity is a print of Renoir's Two Young Girls at the Piano. He had bought it himself in a rare moment of adventure, following his wife's criticism of the sterility of the room.

She had hoped that he would put a picture of herself on his desk, but instead he had noticed an art shop close to their home in Rickmansworth. He had chosen the print himself without assistance from his wife and had carried it into work under his arm, at some inconvenience, on the Metropolitan branch of the Underground Railway. The Office manager had provided the hammer. If one asked him what he liked about the picture, he might have muttered about the demureness of the girls' attention to their task. He would have been unlikely to mention his great desire to stroke the strawberry blonde hair of the older girl seated at the piano.

'Oh.' He had made his grunting acknowledgment as hostile as possible, but it was ignored by Drayson, whose own father was like this in the morning with the Times' crossword. Alan Drayson suspected that the decision by the editor of the Times to commence a daily crossword in 1930 was the single cause of the failure of family breakfast conversations in millions of English households, and probably of the alarming increase in the divorce rate over the last two years.

'The letter is from Amit Jaipur. Do you remember him?' Not a sound came from the lips of the Captain. Alan Drayson was a man who, having not only a difficult father but also a trying mother, had learnt early in his life that success with others often depended on strategies, and sometimes rather unsubtle strategies.

'May I help you with the clue, sir?' The Captain looked up at his junior, and gave a glimmer of a smile.

'Nice summer follows start of this puzzle at the island. Five letters.'

'Crete,' Drayson replied without a moment's hesitation. A blank look remained on the senior man's face.

'Well, sir, this is a crossword puzzle; the 'starting letters of the word 'crossword' are the letters CR. Nice is a town in the country where summer is spelt ETE, and CRETE is of course…'

'… an island in the med. Don't know where I would be without you, Drayson.'

'May I speak about this letter, sir?' At that moment two rays of sunshine appeared in the first floor office of 54, Broadway. The first arrived from the sun itself getting a ray in edgeways following the over-night drizzle which had at last cleared, giving the occupants of the Headquarters of the Special Intelligence Services a pleasantly verdant view past the underground station and into Green Park. The second was the arrival of Sarah Grandison, who popped her cheery face around the door.

'Anyone for a drink?' was the suggestion. A duet of requests for tea in tenor and baritone warmed the air.

Alan waited until she returned.

'Thank you, Sarah, and you had better hear this too.' She sat.

'This letter was sitting on my desk in this morning's post, presumably courtesy of our Mrs. Maple. The envelope is dated only a week ago and is from Cape Town, South Africa. It has rather exciting stamps of South Africa and is overprinted by Imperial Airways, and which incidentally I would like to keep…' Shuttleworth, also a stamp collector, looks darkly at this suggestion but says nothing.

'So this missive appears to have come,' he continues, 'via their new regular air postal service from the Cape, which explains its rapid arrival. The signature is that of Amit

Jaipur whom you may recall, sir.' A blank look crosses the Captain's face.

'You must remember him, sir. We eventually decided that he was probably not suitable for work in our department. He was a chemistry student in Leipzig, son of a high-up prince in one of the Indian states, who came over to London in one of the summer vacations and offered his services. A clever man, well educated, who spoke a number of languages including almost perfect High German so we started him off on the training course at the centre in Pitlochrie. But we decided after a month or so that he was a bit, how can I say, slightly out of touch with reality. Kept asking interesting but irrelevant questions. He was mostly easy to train, the craft etc. But just a bit too, what can I say, too philosophical.' And he smiled wanly.

'I remember his intelligence,' added Sarah.

'Can't recall the chappie at all,'

'You must remember him, sir. We don't look at many brown chaps.'

'Aha, why didn't you say that he was brown? Yes I remember. So he has written to you.'

'Perhaps it would be quickest if I read it to you both?' Nodding heads could be seen.

'It is headed – German Embassy, Cape Town, Union of South Africa and dated March 20th 1933.

Dear Lt. Drayson,

I hope that you can remember my smiling face from that time in London and Pitlochrie when you attempted to instil the art of matters of secrecy into my thick skull, back in the summer of 1929?'

'Rash of him to mention training in Pitlochrie in a letter. No wonder we weren't very keen on him.' The Captain grimaces a little.

'I am now in South Africa by a remarkable chain of events. Suffice it to say that I have been recruited as Head Chef to the German embassy here, having had a few adventures since graduating from the Leipzig University. Despite their obvious feelings that my brown skin hardly qualifies me for human status – they use the word 'Unter-mensch' when they think that I am not listening – never-theless I have been welcomed and indeed, to my amazement, am now completely trusted.

I wondered whether I might be of service to you and to England?

Yours sincerely

Amit Jaipur.'

A brief silence fills the room when Alan finishes reading, broken eventually by Sarah.

'Well boss I would say that this seems on the face of it to be rather a stroke of good fortune.'

Shuttleworth looked at her with a somewhat neutral expression and was silent again. A fly buzzed aimlessly in the far corner of the room.

'I think we will have to be a little circumspect here. Alan, let me ask you a question: 'what did we tell this chappie when we failed to take him on?"

'I suspect we gave him the usual formula, telling him that we would not be using him in the immediate future but we might call upon him at a later date. It's the best form of words, sir, as it means that they don't think that they have failed.'

'Yes, indeed. And hopefully prevents them getting bitter and going to the opposition, whoever they may be?' Shuttleworth pronounces.

'Well, in answer to your last point, sir, I would have thought now that it was pretty obvious that the opposition have become the Germans again. The fascists there seem very aggressive and that Hitler bloke has just won their election,' she replied.

The light from the window just touches Sarah's cheek and Alan observes the gentle glow from her skin. He has always liked her. She managed always to be positive even when the office had had a problem or even a disaster. The previous year one of their recruited agents in Russia had turned out to be a double agent. He had been a secretary in the offices of Vyacheslav Mikhaelovich Molotov, an up and coming political commissar. He had been feeding them false information for two years before they realised. The Prime Minister had been furious and everyone in the office had had their pay cut by the Home Secretary.

Months ago, Alan remembered, he and Sarah had walked through Hyde Park in their lunch break. She had told him of her upbringing in Weybridge and her initially successful school career. She had been the star of the local tennis club and had been given tickets for Wimbledon a couple of years ago and seen the German star Aussem defeat another German Hilde Krahwinkle in the Ladies Final. She still lived in her family home as they were short of money after her father had lost his job in the Crash but her mother still had a job in a shop so they had something. She had told him of her father's humiliation at having no work, and his turning to drink. In the end her father had died the previous year and she and her mother were coping on their own, she had told him.

'Indeed, Sarah, there appears to be a steady increase of tension from that nation again and of course the communists in Russia are not such a wonderful lot either,' the boss continued. 'I'm sure there will be plenty of work for us soon but in the meantime to have someone inside an embassy is never a bad thing.'

'But we'll need to be sure that he's working for us of course. After all, he might've told the Germans that he was 'rejected' by us and they may have thought of setting him up to feed us false news, with or without his connivance.' Alan looks at the desultory remains of his coffee, and stray thoughts of home and his mother eased their way into his mind. The dreams floated in and out of focus in a multi-hued rainbow, taking on myriad shapes and forms, having evil semblances and kinder apparitions. He drags himself back in time to hear his boss say:

'Well, I think that one of you should.'

'What? What?' he wanted to shout out, and looked from

53

one to the other. In turn, they were both looking vaguely accusingly at him. Shuttleworth surveys him hostilely with that beetling of his eyebrows that Alan always found distressing.

'Try to listen, Drayson. I was saying that we need someone to pop down to the Cape to suss this chappie out. Why on earth should he be wanting to spy for us? He has a university degree from Germany, and now he is suddenly inside one of their Embassies. The Abwehr could easily have recruited him while he was in Leipzig for those three years. They might have discovered that he had volunteered to work for us, and pressured him to join them, knowing that he could be a double agent. Maybe they have a hold on him – something that his daddy in Jaipur might not want to know.' Someone heavy-footed walks past the door and they stopped talking momentarily.

'And it's all a bit neat if you ask me,' he continues. 'The chap disappears and four years later he turns up in their Embassy in Cape Town. How did that happen?' There was silence in the room while they considered the possibilities.

'And he *is* an Indian national. We haven't exactly been tripping over ourselves to ingratiate ourselves to the population over there. At least the East India Company has stopped stealing most of their resources now but it's no secret that most of the locals want us out. This Gandhi chap keeps stirring them up. Look at those Salt marches a couple of years back. Nearly raised the roof and only stopped by some sharp action by the Governor. So it's no good us sitting here hoping that he's on the side of the angels. We will need a proper assessment of his reliability before we accept any information from him. And I was just asking for volunteers when you left us for one of your small mental sojourns away from the office.'

'Yes, sir, I apologise. So, you are suggesting that one of us goes down there to look him over?'

'Indeed, Drayson. That is exactly what I am suggesting. There's a regular flight now to the Cape. Nice weather at this time of year. Go down and spend a few days there to ascertain whether he is doing this for the right reasons.' Sarah and Alan look at each other.

'I think that Alan should go,' Sarah speaks slowly, weighing her words with some care. 'There are difficulties down there between the races and in particular between men and women of differing races. It might be a problem for me to spend enough of the time in Amit's company that would be needed to assess his reliability.' Both men think this through for a minute.

'She is right,' Alan acknowledges. 'I will go.' Although he hated to think what his new girl-friend would make of it, at last he was to get a foreign assignment. Frankly he was getting sick of moving around the Home Counties interviewing refugees from Europe, looking for possible candidates for the service, under the pretence of checking their credentials. He chuckled inwardly recalling the middle-aged man from Poznan, apparently a Professor of Philosophy in his home city, now living in a flat in the middle of a small town in Sussex, who had seemed quite stark staringly mad to him. The man had wittered on about how scientific knowledge was the only kind of factual knowledge and that all traditional metaphysical doctrines must be rejected as meaningless, whilst he himself was living in the messiest, most cluttered flat that Alan had ever seen. They had drunk tea, or he had hoped that it was tea, while both were seated upon piles of old newspapers. The man had only been in the country for six months, but the papers appeared to date back many years. He was sporting an enormous moustache that completely obscured his mouth, and which seemed to act as a kind of filter when he drank. Perhaps, Alan had mused, it was a necessary hygiene tool to keep lumps of mould and unwanted food out of his digestive system. This man would be so noticeable wherever he went that he would be totally useless as any sort of spy.

The reality was that, during the whole of this mission, he had met just the one man in his travels who would have been a 'possible.' This man, named Dmitri, was from a small town in the Ukraine. He was young, in his twenties, with a full head of light brown hair, of medium height with a rather flat unmoving face and spoke in a monotonous voice with near perfect English. Apparently he had been an English graduate from the University at Kiev. He was vaguely good-looking but not outstandingly so. He would easily blend into a roomful of people and not be noticed. Dmitri had spotted all of the observational traps that Alan routinely set for his interviewees – the Eton tie, the briefcase with the wrong initials on the leather, the American fountain pen, the misuse of an old English word. He had left his wallet on the chair when he went to the toilet – nothing had been touched. He had corrected a small error in Alan's quote from Virgil. The man had been perfect, and Alan had recommended that he be further investigated.

Alan's own recruitment had been very different. He had been sitting in the small family garden of his parents' house in Holt on a warm summer's day. They had lived in a small cul-de-sac not far from the station. The terrace was warm and his father had fallen asleep in a deck chair. His father's brother, Uncle John, was a crisp, rather cheery man very different from his father. His uncle had fought in the Boer war and was full of great yarns about battles with the natives and the Afrikaaners, which had kept the young Alan enthralled through his childhood. Alan had just drawn his uncle's attention to a Firecrest sitting in the hedge on the right of the garden. His uncle had been impressed. 'Well spotted. Very rare bird in this country – see quite a few in southern France.' Apparently the conversation had stirred something in his uncle's mind. He had looked over at the sleeping and softly snoring father and had asked Alan quietly what career he intended.

Alan, being young, male, and mildly dreamy by nature had been non-committal, not having given the subject much consideration.

'Thought you might be rather suitable to join us in the Service.' Alan had felt horrified at the thought of a military career and clearly his expression had shown it. 'Not that sort of service,' his uncle had laughed. 'I work for the Intelligence Service. Mostly rather boring desk work but occasional nice travel opportunities. Opportunities to spot birds in foreign countries. All that sort of thing, you know.' Alan had always enjoyed his uncle's clipped military

57

manner of speaking. And that had been that.

A week later Alan had presented himself to the slightly shabby building in Piccadilly, travelling up from Holt to Liverpool Street station and taking the underground train to Piccadilly. He had been interviewed and started work the following month, interspersed with trips to the Highlands for training. His reminiscences ended when he was brought back to earth by the slight raising of the tone of Shuttleworth's voice.

'By the way, bit of news that I received last week from our man at Croydon airport. He called me to let me know that one of our known German chappies passed through on his way home to Berlin. Apparently this German fellow had been to southern Africa just for a couple of days. In fact he had stopped at Livingstone in Northern Rhodesia, and came back on the next flight according to Smyth. No idea what he was up to, and Smyth didn't even know that he had gone. Apparently he was travelling on a false passport and Smyth just happened to be on duty and recognised him as the chap walked through Immigration. Chap's name is Peter Shroeder and he is part of the Africa section of the Abwehr. We don't know much about that bit of the Abwehr and we certainly don't know why one their men might fly all the way to Livingstone and then come straight back.'

'Maybe he gave instructions to someone, or delivered something that could not go by post?' They both looked at her and she blushed slightly. Alan was entranced.

'Yes, well, either of those ideas sounds plausible. But it would have had to be something pretty big. On your way down to the south Alan, I suggest that you stop off at Livingstone and find out what he was up to.' Alan nodded.

'The flights only go twice a week, so you will have three days stay in Livingstone to suss matters out before you can catch the next flight southwards. There can't have been too many Abwehr officers swanning around a little town like that managing to keep much secret from the locals.' A short pause. 'Now you have a successful trip. Sheila will sort out flights to Cape Town for you. I will cable the High Commission in Cape Town so that they will put you up for as long as you need and Sheila will get the High Commission to meet you at the airport. James Pringle is our S.I.S. man in the South but he is pretty useless frankly. Might be capable of providing a bus ticket but little else. Don't count on him. But the Head of S.I.S. for southern Africa is much better. She's called Gloria Simpson; she will find you.' Alan searched for any other questions before the meeting broke up.

'Oh, and Alan. While you are there, there is another little problem.' They both watched him with care. Shuttleworth was at his most circumspect whenever he started a sentence 'Oh, and...'

'We had a small bit of news from a friend of ours in the civil service in Germany. The folk over there are just a tiny bit troubled about the machine-tools in their factories. Seems they can't get enough diamonds to run these tools. There has been talk at the highest levels about acquiring rather a lot of diamonds, but needless to say without telling anyone.' They wait. Eventually Alan can stand it no longer.

'I am sorry, sir but why can't they buy the diamonds

from Antwerp like everyone else does?'

He looked at Alan and gave a little laugh. 'Yes, that was what I asked. Apparently diamonds are needed for making the cutting surface of machine tools and cut most metals. But particularly they are essential in the manufacture of rifles and other armaments. Apparently the German High Command is keen on having a lot of these arms – but not telling us that they are making them. Obviously the Treaties after the last war were meant to stop the Germans making that sort of thing. And where do most of the diamonds in the world come from?' The question hung, but the answer floated through the dusty Piccadilly air.

'So be a good chap and while you are down there, find out what is going on.' They both rose, and as they were leaving the Captain stopped him.

'Just one last thing, Alan, try not to get caught doing anything too bad. It is our colony but the locals can be a tad sticky. I couldn't promise to rescue you in a crisis.'

Chapter Five

The nature of the scheming

Alan arrives in Livingstone battered and damaged by his four days and four nights of travelling in cold noisy aeroplanes. He stays fortuitously at the same hotel where Peter Shroeder had stayed, but of course in reality there just was no other building in town that could be justified in having the epithet of *Hotel* honestly applied to it.

He slumps on his bed and sleeps for a few hours and dreams; how he dreams.

He is in the plane low over a herd of elephants. The lead elephant stops and demands that he descend from the strange craft and fight like a man. Alan demurs saying that he would feel unsafe due to the elephant's tusks. The elephant removes his tusks and passes them to another of the herd, and repeats the challenge. Alan tells the pilot to rise up into the deep blue sky. At that moment a large cloud appears and spits lightning and hailstones at the aircraft, and a terrible banging can be heard.

He jolts awake and realises that the banging is coming from the door of his room.

'Breakfast is just finishing in the dining room,' says an

61

unseen voice. He dresses in haste and takes the rather elegant hotel stairs two at a time in his desire for food. He slows his pace and wanders into a virtually empty dining room. There are two middle-aged men, dressed like travelling salesmen, seated at the far end and two elaborately dressed waiters standing close to some intriguing silver salvers. He lifts the hood of the first salver and sees a solid block of what might once have been scrambled eggs. He goes down the line, arrives at number five and observes a congealed mass of fish and rice.

'Bwana would like?' asks the waiter hopefully.

'Bwana would like a cup of tea and some toast and marmalade.'

The waiter disappears, looking disappointed. Alan sits where he can observe the two men at the far end. He looks out onto the terrace and garden beyond, and his eye is caught by an orange movement on the extreme left of his vision and turns to observe a vast cat licking its' paws. The cat ceases his licking for a moment and in turn observes Alan. After a moment she decides that he is of little interest and returns to her morning cleansing operation.

'She is called Bronwen.' The waiter is there with his tea and toast. 'She is from Wales.'

'She has a lot to answer for in that case,' he observes, wittily to himself.

'You did not like our cooked breakfasts, Bwana?' the waiter asks somewhat sadly. 'It is not surprising, I fear. Recently we have lost our chef. Our new chef does not have the skill of our previous man, an excellent cook from India. Alan felt a sudden surge of interest in the hotel's previous culinary arrangements.

'What happened to your previous chef, then?'

'Vanished. Taken away by German man. Took him away to the South on the aeroplane.' Alan could already see gold stars for achievement flashing over his mantle back at the office and this was just his first morning. His eagerness got the better of him.

'And what was the name of this chef?'

'Amit, bwana.' This was all too easy. He could see promotion looming. Would he get the boss' office with that nice window looking out onto the park? Reluctantly he decided to change the subject and tap the source of this knowledge at a later time.

'And where are the Falls?' he asked. The waiter lost interest instantly.

'Just follow the noise, bwana; just the noise.' And he gestured out of the hotel towards the garden, clearing the table as he left. Alan sauntered back toward the hotel reception desk. A tall man was seated behind the counter.

'May I help you, Mr Drayson?' Surprised at the use of his name, Alan looked at the man.

'I was here when you arrived last night, sir. I am sure that you didn't notice me as you appeared extraordinarily fatigued. Welcome to Northern Rhodesia. My name is Cundell.'

'Thank you. This is my first trip to this country. It's beautiful.'

'Indeed we are a small backwater but it is my pleasure to run a fine old hotel in this long-established town.'

'Thank you for your offer of help. I have come here to

look for an old friend of mine, a cook named Amit Jaipur. I've had a letter from him saying that he was in Livingstone and I've stopped here to try to find him. Is it true that he is no longer here?'

'Indeed to our great sadness. Amit was the best cook that the hotel has ever had. He was stolen from me by a man from the German embassy in the Cape. No doubt you are anyway travelling on to Cape Town. I am sure that you will find him at the German embassy there. To my memory, the embassy is close to the harbour.' Alan did his best to appear disappointed.

'I am indeed going on to the Cape so thank you for that.' He paused to turn away and then appeared to think of something else. 'And could you tell me the name of this German who stole your cook?'

'One minute and I will check in the register. There were of course two Germans.'

'Really?'

'Oh, yes. One came from London and one from the Cape and they stayed a couple of days and then flew away, the one from the Cape taking our Amit. Let me see on the register. The one from the south was called Carl Hans von Wasserburg. His friend who returned to London was Peter Shroeder.'

Alan managed to control his excitement. Ten gold stars; even maybe Alpha Plus for Drayson. Promotion would not be far off. He would decorate Shuttleworth's office properly. There would be none of this Impressionist nonsense on the walls. Cubism was the rage; cubism was his love; and cubism would be on his walls. He loved Picasso but his real favourite was this French chap Braque. He might even be brave and put a bit of Fauvism on display. That would shock old Shuttleworth.

He rushed over to the hotel's office and sent a coded telegram to Sarah giving the details of what he had learnt. Now he had two days until the southbound Imperial flight would be here. What could Carl von Wasserburg and Peter Shroeder have spoken about while they were here? Sarah had been right that it had to have been something of importance for someone from the Abwehr to have come all this way – but it was not clear to him as to how he might find out what they had discussed – unless of course someone at the hotel had overheard them – or maybe had seen something. He needed to have another chat to that hotel manager. And who else would have heard or seen anything? Maybe those waiters in the dining room. Possibly someone who cleaned the hotel rooms. Two days was plenty of time to find out more about those two German men. First though he would read a little.

Before he had left he had bought a copy of Livingstone's Diaries and he went off to immerse himself by the cloud of noise, seated on the lawn of the hotel in one of the two slightly incongruously deckchairs placed there. The deckchairs would not have been out of place on the beach at Scarborough where he had stayed as a lad with his aunt and uncle who had owned a Boarding House near the pier. The deckchairs here were worn and slightly grimy, and gave the impression of imminent collapse if you dared to sit in them. Having summoned up his courage, he was relieved to find on lowering himself, that his buttocks remained at least six inches above ground level.

Later he strolled up the river bank, returning to dine on ghastly hotel food and afterwards he had sat in the bar drinking a malt whisky. The bar was long and wooden, seemingly hand-painted with an assortment of animals, and lined with high stools standing ready for hotel guests. He sat on a stool and the barman, having taken his order for a beer, was happy to chat as there were no other customers. After some trivia about London, they got on to the subject of politics.

'Of course you Europeans have your hands full of the new Germany, I hear.' Alan looked at the barman. The remark had been dropped casually but it felt as if there was more to come. There was.

'We had two Germans in here recently. Nice men but a bit noisy.' Again a pause. 'Sat right at that table over there,' and he pointed to a far table in a corner of the room.

Alan wondered vaguely as to whether his good luck was still holding.

'Noisy, you said?'

'Talked more and more loudly the more beer they drank.'

Alan moved a little closer to the bar. 'And maybe you heard what they were talking about?'

'It is possible that I might have heard some of the things that they talked about.' Alan's attention was suddenly sharply focussed. The barman was not looking at him, just muttering.

'Of course my memory of what I might have heard is not so good.'

'Could I help your memory?' Alan asked cautiously.

'It is true that my memory is sometimes capable of improvement in these most difficult of times.' A crisp one pound note appeared on the counter. Both men observed it but only one picked it up and pocketed it. That man looked around with some care to ensure that no-one was close enough, as two or three customers had strolled in since Alan had first arrived.

'The name that I heard was that of Ernest Oppenheimer,' and he went to the other end of the bar to serve yet another customer who had just strolled in.

'Ernest Oppenheimer.' The name was not unfamiliar, but although it felt as if he had read it somewhere, Alan could not quite put his finger on it. The more he tried to remember where he had seen it, the further away the answer seemed to be. He spent the next two days hoping to stumble across more leads but it seemed that his spell of good luck was over. When he caught the flight to Cape Town, his information appeared to have ended with those three names: Carl Hans von Wasserburg, Peter Shroeder and Ernest Oppenheimer.

Chapter Six

A chef is examined

James Pringle met him at Cape Town airport in a Rolls-Royce Phantom 11 Continental.

'Pringle, the idea is not to announce my arrival to the whole world.'

'I'm sorry, sir. I thought you would like to ride in a Continental.'

'Of course I would like to ride in a Continental, but my visit is supposed to be moderately secret. Whose is the car anyway?'

'It's the High Commissioner's. He had Rolls-Royce ship it out here last year. He lets me drive it around when we have important people to meet at the airport.' Alan remembers his boss' parting words describing Pringle as – 'pretty useless really.' This seemed to sum him up rather well. The conversation was brief. On the way in from the airport, Alan watched the beauty of the scenery of the Cape passing before him.

'Please drive me past the German Embassy, and nice and slowly so that I can get a feel for the place.' Eventually they arrived and Alan noted the fineness of the Embassy's exterior, and its proximity to its British equivalent. He would be able to walk between the two with ease.

He was taken to the High Commissioner on arrival. Sir Robert Lancaster was a tall slim man with red cheeks and a small moustache, not dissimilar in appearance, he couldn't help but feel, to that sported by the new German Chancellor. And it rapidly became apparent that Sir Robert's political sympathies were not far from the Fuhrer's also. After a short welcoming speech, Sir Robert had asked him

'So just explain to me what you are doing here.'

'It might be for the best, sir, if I didn't tell you too much.' The High Commissioner looked at him with an expression of some irritation.

'Why the devil not? This is my place and you are responsible to me. I cannot possibly have my staff swanning around upsetting people, doing illegal things, fraternising with the natives and so on.' Alan winced and looked at his feet, not wishing for his eyes to betray his thoughts. When he looked up, Sir Robert's eyes were boring into him with marked hostility. He knew that a statement was due but had no wish to be bullied.

'The situation is delicate, sir. It is possible that some illegalities are about to be perpetrated here by the representatives of another European country. These illegalities might have implications for our national security.' He paused for the importance of his phrases to sink in. No effect was apparent. He had little option but to plough on.

'I need to investigate exactly what may be about to

happen, and if necessary obstruct or prevent these actions. I regret, sir, that I cannot give you any more details.' The High Commissioner's face had reddened even further and a small drop of saliva appeared at the corner of his mouth.

'And it would be best for the integrity of the High Commission if you could deny any knowledge of the details of my activity.' Alan was grateful that there were no others present to hear the humiliation of the representative of the British nation. He decided that he had better get it over with.

'And I will need your help sir; from some of your staff.'

'What staff?' It was a whisper curling through the air with fire at its edges.

'James Pringle.' The High Commissioner nearly smiled.

'You are welcome. Pathetic and useless.' Alan vaguely wondered how Pringle had managed to give the same impression to two such widely different men as his boss and this man, and made a note to think it through later.

'And Gloria Simpson.' The eyes watched him again.

'Until this moment it had been my belief that Miss Simpson was a simple clerk in our personnel section.' Alan said nothing. Time stood very still as he watched Sir Robert's eyes flick to the side and then slowly back to him.

'I see. Not so simple then.'

'Indeed not, sir.'

'I don't even know what's going on in my own bloody High Commission then. Marvellous, bloody marvellous. Just get out, Drayson, and try not to upset me anymore. Let me know when you leave the country.' Alan couldn't prevent a wry smile as he left the room to find Pringle waiting outside the office. Pringle showed him to his room which was surprisingly large and comfortable with a view north towards the harbour. He took in the sun-strewn sight of naval ships at anchor and gazed at the never-ending movement of a great harbour. A large warship was being dragged by three tugs out of the harbour entrance, its greyness slipping through the calm jade waters towards the blue skies of the horizon. Small wisps of smoke emerged from its funnel. Men in white naval uniforms, small as grains of rice, scurried over its decks; the British flag trailing from its rear mast; a Blue Peter flag also present, signalling the ship's immediate departure.

He recalled his scout leader teaching him and the other boys at his school of the naval code signals; he had been a diligent student and had learned them all. Somehow the Blue Peter had resonated most with him. As he watched, the flag was lowered, leaving the Union Jack with a small South African courtesy ensign fluttering in the breeze. The jade colour of the sea was hardly ruffled by the ship's progress. Alan found that the beauty made him yearn for his violin. He had learnt the violin when young and found that he had a talent. The school had encouraged him and he had played with the school orchestra from his outset at secondary school. And now the fluttering of the flags made him think of cadenzas. Perhaps he would buy a violin for his stay here; he had seen a musical instrument shop on his way in from the airport.

*

71

He could not know that at that very moment, in a building a short distance away, a slight man of Indian origin was taking in the exact same view. When this man had been young, his father had taken him down one of their jade mines. He had hated the noise and the heat and wondered at the darkness of the walls of the mine. He had been frightened and anxious and wanted the warmth of the up-side of the earth, but did not wish to appear cowardly to his father, that strong man, the Maharajah. This jade colour of the sea showed no sign of the trauma of bringing those jade stones to the surface; this was a calm, soft, peaceful hue dedicated to the beauty of a quiet world.

An hour later, there was a knock at Amit's door, high in the roof of the German Embassy. One of the servants brought him an envelope, with his name written upon it in green ink. He regarded it with some surprise as he could not understand who would write him a note since he hardly knew anyone in the town. This green of the ink was the green of the emerald stone, a fervent acid green, not that of jade. He turned the envelope over in his hand, looked at it in some wonder and then dived in and read the brief note inside.

Slowly he opened the door to his room and slipped out into the corridor, down the stairs and into the street. He walked slowly towards the harbour and yes there it was; The Cape Café scrawled in rather garish letters over the front picture window. He entered and looked around. The clientele was overwhelmingly white, making him retreat slightly, until he spotted a family that reminded him somewhat of his own sitting near the back and tucking nonchalantly into their cake and drinks. The tables extended far into the back of the room. On one of the back tables he could see a man in a grey suit waving gently to him. He was young, light skinned but slightly handsome with paradoxically dark hair, as the note had said.

Amit sat and looked around. Nobody seemed to be interested in them.

'Mr Drayson?' he asked.

'Indeed.' The man had replied equally gently and had smiled a soft, pink, easy smile. When their teas had arrived, the man had turned to him and said,

'We were rather pleased to get your letter in London. I have arrived here to see whether you would like to help us with a few small matters.' Amit vaguely remembered him from his stay in England, but was sure that he'd had a different name.

'But first there is some catching up to be done. You have travelled a long way since our days with you in London and the Highlands of Scotland?' The man was obviously asking a question so Amit set out his journeys from Germany on a steamer through the Mediterranean; his wonder at the voyage across the Egyptian desert on the waters of the Suez Canal and his leaving of the ship in British East Africa whence it was returning to Europe. He had enjoyed the excitement of the port of Dar-es-Salaam, but the continual heat and humidity had eventually worn him away. He had spent some days at the beach gazing across the vast expanse of peaceful Indian Ocean. His family felt close. He felt that if he listened hard he would be able to hear his mother scolding a kitchen maid. His father would be in his study poring over papers. The attraction was great and he felt a great magnetic force dragging him back to the comfort of the family. It would be so easy. His life could be comfortable again, but the adult in him knew that this would then be too easy. How could he develop his humanity in such an environment? He needed the bruising world to buffer him.

One morning he met an Englishman named Cundell, shopping in the town for spices from Zanzibar, and Amit had been curious as the man was buying large quantities of everything. Apparently, the man owned a hotel somewhere in the middle of the continent and was doing his biennial stocking up. He had almost filled his lorry and was about to return home. When the man discovered Amit's cooking abilities, he had immediately offered Amit a position at his hotel. Amit had decided on the spur of the moment to accept, although he had no idea where the town of Livingstone was. The journey had taken for ever and Amit had been taken aback by the apparently vast expanse of the dusty plains and deep forests that they passed through. Every now and then they would pass a small village where a few huts were made of wattle and covered in hardened mud and the children ran naked around them. He had begun to wonder what he had let himself in for.

At last they had arrived and Amit had at first been excited beyond belief by the Victoria Falls and his new job in the hotel. But slowly, slowly, he had lost his vitality in the numbing heat of the dry season and the ordinariness of small town central African life. He told Alan of the arrival of the Germans and his subsequent escape from the tedium.

Alan listened in silence to the chef's tale of wanderings and when the tale had finished, two cups of tea down, had interjected,

'And tell me about your life now as cook for the Embassy.'

'Tonight I am cooking Babootie for my German hosts. The Ambassador is a great man for his food and so I have been trying to find the most typical South African food and prepare it well. One day I was out strolling and met a fine man, apparently a writer and a doctor, and we started a conversation. When he discovered that I was a chef, he took me to his house and gave me a copy of his just published recipe book. And in it was this recipe for this dish Babootie, which is said to be a local dish. My new friend, named Louis du Plessis, says that this is rubbish and that it is a dish brought here by the Malay population who settled long ago in the Cape.' He paused and leant back in his chair before continuing,

'This recipe is most exciting. There is fried mincemeat and breadcrumbs and onion and butter. It is mixed into a curry sauce made with chilli pepper, spices and plenty of lemon juice. Then it is baked with a topping of egg and milk. Truly yummy, sahib. Most scrumptious.'

'And your friend, is he an Indian too?'

'Oh no, he is an Afrikaaner, sahib and is a most unusual and intelligent man. He is paediatric doctor, well-known poet and he writes books too but refused to show me. He says that no-one may see them yet or his friends would be angry with him. Because they are books about the history of the Afrikaaner peoples, but they are most sympathetic to the native peoples.'

'And his friends are not?'

'Apparently so, sahib.' They both considered this matter for a little.

'And how is your life now Amit, here in Cape Town.'

'Oh, sahib…'

'You know, Amit,' he interrupted. 'We are not now in India, nor are we in London. Please call me Alan, or even Mr Drayson, if you must.'

'Indeed, I shall need to think, sah…' He laughed ruefully. 'My cultural conditioning, I fear.' They both smiled in recognition.

'Alan,' he savoured the word slowly, like the juice of a good peach in the mouth. 'Alan, it is most pleasant living with the Germans. I have a good salary, plenty of free time and my bosses are mostly normal people. What's more, they've given me free lodging in a lovely room looking down to the harbour.' Alan made a mental note of his understanding of the similarity of outlook of their two rooms.

'So now, Amit,' he said. 'I have some difficulty with what made you contact us. My problem is that, should I be in your position, I would feel rather well disposed towards Germany and the Germans. Firstly they gave you hospitality and I suspect a first class education at Leipzig. Secondly they have plucked you out of a dead-end place in the centre of Africa. Thirdly, they have given you a good job with a reasonable salary and accommodation in a vibrant city. Whereas all we English have done for you is to not employ you at the end of your training,' and here he paused for a touch of drama. He also wanted to spring a thought on Amit. Doubtless Amit would have known that he would have to explain these points away and had already thought up a plausible answer, but maybe there was another more pressing point about Amit's background that would need careful probing. In his preliminary discussions with Sarah back in London they had decided that the best strategy would be to throw everything at Amit at once and not allow the man space to deal with the points one by one.

'And,' and here a short pause, 'we English have taken over your nation and your father's State. So I fail to understand how you can feel well enough disposed towards us to give us important information.'

Back in England before he had flown out, he had also discussed with Sarah the way to try to draw out the man's ideology, resentments, and feelings. They had agreed that family attitudes would be vital. Probing the background politics and the father's feelings towards the British would be key in assessing his innermost loyalties.

He watched Amit and noted the flicker of the eyes to the left and then back, attempting to hold onto the gaze. Amit smiled but there was a tension in the smile.

'Let me tell you about my father, the Maharajah. He is a man for whom the word 'benign' was invented. He is a man of tolerance. He practises his strong, devout Hindu beliefs on this earth, a true disciple, a man for whom gentle persuasion is always the path of progress. I am his son – of course you will know that I am the third son – but still his adoring son. He is a man hardly touched by the evils of this world. My ideal would be to live a life as close as possible to the way set out to me by my father. Except...'

'Except – ', he encouraged. Amit looked deeply into his eyes.

'Except that I am touched by the world. I am touched by its miseries, its inequalities, its poverties.'

'So you are a communist?'

'Alan, I am no communist. Communism is a negative philosophy. It wants always to take – and also, in the end, great chunks of philosophy are not for me. For me the way forward is in the mind and the actions of the individual, not the mind and actions of the masses. I can no more be a communist, a fascist or any other –ist. I am Amit and I focus on ensuring that Amit's behaviour is correct,' and he sat smiling from behind his mug of tea in a small café in a strange warm country. And Alan was very nearly convinced. They talked on of many things. His childhood had been happy; his large loving family and servants surrounded him with a love of knowledge and a great security, only degraded mildly by his experiences in Germany where he came across abuse from the fascists.

'And you had no abuse from the English at home?'

'Perhaps because I was my father's son, I was always treated with care by the English. And even in England, I was not really abused by the ordinary people for my colour. But in Germany I was attacked both physically and mentally. One day I was beaten by two Nazi thugs. In the streets. In the streets of Leipzig. For no reason other than the colour of my skin. They broke my arm.'

'So maybe that explains why at the end of my time in Leipzig I decided to offer myself to the British, whom I perceive as a people of energy and dynamism. And so does my father, to answer your question. He was always quick to praise the English. He had little time for nationalism or Mr Gandhi or protests.' The waitress returned to see if they needed more tea. Both were sated with drink, so they left and wandered down to the harbour. The sun was setting and as the port faced more west than any direction, it fell towards the sea ahead of them as they strolled along, colouring the little waves a sparkly red colour. The sun set more rapidly than in England and Alan was surprised to find it dark so quickly. Eventually they walked slowly back towards their respective homes and parted with care. They arranged to meet again two days later on the Wednesday when Amit had plenty of free time.

Chapter Seven

Gloria – in excelsis deo?

A lan Drayson was truly shocked by Gloria Simpson. He had received a note at breakfast asking him to attend her office at 9 a.m. and had knocked promptly on the appropriately labelled door.

'Come in.'

Behind the door he found a very young woman smiling from behind a typewriter and assumed that this was Miss Simpson's secretary.

'I was looking for Miss Simpson.'

'How nice to meet you, Mr Drayson.' She strode forward, hand out. Clearly an inaccurate assumption then. But how could a woman as young as this be Head of S.I.S. for southern Africa? He was mystified. His face clearly showed it and she had little difficulty in reading his thoughts.

'Well Mr. Drayson. I'm the Head of S.I.S. here but there are not so many of us, which is why they felt they could entrust the area to a woman.' She laughed, and her brown shoulder-length curls shook attractively. He was lost – not only an appallingly bad start by him, but she was so beautiful too. Her slim figure and blue eyes entranced him. What a disaster.

'Now Mr. Drayson, I have an important question for you?' Needless to say he was expecting discussion on the rise of fascism, or even possibly some aspect of internal S.I.S. politics. He was to be wrong-footed again.

'Are you an expert in making cocktails?' Alan looked aghast. This first, and so important meeting, appeared to be sliding completely out of his control.

'Weeeell,' the word was somewhat slurred. 'I don't think that 'expert' would be the right word.'

'Pity. May I call you Alan?' But the question did not appear to need an answer as she breezed on without waiting for a reply. 'The Embassy is hosting a cocktail party tonight and I seem to have been delegated by His Highness to be overseeing the bar. I believe that you have met our leader here in the High Commission. I am afraid that we all call him 'HH' slightly mockingly. A bit naughty, I fear, but it's sort of caught on. A man of strong views as you may have realised.'

'Yes I did notice.'

'Well,' she continued, 'he is not married, a touch unsurprising don't you think, Alan? Anyway, back to tonight, we will be serving cocktails. I do have Sarah Coleman's wonderful book as a guide. Of course she is still at The Savoy. At least I hope she is, but I haven't been home for a year. My chums and I used to go there all the time. Do you know her, Alan?' Enough of a pause occurred for Alan to slip in a couple of syllables to break up the monologue.

'I don't think…' and she was off again.

'Well the book is called 'The Savoy Cocktail Book' and did you know that it has two thousand recipes, Alan?' He shook his head.

'But enough of my prattling. We had better discuss work. And first you must tell me why you are here?' So he told her about Amit, the German embassy and the diamonds. He could tell that she was a bit surprised.

'Well, this is all rather shocking. When I was posted down here last year, I think that they sent me to get me out of the way. No-one anticipated that there would be anything for our department out here to do as it's all rather peaceful. An occasional march by the natives, that sort of thing, but no clandestine activity of any sort really. They called me Head of southern Africa to give me a title but there's really only me and James. You've met him of course. Pathetic and useless.'

'I can't believe it,' he thought. 'The third person to use exactly the same words to describe him.'

'Of course they did it because of daddy.' And a pause, forcing the almost mandatory response of…

'I am sorry I don't think…'

'The Duke of Mundesbury.'

'So you are Lady…'

'I forbid you to call me anything but Gloria, or I will call you Lieutenant Drayson for ever.' Alan knew when he was beaten.

'I surrender, Gloria.'

'Good boy. Now back to Amit Jaipur. Funnily enough I met the Maharajah some time ago because he came to discuss business with daddy. A lovely man, the Mah, so courteous. So, can you tell what game Amit is playing? We have to think through whether his treatment in Germany can be the motivation. In general it's often suspicious when they offer themselves to us off the street. Did his original record say anything when he first came in?' And suddenly she had transformed herself from a chatter-being-daddy's-daughter to a thoughtful member of S.I.S.

'There was nothing. But to be honest, the initial recruitment record was not very good. It was four years ago and we weren't as thorough in those days. Nowadays there would have been more checks done, and especially of that time he spent in Germany. Of course four years ago no-one would have considered that Germany could rise again to be our foe so it just wasn't considered a factor.'

'And do we know what the Germans might be up to?'

'Not really. We know that they are up to something important as they sent a man all the way down here. He had a meeting in Livingstone with this Carl von Wasserburg from their embassy here. It appears possible that it has something to do with diamonds but we really don't know for certain.'

'Well now that's an excellent co-incidence as Carl is going to be at the cocktail party this evening. I will introduce you. At one time we did wonder whether Carl worked for the Abwehr, as we cannot seem to find anyone else here who does. But we never found any trace. So we still don't know whether the Abwehr have anyone in their Embassy.'

'I would be happy to meet him but if you know him, it

would probably be best for you to talk to him and see what you can discover. How do you know him, anyway?'

'Oh diplomatic circles are rather small down here. Mostly we all know each other. And anyway he's rather dishy,' and she laughed. He felt just a tiny tinge of something that he would prefer not to have thought. She was watching him.

'What is your excuse for being here, Alan? People from the other embassies will ask and I can't just say 'I don't know' can I?'

'The story relates to gold. You will know that the British government has just taken the currency off the Gold Standard and that the price of gold has started to rise. I am here on behalf of the British government to have discussions with mining companies about this. We thought that it would allow me access to mines, and thus to the question of diamonds, without it being too obvious.'

'So, no further ideas about the Germans' games?'

'Only that, when I was in Livingstone, a bartender told me that he had heard the name Oppenheimer used in conversation. Ring any bells?'

'Ring any bells?' And she looked at him with some incredulity. 'Do you mean Ernest Oppenheimer, the Member of Parliament for Kimberley and Chairman of De Beers diamond mining company? You've never heard of him?'

'Well the name did ring a bell but I could not quite recall...' he tailed off in some embarrassment. 'But of course that would fit with the theory that this is all about diamonds.'

'But there might be a few confounders there. Mr. Oppenheimer was born in Germany and is, by birth, Jewish,' she told him.

'Well he is not likely to be sympathetic to the Fuhrer and his ideals then,' he said.

'Probably right, but apparently Oppenheimer is now an Anglican, and a citizen of South Africa.'

'Oh. Then the question of his allegiance may be complicated.'

'Indeed,' and she sat gently back into her seat. He thought about all these matters and stopped himself looking at her so that he could think without distraction. He forced his eyes away and for the first time looked around her office. Full of rather utilitarian things he noted. No photos on her desk anyway. And he remembered his girl-friend at home.

'So this evening I will see what I can prise from the Germans and will also of course introduce you to all sorts of interesting people.'

'Is it likely that Amit will have been invited?'

She looked at him. 'No, Alan. This is South Africa. We British are generally relaxed about issues of skin colour but we make sure that we don't upset our hosts in the government by going out of our way to irritate them. It's called politics. Perhaps that is an area that you have not too much experience in.' He was suitably admonished.

'Now,' she started brightly, 'about the cocktails. 'Do you know what a Hanky-Panky is?'

'No idea.'

'Oh dear. Not got around much then have you?' He

managed to smile wanly in agreement. 'Well as I said previously, when I was a girl, daddy introduced me to this marvellous woman called Coley who was the barmaid at the Savoy. She was lovely with us kids. Daddy said she was the best cocktail mixer in London and she had invented a special cocktail for Charlie Hawtry. Now you have heard of *him*, surely?'

'The actor?'

'Hurrah. Well, Charlie loved his cocktails and in particular his sweet Vermouth. So she made this cocktail with the Vermouth, gin, Fernet Branca and orange juice. When she made it for him, he had a good swig of it and said 'By Jove! That is the real hanky-panky.' And the name stuck.'

'Great story,' he admitted.

'So tonight we will have plenty of them and a few others. Maybe a French 75 as it's important to have at least one champagne-based, don't you think?'

'Oh, absolutely.' He was getting into the swing of all this party-talk.

'The High Commissioner loves his little luxuries, you may have noticed.'

'Like the Rolls-Royce?'

'Exactly.' They both laughed. He rose.

'Well, till tonight then? What time?'

'Seven o'clock. Don't be late' And he gave her a little bow and left.

Chapter Eight

An informative cocktail party

At 6.59 p.m., not daring to be late, Alan presented himself at the embassy's largest room which appeared to double as conference hall, reception venue or indeed anything that required a large space. He had dressed in a tuxedo and wing-tip shirt and prayed that this was the correct dress for the fashionable South African party. Apparently it was. Gloria had looked him up and down and muttered 'delicious' but not so under her breath that he didn't hear, deliberately he suspected.

She was wearing a light green silk dress which shimmered as she moved. The shoulders were padded and the sleeves short.

'You look lovely, so like Jean Harlow,' he had told her. She had smiled at him.

'Now what can I do to help?' He looked around, noting the bar at the far end with two bartenders, one of whom was busy mixing cocktails, and a raised dais to the left on which musicians were unveiling instruments and adjusting seats.

'I assume that you can't mix a French 75?'

'Correct, although I know there is champagne in it somewhere.'

'Come with me,' and she walked him towards the bar.

'Jacob, please show Mr. Drayson how to make the best French 75 in the world.'

'Best 75 coming up, Miss Simpson.'

'So, Mr. Drayson,' began Jacob, a tall black man with a wide mouth and slightly stooped shoulders, 'welcome to the home of the South African cocktail industry centred around the person of the lovely Miss Simpson of Great Britain – our hostess with the mostest.' Both men grinned slightly inanely.

'Now watch carefully. Just the one lesson, and the next time that Miss Simpson's glass is empty, you have to make it by yourself.' Alan was suddenly attentive and focused.

'So, for the French 75 cocktail, Miss Simpson likes us to use the old Moor London Dry Lemon gin. She correctly says that it has a little suspicion of the bite of the lemon, so lacking in the Gordon's Distilled that we use for the simple other gin-based drinks, such as the gin and tonic.' He paused. 'Now, to one and a half ounces of the gin we add half an ounce of fresh lemon juice, made from lemons picked from the embassy's trees this very morning, best picked of course just as the sun rises, to maximise that flavour. My friend Alphonse here does the picking himself' – and Alphonse, also a tall black man, threw a wide grin of acknowledgement at the pair. 'Then a teaspoon of this simple sugar syrup and finally we add it to six ounces of champagne. Everything in my shaker and then I fill the shaker with ice,' and Alan watched in admiration as Jacob shook the drink with such fluid rhythm that it almost looked as though he were dancing.

'We pour it into this beautiful champagne flute, add a little piece of the peel of the afore-mentioned freshly picked lemon and transport it to Miss Simpson's hand.' Alan picked up the drink and carried it carefully to Gloria, who cast him – or perhaps the drink – a look of delight. Somewhat to his surprise, the room had filled up during his cocktail masterclass with Jacob.

'Come and meet the Germans,' she said, slightly ominously, and she threaded her arm through his and eased him across to where three people were standing, looking slightly lost. Their faces lit up when they saw her.

'Ambassador von Bauer and Carl, how lovely of you to come. And this is?' and she paused opposite the third member, a young woman with fair hair, blue eyes, and a smiling face.

'Fraulein Helmholtz is the new cultural attache to our embassy,' the Ambassador explained. 'Fraulein Helmholtz, Miss Simpson, the star of the British embassy.'

'Don't let our High Commissioner hear you say that, Gerhard,' she said, and they laughed, the ice broken.

'Oh and I have shamefully not introduced Alan Drayson from the British civil service in London, just newly arrived here. Ambassador von Bauer, Mr. Carl von Wasserburg.' Alan bowed just an inch or two.

'Welcome Mr. Drayson and what brings you to this beautiful land?' The ambassador had raised his eyebrows just a little.

'My government is keen to explore ways to increase the flow of gold to Great Britain, so I am here to have discussions with the mine owners and other interested parties.'

'And why would His Majesty's government want to do that, especially as Great Britain has allowed its currency to abandon the Gold Standard for the pound?' Carl wondered aloud.

'Indeed, I too wondered that,' said Alan, 'but they told me that that was above my pay-grade and that I was just to get on and do it.' This caused some amusement amongst the Germans.

'Oh our civil service is just like that too,' said the ambassador but Alan noticed that Carl was watching him now with some care. The band had struck up and Gloria took the opportunity to whisk Carl off to the dance floor. Alan wandered desultorily off back to the bar and brought her a personally made '75' when he saw her, much later. By then she was having what was clearly a fairly intense conversation with Carl and he chose not to interrupt them. At that moment, he himself was approached by Judit Helmholtz, who not only seemed to have a determined gleam in her eye but also proved to be a proficient and inexhaustible dance partner. By the end of the party, Alan was delighted to find his bedroom, collapsing into a deep and dreamless sleep.

The next morning he descended somewhat blearily to breakfast. Gloria and a few others were there and they chatted idly about the previous evening's party. They retreated to her office, which was bathed in an early morning glow.

'Well I am sure you want to know what I extracted from the dishy Carl.' He appreciated that she had noticed his previous twitch and had deliberately used the same adjective to stir him. He tried to show nothing.

'In fact I extracted remarkably little. So much so, that I am sure that something is up. He is normally very relaxed with me.' Again that look to provoke. 'But he was quite guarded when we talked. He chose his words with some care. He made his drinks last a loooong time,' she said drawing the word out, 'And he is never like that with me. Finally he kept changing the conversation back to me – and he is not that sort of conversationalist. So my view is that they are definitely up to something, but I learnt nothing specific. The only extra thing is that when I mentioned that I had heard that they had acquired a new chef, he sat up straight, looking rather shocked. I passed it off as girl's gossip and eventually he relaxed. But there is something there.'

Alan thought on this. The question about the reliability of Amit was becoming more complicated, and little closer to resolution. He decided to explore a different aspect.

'Do you know of anyone named Louis du Plessis, a writer and children's doctor here in Cape Town?' he asked her.

'Well I know of him, but we've never met. It's the sort of information that James the Useless might have.' And remarkably, as it transpired, James the Useless failed to live up to his nickname by not only knowing the man, but even having his address. James telephoned and made an appointment for him for later that morning, so Alan walked out into the balmy Cape blueness and strolled gently towards the harbour, deliberately allowing his tail a simple task.

Chapter Nine

An Afrikaaner promises assistance

Alan had spotted the tail with some ease as soon as he left the High Commission on Riebeck Street. He had always been good at that aspect of tradecraft and either the man was careless at his job, or he had wanted Alan to know. The man was a native and relatively tall, always a disadvantage in the game of following. Alan had routinely done the usual sudden lace-tying or window-shopping and the man had been slow at evasion tactics. Alan looked carefully for another tail – the man ahead or back on the opposite side of the street but saw no-one. Being followed in a strange town meant that losing the man would be a little more complicated but not impossible. He studied his map with some care and noted the street configuration. He sauntered slowly along as if on a sight-seeing tour, staring at buildings and shops. At last he arrived at Rose Street which he strolled down. As soon as he turned into Castle Street he ran and turned immediately left into Rose Lane and sprinted along taking the first left into Chiappini Street and quickly entered a wholesalers from where he watched the window and stayed a few minutes browsing, keeping concealed behind a rack of coats, with one eye on the street.

No-one appeared. He emerged cautiously but the street was clear, and he walked casually back in the opposite direction. He turned over thoughts about by whom and why he was being followed. Presumably the Germans were interested in him but if it was not them, he was unsure who it might be. He allowed possibilities to float through his mind but emerged without certainties. The fact of his being followed undoubtedly had raised the stakes. He was a person of interest to someone.

The house was large, even in a street of large houses. The front door was befitting to the house – elegant but unpretentious in its dark hued wood. He was admitted and Louis appeared. The man was tall, gentle and courteous in demeanour with a smiling face, a small beard and a large eager nose. He led Alan onto a wide veranda set out above a garden in full bloom with double borders curving around a wide path, and leading in the distance to a rectangular pool surrounded by statues in an Italianate style.

A servant brought lemonade and Alan noted the strength and colours of the planting of the borders, but with some difficulty as he was unable to recognise many of the flowers. He had already admired the beauty of the Cape in general and the gardens in particular.

'Easy,' was the word that Louis had used. 'The plants here are wondrous easy; the Lord and my servants water them regularly and the sun bakes them,' he had said.

That Alan worked at the British embassy appeared not

to interest the man, but the fact that he was acquainted with Amit sparked an immediate and obvious pleasure.

'Such wisdom and such breadth of knowledge. No sooner were we talking about recipes than we had turned to the romantic poets and somehow immediately off into German philosophy,' Louis had told him. And slowly, slowly Alan had moved the conversation on to the reason for his visit.

'I know nothing of gold or diamonds or stones, but I do know of people who work with them. I am a people person, Alan. May I call you that?' But he did not stop for an answer. 'You must understand that the people of our land are what excites me. All of them – the white and the black and the brown; the Brits, the Afrikaaners, the Zulu, the Hindu. We are a cooking pot and my aim is to make the recipe such that the ingredients complement each other. If we do not work to that aim, I fear the overall taste will not be of delicacy.'

'I am rather new to all of this.'

'Indeed you are but perhaps like Amit you are an observer. He used the recipe for kedgeree to show me an analogy.' Alan grinned in recognition. And indeed a recognisably fishy smell had permeated the veranda. 'While he was here he taught my cook a few of the secrets and by your especially good timing and fortune, you are about to be regaled with the results.' And indeed it was so. A bustle of activity ensured that plates and cutlery arrived and they sat with a vast mound of steam rising above a pile of fish and spices and rice.

After a few mouthfuls Louis observed 'He has done well

the Amit person. By the way, who is he?' Alan looked at him with care, not quite understanding the question being asked. So he went through the details of Amit's upbringing and education and paused.

'Yes, of course I know these things. I suppose that I was asking a deeper question. Maybe, what is he to you and the British?' Alan had of course prepared an answer to this question but somehow sitting in the peace and beauty of this tranquil space, his dissembling reply appeared lacking in elements. He somehow doubted that this thoughtful man would buy into it and he clearly didn't. Louis' eyes moved aside and he laughed.

'Come and see my borders. I am very proud of them. Maybe your English Miss Jekyll would like them?'

'She has just died, I fear.'

'Yes, I read. An enormous loss to the world of gardens. But let us pretend that she stands at our elbows now.' And with that charming thought they wandered through his mass of exotica; the Agapathuses, the Baberton daisies, the Alstroemerias, the Canna Lilies, the Orchids, the Proteas and the roses. And eventually they emerged into the Italianate garden with its rectangular pool, full of carp it transpired. They sat on the bench at the far end.

'My workplace. I come here to contemplate the idiocy of my fellow man amongst other matters,' and he laughed wryly. 'You will discover, Alan, that some of us believe that we are headed for trouble here in the far end of the world. If my fellow Afrikaaners get their way, the races will be totally separated. Madness, madness – and certainly no permanent solution.'

'What is the permanent solution?'

'We need to integrate, not separate. We need to bring the natives up to our level. First education. We must start with education. There are some missionaries running an excellent secondary school in the Transvaal. We must copy them. Next, business. They must be taught to run businesses. And so on and so on.'

'And what of language?'

'Oh that too. We now have a language – Afrikaans – which has suddenly blossomed. It arrived here as the language of 17th century Holland, the language of the rough and simple Boer. Now suddenly here in the 20th century it has taken off, metamorphosed into a first-rate literary language. It has taken into its domain all the best ideas of English, German and Dutch and melded them into a new dynamic literature. Even the poetry has moved smoothly on. Overall, it is now a progressing language, indeed a medium for expressing the processes of thought. It can maintain itself against any European language. One day, Alan, when we know each other better, I will let you have some of my writings in Afrikaans, but for today we will keep to English.' And they both laughed.

'Laughter is so marvellous. I have some friends who do not know how to laugh. And of course there are the joking relationship of the Bantu.' Alan had no idea what Louis was talking about and must have showed it.

'Centuries ago the tribes here used to have constant wars against each other. Then far in the North up near the Zambezi, two of the tribes began the custom of joke-telling. The Ba-Tonga and the Ndebeli apparently began it.

There is some tale that the women got fed up with the continual warring. So – every new moon the tribes would sit in a vast circle and the best in each tribe would tell jokes. And, surprise, surprise, the wars stopped.'

'But the Boers are not known here for their sense of humour, surely?'

'My family are of Huguenot descent – I am not a Boer. They stopped speaking French and assimilated the Afrikaaner – speak.'

'So you spoke Afrikaans at home when you were a child?'

'Oh yes. The family left France long ago as Huguenots, French Protestants, were treated very badly by the Catholics in France in the seventeenth century. My family had settled in Brittany long ago where they farmed. We still kept vestiges of our Breton life, so I was brought up here to Breton tales and stories which have been a blessing to me. My father would sit and tell us all some of the stories. In Brittany during the Black months, there is a tradition of story-telling, probably with their origins from the Druids'

'The Black months?'

'November is the first Black month and December the Very Black month, and of course in France those months are ideal for story-telling when the evenings are long. The family would sit by the fire and tell the tales focused on the menhirs or standing stones in our village of Beg-meil on the western coast, not far from Finistere and the Pointe du Raz, the westernmost tip of France, the French Land's End. The story-telling would start at All Saints Day on November the first, and centre on Toussaint, who becomes a character. The tales are weird and exciting for a child. They tell of ghostly appearances, of mermaids and serpents, of dead children and angels. And of course centre on the ever-present sea. The whole village would sometimes come to our house to listen to my forebear, apparently the finest story-teller in the village. I am translating some of these Breton tales into Afrikaans but of course they will not be the same.'

'Why?'

'The power of the spoken word, I think, Alan. The Druids believed that the spoken word was the breath of life but that writing was a form of death.'

'Anyway let me see what I can do to help you,' Louis continued. 'I have a friend high up in De Beers. He is of Scottish extraction. Perhaps he will help you with whatever it is that you are up to.' Eventually Alan stood and left and the wide gentle front door closed, leaving its occupier thinking deeply. He had of course seen the colours on Alan. He had bathed in the man's green haloes. His feelings had been touched by the purity of the flickers and he had been moved by the auroras. Such auroras, such exquisite pleasure. A man to be trusted – mostly.

Chapter Ten

In which a trap is set

A mit had received a note. He met Alan at a new place – the Waterside café which was as advertised, with a fine view of the harbour. An old-fashioned sailing ship was bustling with activity, seemingly right outside their balcony seats. It had seemed more private to Alan to sit upstairs and the view was certainly designed to relax and assuage any fears or anxieties as they sat in the warmth of the afternoon sun sipping their teas. Alan watched the ship, presumably at one time a slaver, but now sailing the high seas mostly for pleasure, he guessed, although maybe some trading of a different kind was being done as there were stevedores loading heavy-looking boxes into the hold.

His reverie was interrupted by Amit's last sentence.

'So I took the dinner to the Ambassador's bedroom. He was clearly ill, with perspiration on his forehead and a sallow glare to his face. I knew of course that he was unwell, as he had just asked for some toast and scrambled eggs in his room. Normally, being a sociable man and good at conversation, he would dine with at least a couple of members of the embassy staff. The ambassador was sitting up in bed, so I placed the tray as delicately as possible, balanced on his legs, and retreated. When I returned an hour later, the tray was by his bed and he was deeply asleep, snoring loudly. As I was removing the tray as quietly as possible, I noticed a letter on his desk, headed *Top Secret. For Ambassador von Bauer's eyes only*. It was signed by Herr von Wasserburg. I read the document twice, returned to the kitchen with the tray and sat at my desk writing the details of the letter on a sheet of writing paper.' He looked around with care and, noting their privacy, produced a sheet with writing on it from his inside pocket.

'I will tell you the gist of the matter from memory and use the sheet for the details if that is good for you, sahib.'

'You must stop this sahib nonsense, Amit.' He looked embarrassed.

'Thank you, Alan. The habits of childhood in the Raj are not immediately unlearnt in the weary travellers mind.' He had this fine turn of phrase which brought Alan such a sense of well-being.

'So I want to tell you the plan of the Wasserburgian brain. It concerns the purchase of diamonds.' And he paused, looking at Alan meaningfully. Alan's eyes were immediately drawn back to their little table.

'Does it indeed?' Every neurone was alert.

'The plan as set out in the documents was that an approach was to be made to De Beers to procure a steady monthly supply of industrial-grade diamonds. No mention was made of quantities or cost, nor of the overall purpose of the operation. There was an interesting short appendix saying that attention must be paid to the method of getting the diamonds out of the country. In fact it was argued that this was the single most important part of the plan because without a secure method of exporting the diamonds, the plan would collapse and that the Reich would have wasted all the money.'

Alan considered all of this, seeing the activity on the sailing ship in his eyes but losing it in his brain, which was by now fully involved with the news of the diamonds. It occurred to him that he might be being fed information but he could see little advantage to the Germans to give him this secret. He watched Amit's eyes but they seemed as clear and direct as the sun sparkling outside on the waters of the harbour.

'And was there any more in the document?' Alan asked.

'Well there was the name of a potential contact at De Beers. Mr Oppenheimer was mentioned but some doubts expressed because of his known Jewish status. It was doubted that he would have enough loyalty to the Reich despite his German birth. And it was noted that he had a political role within the government and that this too would be a barrier to any approach. There would be a serious risk of Oppenheimer denouncing the scheme publicly, which would be totally unacceptable to the Reich and might have severe long-term international consequences.'

'Yes I can imagine,' murmured Alan.

'But the plan mentioned one Roderick Patterson, Deputy Head of Contracts at De Beers. The document says that this is the man who makes all the decisions about big deals at the firm. Wasserburg knows him and described him in the document as a personal friend, but not necessarily a friend of Germany, so the approach would have to be made with care. Apparently Patterson told Wasserburg over drinks last year that his grandparents had been Scots with no love for the English.'

'Well,' said Alan, 'I'm sure there's no love lost between the Scots and the English, but would a Scotsman really side with the Germans against us?'

'Indeed, Alan,' said Amit pronouncing his name with care, 'That would be a rather important question. It seemed that this Patterson was talking about something called the Highland Clearances, where his great grandparents lost everything that they owned and had to move to Africa. It did not mention why the English were to blame, but apparently Patterson's family had held a grudge against the English ever since.'

Alan thought about this. The whole thing seemed to be a nonsense to him. After all these 'Clearances' were surely conducted by a Scot, the Duke of Sutherland. And were they not more than a hundred years ago? Was it possible to hold grudges for so long? And then he remembered that his own grandparents had held Napoleon responsible for many of the catastrophes that befell England and would never visit France as a consequence. And that of course was long ago too.

But the real question here for Alan seemed to be as to whether or not Amit was a double agent and luring him into a trap? Which in turn led to the question of whether Amit was committed to the English cause? Maybe the Germans knew that Amit was in contact with Alan, and that the document had deliberately been left open in the Ambassador's room for Amit to transmit, and create a subterfuge. Alan decided that this was too complex for him to resolve, but that he must discuss it with Gloria later.

'And you should also know, Alan,' Amit was talking again, 'that Herr von Wasserburg told me this morning that he would not be at dinner for the next few days. He did not mention why.' Alan pondered this extra information. So maybe Carl was going to see his friend at De Beers.

'It would be important for you to find out what von Wasserburg is up to. Presumably he's travelling. If so, we need details of his travel, where he's going, when he's leaving, and whether he's flying, going by car or train.'

'Certainly, Alan. How shall I communicate with you at the Embassy?'

'Yes. We need to stop these open meetings. If they're suspicious of you, they'll follow you and then I would fear for your safety. If you have an urgent communication for me, pay a street boy to deliver the letter. Don't bring it yourself. And for anything else we must devise a safe drop. I will find a place and be in touch. This must be our last meeting for a while, I fear.'

Alan hurried back to the Embassy to find that Gloria was with the High Commissioner. He kicked his heels for half an hour until she had finished when she came up to his office so that they were not interrupted. He told her of his meeting with Amit and the possible departure of von Wasserburg. Gloria was excited.

'So, as Holmes would say "the game's afoot".'

'This is not a game, Gloria. Amit might well be in big

trouble if they discover what he is up to now. After all, the transmission of the contents of one of their documents to me endangers him. It raises the stakes from his point of view too. There must also be a question as to whether they deliberately let him see this document, or possibly whether he is working for them too and they are feeding him this stuff for us.'

They looked at each other.

'How can we sort this out?' he asked.

'Maybe we could feed him something false and watch for them to react. If they do, then we will know and can cut him loose. If they don't, it's good news. So, be prepared to communicate with Amit later today. By then I will have a juicy titbit for you and him. In the meantime, I think that it is time for me to graciously accept the dinner date that Carl has been tempting me with for the last month.' She watched him, and saw the small flicker of his eyes. He left, and returning to his office, considered what information to feed Amit and maybe thus Carl. He carelessly opened the day's mail and the solution to the problem was there, sitting in a letter from Sarah Grandison from London.

Dinner that evening seemed tiresomely long to Alan. The High Commissioner was full of the financial events in the United States and the American government's refusal to stabilise the dollar, a subject that Alan found tedious.

It was not until after the end of the meal that he and Gloria had the chance for a quiet moment. He showed her the letter from Sarah. She loved its contents and agreed that the scandal within it would be ideal to feed to Amit.

'So, as I understand it, the proprietor of the Saturday Review, one Lucy, Lady Houston, has copies of love letters written by the P.M. to Lady Margaret Sackville with intimate details of their relationship. Not only that but they contain proposals of marriage. And for reasons that are not quite clear, S.I.S. is busy trying to prevent this publication, apparently seeing it as a threat to British national security.'

'That seems to be the long and short of it.'

'Bit naughty of Sarah to put it down in a letter to you, wasn't it?'

'Yes, maybe my fault. About three years ago, I shared a similar series of letters with her about another public person that we had to 'retrieve' from its owner in the 'national interest.' It rather cemented my relationship with Sarah.' He suppressed a smile as Gloria frowned briefly, before replying as if unmoved:

'And if this was to be public knowledge, would there be damage to the P.M.?'

'Bound to be. Even in these so-called modern times, an affair, let alone a marriage to a Catholic, would be bad political news.'

'Even though the PM's wife has been dead for a while?'

'Absolutely.'

'So we could feed this to Amit and wait to see whether he tells the Germans?'

'Exactly. It's dangerous political news. We could watch how far it travels, and yet the source is totally deniable. A perfect fishing net for us.' Alan smiled at his own wit.

'I'll be accepting a dinner date for a few days' time and meanwhile you'll tell this all to Amit tomorrow.'

'A great plan. Goodnight Gloria.'

Before he fell asleep, Alan composed a note for Amit which set out the scandal he and Gloria had discussed and the following morning he left the High Commission with the intent of putting their plan into action. First, he would find a safe dead-letter drop box, and then he would give a note of its location for Amit to one of the street boys to deliver.

The following morning, he had just left the front door when he noticed his stalker of the previous week loitering unobtrusively outside the gates. Alan turned on his heel and went back inside to have a moment's thought and then descended to Gloria's office, where he explained the situation.

'You can slip out of the rear entrance,' she pointed out.

'Well, they'll be fools if they've not got that covered too,' he said. She thought again.

'Well by chance the laundryman is here at this moment. His van is parked in the embassy's back courtyard and he's bound to be leaving shortly. How about travelling in the back of his van with the linen?' He laughed, but a few minutes later found himself sitting uncomfortably on a tall pile of soiled shirts. The driver stopped around the corner and he got out and re-traced his steps so that he could observe the rear exit to the embassy. Sure enough there was a nondescript man there, pretending to look in the window of the bookshop opposite. He mulled over whether the Germans had set up these tails. But what could they know? Possibly nothing, but maybe Carl had been made suspicious at the cocktail party. Unless of course there was some other party who might be interested in Alan's movements, but he couldn't think of anyone else who might be a threat.

Alan realised that under no circumstances could he have any physical contact with Amit for a while. He wandered down towards the sea, searching for an ideal site for a 'drop.' He eventually found a place concealed behind a large pipe that had been fixed to the wall of a warehouse, down near the harbour. There would be enough room to conceal a letter or thin package behind it without it being obvious to passers-by. He drew a map of the location and sent it to Amit, suggesting that they both look there regularly, even daily if possible. His letter also pointed out that he himself may be under observation, and that Amit should also watch for tails. In particular Amit needed to be careful not to approach the drop site if being observed.

When next day he wandered down to the drop point he found, to his delight, that there was a note from Amit. It read –

'*C. flies to Kimberley on Imperial Airways tomorrow morning.*' Alan hurried back to the embassy to discuss the matter with Gloria, who arranged for Carl to be tailed from Kimberley airport.

Chapter Eleven

A trip to the mines

The next morning a note arrived from Louis. He had been as good as his word and arranged for Alan to meet a senior member of De Beers at Kimberley two days later. Louis had arranged for him to meet his contact there, Roderick Patterson, and Alan had realised of course that both he and Carl could be due to meet the same man.

Alan sat at the breakfast table looking at Gloria, allowing the aroma of the coffee to surround his thoughts. Today she wore a deep green velvet suit setting off her light brown hair and those blue eyes. He was unable to decide whether green suited her. She had asked him a question, of that he was certain, and as so often in his life he was caught in the self-inflicted trap of his own dreaminess.

'You were not with me, Alan.'

'I can only apologise. I fear that sometimes I drift…' and he could not find the words to finish the sentence.

'Indeed.' She paused and, he shifted uncomfortably in his seat.

'I had asked whether we needed to go to Kimberley by

plane or by car? It's rather a long way, and would take two days by car or alternatively overnight by train.' She crossed her legs and Alan found himself once again distracted. When he looked back up, her face remained impassive.

'You can advise me. For myself, I think that there is a certain amount of urgency,' although in his heart a long car journey with her exploring a new country sounded ideal. 'And money is not a problem, of course.' Before he had left England, Shuttleworth had made it clear that the uncertainty of the German behaviour was causing anxiety of such importance to the Foreign Secretary that Alan would have a wide latitude for expenses. Recently the new Foreign Secretary, Sir John Simon, had attracted serious criticism for failing to condemn the Japanese invasion of Manchuria. Apparently Shuttleworth's boss was concerned lest a failure to keep a close eye on any German plotting might undermine Sir John's political position even further with his colleagues in the National Government.

After discovering that the cost of the flight to Kimberley would be £13 for each of them, they agreed to fly and caught the Imperial Airways flight two days later. The stewardess, a pretty girl with auburn hair, had discovered that they were attached to the High Commission and apparently informed the pilot. She brought a message from the cockpit asking if they would like to 'come up front for a while?' Gloria had declined, pleading terror, an excuse he felt was improbable. The stewardess escorted him to the front and motioned to a seat alongside the pilot, a middle-aged man who it transpired was named Farthing. They chatted with difficulty due to the great noise of the engines while the countryside passed below, but Alan enjoyed the excitement. At one point he pointed down as they crossed a large river.

'The Knuvu,' Farthing had said and Alan saw the great river meandering below. 'About half way there now.'

They arrived at Kimberley and were escorted to their hotel from the airport by a part-time retired English teacher, the embassy's man for the area, who drove them into the centre of town where he had pre-booked hotel rooms. On the way he updated them on German activity. Carl had arrived yesterday and been driven directly to De Beers where he had had a two-hour long meeting. Apparently Carl had then taken the over-night sleeper train back to Cape Town.

The hotel was comfortable and they eat well. She pleaded tiredness after the meal and retired to her room so he wandered into the hotel's ornate bar. To his delight, the pilot Farthing was sitting at a table near the bar. Farthing called him over, bought Alan a double whisky on the rocks, and chatted about the flying.

'I was just doing the first leg this time. It seems to vary according to some mad schedule dreamed up by headquarters. Sometimes I go as far as Livingstone or further and then turn round and sometimes just up here. When the next plane comes through, I will take it back to the Cape as pilot or second pilot, and someone will get out here. It's quite nice in a way. I get a couple of days seeing a new town, and peace and quiet.' It emerged that he had four children, so home life was busy. 'Any hairy moments?' asked Alan, and immediately regretted it. Farthing grinned.

'Had one last month actually. We ran out of fuel just south of Livingstone on the way down. Not quite sure why but we had had strong head winds, and maybe the lazy bastards at Broken Hill hadn't filled us up properly. Anyway we had to make an impromptu landing, so to speak. I spotted a wonderful lawn below and I just managed to stop before we ruined the people's hedge at its far end.' And he stopped for a swig of whisky.

'The people came out of their house and were frankly rather shocked at seeing our enormous plane sitting in their garden. Mercifully I had managed to avoid their rose-beds or they might not have been so charming. Anyway they had a vast mansion of a house and put us all up for the night, while my co-pilot rummaged around and got us more fuel. All of us, passengers and crew, were given a sumptuous evening meal. They were so charming and British about it all, it was almost as if we had been expected! And next morning, I managed to get the bird off the ground with plenty of room to spare. I am not sure what the tires did to their lovely lawn though.' Alan was somewhat staggered at this marvellous story. Farthing was a good raconteur and an experienced pilot, who had flown at the end of the world war before becoming one of Imperial Airways senior pilots. He reminisced about fighting the Germans.

'Bloody good the Germans were. Don't tell too many but I thought they were better than us in the air. Better on tactics you know, old boy. Always managing to get up our backsides when we didn't know they were coming. Got the business of flying out of the sun better than we did, so we didn't see them coming till the last minute. That Rich-thofen and his pack were marvellous pilots. Fought them a couple of times. They were all over us. Of course they are building up an air force again,' he threw out almost as an after-thought.

'Surely that is forbidden after 1918? Wasn't that a spe-cific clause in the Versailles treaty?' Asked Alan

'Of course it is old boy,' Farthing laughed, 'they are not allowed to build an air force. But no-one said that they can't do a spot of gliding.' Alan looked at him in horror.

'So they are doing it all quietly. They have young men being trained as pilots on the gliders. They have these glider clubs innocuously flying all around the countryside. A little harmless weekend fun in gliders. What can be the harm in that? They have a Glider called the Primary SG38. It's very simple, constructed essentially of wood, metal cables and cloth. The pilot sits on a seat at the front com-pletely open to the elements, and the glider is towed up to a thousand feet or so. Then the cable is released and he has to glide around and then make it back to base. It's a bit hairy but most of them get back alright. We have the same gliders back in Blighty and I went up in one last year at Marston airport – scared the hell out of me.' He smiled, amused at his little memory. 'No, it really did. I went into a bank of cloud at one point and if you have no power and can't see a thing, you need to keep your nerve. Fortunately I came out, could see the runway below me and got down O.K.'

'And they are building aeroplanes in secret factories. An old mate of mine showed me one last year in a forest near

Frankfurt.' Alan was again horrified but tried not to show it this time. He realised that an intelligence seam was opening up in front of him, and could not help wondering why his Department had heard none of this.

'Of course it's all pretty hush-hush,' Farthing continued. 'My friend only showed me because he didn't approve of the Nazis. He told me not to trust any of them, and especially not their chap called Goering, who's apparently in charge of this new non-air force. But of course they don't call him Air Marshall or anything like that.'

'Anyway that's how they are training the future of the German Air Force. Mark my words they will suddenly produce a fully-fledged air force to fight the world when we least expect it.' They had another couple of drinks, the conversation veered onto South African politics and they eventually said good night. Alan returned to his room and made some notes before sinking into a deep sleep. His next transmission to London was going to be long and the content unexpected.

Alan and Gloria's appointment t De Beers was for eleven o'clock and they spent part of the morning walking around the old town, discussing tactics for the meeting.

'The most trying moment will come when he tells us that he has just been visited by the German embassy in the form of Carl, attempting to buy all his diamonds.'

'Well, our advantage is that we are not attempting to buy all of his diamonds, or indeed any of them come to think of it. What we will need is information about where they are going when they leave his headquarters. And of course the dates that they are leaving.'

'And will he tell us?'

'And 'will he tell us without telling the Germans?' is the important question.'

'So what are we to appeal to? His patriotism, his dislike of Germany, his avarice, his desire for a beautiful woman? All of these?' he looked laughingly at Gloria. She pretended to look shocked.

'Well the last is out, unless he is very rich and handsome.' She smiled at him. 'Personally I would think that a mixture of numbers one and two. The trouble is that Carl can be quite charming if he wants. It also must depend a bit on how much in the way of diamonds that Carl told them they wanted.'

They arrived at the Headquarters of De Beers on Stockdale Street by taxi. Gloria wore blue, a colour that suited her better, Alan decided.

They were expected and led to Mr. Patterson's office on the first floor. He was a slight, tall, athletic-looking man with a full head of sand-coloured hair above light blue eyes. They started unsurprisingly with their mutual acquaintance.

'He is a fine man, the Louis.' He began, just the faintest hint of a Scots brogue upon his speech. 'A fine Libertarian with so many skills. Somewhat unusual in your average Afrikaaner in my experience.' Gloria agreed with him while Alan kept quiet in view of his limited experience of the local people. The tea was brought and the conversation drifted around to the economy and how the country was only now just emerging from the knock-on effects of the American Depression, and Britain's departure from the

Gold Standard.

'Of course we produce a bit of gold ourselves. Rather upsetting for the company,' was Roderick's comment. Alan felt that as understatements went, that was rather a good one, and his admiration for the man improved somewhat.

'So, you have presumably come all the way from Cape Town to talk about something somewhat more specific?' And the question was asked in such a kindly avuncular manner that Alan was disarmed for a moment. They had agreed both on the general strategy for the conversation and on some details, but had accepted that it would be hard to know exactly how the discussions would go. There would need to be some 'ad libbing' as Alan had put it.

'Indeed and we need to speak to you on a matter of some confidence.' Alan began. Roderick Patterson managed the tremendous feat of appearing neither to move nor to breathe. Alan decided that the only way was to plough on.

'We wanted to talk to you about diamonds.' And a pause. The diamond man inclined his head just a degree – and appeared to inhale the air around him in a slow languorous breath.

'In fact we wanted to talk to you about someone else's conversation with you about diamonds.'

'Ah, yes. It had occurred to me that that might have been the subject for our chat. It is not often that we get one representative of his country visiting our headquarters. But to be followed the next day by two more is truly remarkable. But please continue. This is most interesting.' He was all charm and attentiveness, and Alan could feel Gloria enjoying the conversation. So Roderick had it all worked out then, and presumably had a response worked out too. Just a gentle lead would be all that was necessary…

'So we hoped to discuss a way forward that might benefit all parties.'

'That would of course be a fine conclusion. When I was considering the matter, I was not quite certain that a resolution of that type would be possible. So of course I would be most interested to hear your view on how we could…' and he paused to consider his words. 'Let's say square the circle.' Another pause. 'Or even better, square the triangle.' And he grinned at his own joke. It served the purpose though and both Gloria and Alan relaxed a little. Alan grinned.

'A mathematician?' Alan asked and Roderick laughed.

'Indeed I did maths at Cape Town, just at the time when the university moved to the campus at Groote Schuur on the slopes of Devil's Peak. What a marvellous site, and my teachers were excellent. But maths doesn't make too much money and I was married with three children by then. I got a job offer from the great man himself after my graduation. There were only two of us with Firsts and he employed us both. So yes, maths was and still is my hobby, but diamonds puts the bread on my family table.' Rather a sweet disarming speech.

'And was the great man Ernest Oppenheimer?' she asked.

'Oh yes. It was graduation day at the university, and he just strode up to me, asked me my name and offered me a job. I could hardly speak. I knew who he was of course. Eventually I told him, "But I don't know much about diamonds, sir. Except the mathematics of carbon molecules." Oppenheimer had laughed and told me that that would be a fat lot of use, but that he would train me in all the important things to do with diamonds. And of course he and the others have taught me everything,' Roderick concluded.

The noises from the street wafted into the office and Alan was reminded of S.I.S. headquarters in Piccadilly, but somehow the warmth and soft smell of the Jacaranda climbing over the walls and around the windows made for a gentler atmosphere.

'But sometimes a mathematician is not as adroit at the politics as a pure-bred businessman.' And Roderick looked at them with care,

'Perhaps it would be for the best if you told me exactly what you seek – and of course exactly what it has to do with my visitor of yesterday.' The time for frank discussion and openness had clearly arrived.

'His Majesty's Government,' Alan began. How else to start. If the cards were to be on the table, they would need to be clearly visible. 'His Majesty's Government wish firstly that everything we should talk to you about would be a matter of the strictest confidence, as we may be talking to you of matters that relate to the security of Great Britain.'

'I understand, and unless there is to be a discussion of matters contrary to the laws of this Dominion, I would agree to your request for absolute confidence.'

'Thank you. We have a concern that a foreign power may be making or about to make a bid for large quantities of industrial diamonds to use in the manufacture of weaponry.' Alan paused as he and Gloria had agreed they would, to gauge his reaction. It was clear that nothing Alan had said had come as a shock to Roderick Patterson so Alan continued,

'We have no intention of asking you to break any contract that you may or may not have with anyone. Nor do we intend to interfere in any way with the working or remuneration of your business. All we will require is information.'

'And why should De Beers give you information, Alan?'

They had reached, rather earlier than expected, the vital point. Gloria shifted in her chair. Roderick Patterson had a smile playing on his lips. He was enjoying this game of cat and mouse.

'His Majesty's Government would greatly value the assistance of your great company in our work to ensure peace between nations. Should you help us in this worthy endeavour, the government of our country would naturally wish to favour your company in any way possible, and Miss Simpson and I would be happy to put your company's requirements to them.' There, it was on the table. Roderick smiled and said,

'It seems likely that I will need advice from my betters on this matter. In order for me to ensure that they are properly informed, perhaps you could tell me of the specific information that you would require from us.' He started to pick up a pen, but then returned it gently to the desk.

'We would like information regarding shipments of diamonds for the German embassy leaving the company offices. We would like to know quantities and types of diamonds, details of their destination and date and time of departure – in advance where possible.' The plot was no longer a secret and a sense of relief filled Alan. It was as if the uncovering had liberated the genie from the lamp into the room.

'Thank you for your honesty. You will understand that this decision will need to be taken elsewhere.' So tactful, that 'elsewhere'. Protecting anyone and everyone. 'I would hope to have some sort of response for you by the end of the day. Perhaps you would care to return at five p.m?'

'It will be our pleasure,' and that appeared to be that for the moment. Alan and Gloria walked out into the warm mildly cloudy day. The Spring rains were slowly ending but a dark shadow in the distant horizon of the Northern sky looked threatening. They decided to walk back through town to the hotel the better to discuss the meeting in some privacy. Gloria began.

'Nice man?'

'Oh yes. Not at all the dour Scot that I was expecting.'

'He played with us for a while. Nothing we said or did was a surprise. Perhaps your friend Louis told him.'

'My so-called friend Louis had no idea what we were up to, I hope. If he did, he didn't hear it from me. But it was odd, while I was with Louis, I had the feeling that he knew everything as well. Like they were both playing us as the trout for dinner on the line.'

'No idea that you were a fisherman,' she commented, rather tartly.

'Not too many fishing opportunities in Green Park.' He

responded in type. 'The authorities don't approve. Unless of course you stand on one leg for hours without furling your feathers, or flap languorously around opening your vast beak.' She smiled at him a touch affectionately, and slipped her arm through his. When they arrived back at their hotel, the cloud had raced in and large tropical raindrops spattered the hotel steps.

'Lunch, I think,' she pronounced. 'And then Mr. Alan Drayson, I shall expect you to entertain me until we meet those De Beers people to hear our sentences.'

Chapter Twelve

Help arrives

A fterwards, Gloria had seemed content enough with her entertainment. They walked back towards the de Beers offices, the ground spattered with the marks of the heavy shower. Somehow her arm in his seemed quite natural. They arrived early but were shown straight up to the office, where another person was seated with the Scottish Roderick. They were motioned to their seats but not introduced. The stranger was a large man in a dark double-breasted suit with black hair slicked back and worn low on his neck. When he spoke he had a slight North American accent. He stood and the conversation was brief.

'De Beers agrees to your request. We shall not be entering into any formal dialogue with you. If we are asked about you and your request, the company will deny that any contact has been made by yourselves. We shall certainly deny that any information has been passed from the company to yourselves or anyone that you may represent. Please now leave this office and do not return.' Roderick Patterson stood in silence and opened the door. They left in a state of some shock. Alan noted that Gloria's face had paled, and she leant on him more than affectionately as they descended the stairs. No-one exchanged eye contact with them as they left. They were as close to non-persons as possible. They hailed a taxi and did not speak until after their return to the hotel.

In the room she had sat, shaking after the experience. Alan felt a similar surge of feeling.

'Once in Morocco I had been shopping in the Kasbah. We had been there whilst I set up a new network for the embassy to report directly to me. There had been a number of episodes of unpleasantness as some of the locals had felt that I was treading on their territory. I was surrounded by three large men clearly all armed with long curved knives. I was hustled into a side-alley where I had a short lecture on the timing of my departure and the consequences of my failure to stick to their time-table. The man who delivered it had been of a similar threatening type of personality; unsmiling, large, and a man of few sentences but full of menace.' Alan's eyes darkened with fear at the memory.

'For me,' said Gloria,' there was that threat of violence behind the words and between the sentences. He was a hatchet-man delivering a statement almost without even a hint of relationship. Simply a command, an order from on high. In a previous posting, I had had a similar moment of near-violence when I was trapped in a car at the border of Russia near the Black Sea. I had thought that I was about to be beaten by the border guards as there appeared to be an error on my visa,' and she shivered. He put his arm around her and she nestled into him. They stayed still and very close for a moment, until her breathing began to slow. She had been very pale but gradually the colour returned to her cheeks.

'Thank you.' As she looked into his eyes, Alan leant gently forward and kissed her, before pulling away swiftly.

'Cocktail?' he asked.

'Oh yes,' Gloria smiled. They wandered downstairs to the hotel bar, a comfortable spot, with gentle jazz from the radio, the setting sun diffusing gold through the windows, and a soft buzz of healing conversation floating around the room. The decor was pastel-themed, blends of greys and greens and pinks. She sat at a table in the corner and watched him talking to the barman. She thought of his empathy, his kindness and the sharing of their fear of the hard men of the diamond trade. She watched his back at the bar as he appeared to be having a laughing conversation with the barman who was fetching various bottles, including champagne. The cork flew up to the ceiling landing harmlessly back behind the bar. She could not quite work out what was happening but it appeared to be causing the two men mirth. At one point they had both looked over at her. He returned carrying two...

'... French 75s made 'specially for you by George and me.'

'The men had been relating over alcohol', she realised, and she beamed her pleasure at him. Maybe this charming handsome man really did care about her, and she realised that she too was starting to care about him, and she understood that maybe it was rather more than she had admitted to herself.

'I have met a number of scary individuals in my shortish life, but he ranks up there with the best of them,' she opined.

'Indeed,' he agreed.

'But it looks as if we won.' Her eyes sought his.

A uniformed hotel messenger boy came to their table and addressed Alan.

'There is a man who wants to speak to you.'

'Where is he, this man?'

'Outside the hotel, boss.'

'Back in a moment.' He told Gloria, but it was a quarter of an hour before he returned.

He had followed the boy out through the hotel doors. There was indeed a man standing on the other side of the street with his hat pulled well down over his head so that Alan was unable to tell who it was. But the man's posture looked familiar. He crossed the street and the stranger turned out to be Roderick Patterson, who had immediately apologised for the abruptness of the meeting. He told Alan that he had been given a hard time by his bosses about even allowing them back onto the premises. Roderick had been told not to let us speak during the meeting and had been as shocked as we had been by the brevity and abruptness of his companion.

Apparently the decision to agree to our request had been taken at 'The Highest Level' of the company. By chance the day before, 'The Highest Level' had received a letter from his niece in Germany. Apparently the teacher of his niece's daughter had been sacked and replaced with a new person who had been making comments about 'rich Jews.' A few weeks after the start of this new teacher, the niece had won the form prize for the best overall class marks, at the end of the Spring Term. The prize had been a new Kodak camera. The girl was so excited. Her teacher had stood up and told the class that the girl could not receive the prize because she was Jewish, and the camera had been given to the girl who had come second in the exams. His niece had come home in tears, and her mother had written to 'The Highest Level' telling him of the girl's humiliation and distress and saying that they would be leaving Germany as soon as possible and 'could they come to South Africa?'

'Apparently T.H.L. had been apoplectic and said that 'he would do his utmost to stop these evil men who stoop so low as to humiliate children.' And then next moment we had arrived with our request. Young Roderick felt that our timing had been impeccable. He left, saying that he would be in touch as soon as he had concrete news and that any messages would be from a Mr. James.'

They had sat in the comfortable armchairs drinking their cocktails and mulling over the meeting. The sun had set in a sudden African burst of excited colours and the dark had reached its fingers over the windows. They returned to their room and he got up to draw the curtains.

'I need to be held,' she had told him and had slipped off her shoes.

Next morning early they had taken the recently upgraded Blue Train south. The journey had been exhilarating. They had of course 'slummed it' in First Class and had been waited on hand and foot. The scenery was marvellously varied; bleak and arid in the middle but gloriously verdant at times. Antelopes, buck and deer everywhere. And a few larger animals; three elephants at a waterhole, and later a family of lions with the very young animals playing quite close to the track and seemingly oblivious of the noisy engine, the smoke and the steam.

Lunch had been an exercise in indulgence. He had had the Tomato soup followed by Ribs of Lamb and Peach Melba. For Madame, the Groentesoup, fillet of Sole and Apple Flan meringues. All washed down with fresh Cape wines. A few clouds blew up later in the afternoon but it was mostly a crisp Spring Southern Hemisphere day. Sometimes he would look out of the window and see her watching him, her face reflected in the glass of the window. They had talked of their lives; hers a life of privilege where doors had mostly opened with ease; her nice girls' boarding school in the Wiltshire countryside; her friends, her love of art and her ability to draw. When still at school she had started to paint portraits, mostly the children of her parents' friends. Then off to Cambridge as she had been 'brainy.' She had been a Girton girl, ostensibly reading History, but with her heart in art and the world of art history. How she had sat in on art history lectures and spent her vacations touring the Tate Museum, the National Gallery and best of all the Wallace Collection. She had loved the Wallace. 'All those beautiful miniatures and the Van Dykes, Alan, the Van Dykes,' she had told him.

But her favourite picture of all time was the Swing by Fragonard, she had explained.

'Do you know Fragonard?' she had asked him. He had had to deny the pleasure. 'When we return to London, we

127

will go together to Manchester Square and I will entertain you with the delights of Fragonard. And of course upstairs the painting of Francesca da Rimini and her lover by Scheffer. So beautiful, so beautiful. Even more erotic than the Fragonard,' she had told him, watching his eyes with great attention, those eyes stopping him from looking away in embarrassment, daring him to keep contacted.

He had understood that this fluttering, chattering woman was full of danger but, too late, he was beginning to realise that he was enchanted, trapped in that danger.

And in the summer before her last year her father had sent her with a girl-friend on a tour of Europe and its art. 'Like Byron and Shelley on the Grand tour, Alan, you know.' Alan had no idea what she was talking about, but chose not to inform her. She had loved Paris but hated the Louvre, she had told him; 'having to wade through oodles of tedious French paintings before you came across one decent Italian,' were her words.

One day arriving at her tutor's room on a cold January day in her final year, she discovered that they were not to be alone for this tutorial. Another middle-aged man had been sitting in her tutor's comfortable leather chair warming his hands on the fire in the hearth, while her tutor sat at the chair at his desk. Her tutor had introduced them and the man had turned out to work for S.I.S. and to be rather cheery. After an hour of chat, he had offered her a job to start in the summer, and she, delighted to be having a job back in London where she could be with her family, had accepted on the spot. Her first year at H.Q. had passed quickly – 'So much to learn, Alan' – and finally last year she had been posted to what she assumed would be a cosy backwater.

'And it was, until you arrived, Alan.' She had smiled at him and had looked out of the window. They passed through a small town with a one-platform station without stopping. The sun was falling and they would be back in Cape Town at 8p.m. He wondered what the future held for him and whether it included her.

Chapter Thirteen

Alan takes some steps on high

On his return to the Embassy there was a note from Morris Shuttleworth in London telling Alan to get in touch. Gloria had set up the radio transmitter and the three of them discussed the current developments with Alan explaining everything except a few of the more intimate bits of his developing relationship with Gloria. He received permission to stay in the Cape for a while longer, along with a welcome 'congratulations' for the tip-offs concerning the training of German pilots. The Foreign Secretary had been 'extremely concerned.'

When the transmission had finished, Alan and Gloria agreed that there was little to do now but wait. In the meantime Alan felt that it was time to make more contact with Amit and to try to establish with more certainty how much they would be able to rely upon him in the future. Having left a note in the drop slot behind the pipe, Alan met Amit upstairs at the Waterside Café. The chef was looking morose. His curry last night had not been well received. 'Too many vegetables and not enough meat' had been the verdict.

'You see, Alan, these gentlemen are raised on things that roam the fields, like pork and game whereas our cuisine relies more on things that grow in the ground.'

'So tell me is Carl back from his travels yet?' Amit nodded.

'He came back yesterday and seemed mighty pleased with himself. In between criticising my not-meaty-enough curry, he and the ambassador were discussing something important over dinner but they were unusually quiet around us when we served them, so I only heard a few snippets of their conversation. They mentioned something about how they were going to *do the exporting.* '

Alan felt his heartbeat quicken. Was this about to be another breakthrough? Was Amit about to prove himself a worthwhile risk?

'Any details?' Alan tried to contain the eagerness in his voice but Amit shook his head.

'Nothing, Alan. As I said, as soon as I entered, there was mostly silence. Except for words of unkindness concerning my curry.' For a ghastly moment, Alan felt a rush of panic, not for lack of intelligence from Amit but of fear that the man was going to cry, and he had not a clue what he would do if that were the case. Mercifully no emotional barriers were breached overtly although Amit's sensitivities had clearly been sorely tried. 'You see, Alan I could have put up with a discussion about the balance of spices, but the crudity of simply wanting more meat, was more than my culinary heart could stand. As Conrad would have said *The horror, the horror.* '

Alan frowned.

'Steady on, old boy. Conrad used those words to discuss the predicament of Kurtz up a river with natives in the centre of this apparently benighted continent. It hardly compares with the lack of meaty stuff in your food.' At that, Amit laughed, seemingly back to himself again.

'Alan, you are right. I'm becoming immersed in the soup of my own ego. But how remarkable is it that I should discuss Mr. Conrad's book with you as well as with the German Ambassador?'

''Remarkable' may or may not be the word to use. That would depend on whether you or the Ambassador raised the subject?'

Amit waved his hand casually at Alan, who found himself comforted by the action. Slowly, Amit was starting to become more at ease, and his increasingly relaxed nature with Alan reassured him that Amit's information may be reliable after all. But still, Alan needed to gauge Amit's true feelings towards the British. Discussing academia one-on-one was not a sure-fire way of establishing any sort of true loyalty, especially not if he'd done it with both Alan and the German Ambassador.

'I don't remember,' he replied and then paused, 'actually, no, that isn't true. The Ambassador raised the subject. He wanted to know whether I was Kurtz or Marlowe. That is, whether I approved of applying our European definition of civilisation to the subjection of the natives.' Alan looked at him, his head tilted slightly to one side in curiosity. They were heading in the right direction now.

'And do you, my philosophically-steeped chef, do you?'

'It's not a new thought, Alan. After all, the Romans knew that they were bringing *civilisation* to barbaric peoples when they conquered them. And how about those Spanish conquistadores, the men of extreme violence, the men led by Cortes and later by Pizarro. The men who butchered and pillaged in the name of Jesus and the civilisation of Seville. What did Montezuma feel of the *civilisation* brought to his Inca peoples when he was garrotted in his prison cell?'

This was more like it. They were getting closer and closer to the trap that Alan hoped was emerging from the mists.

'Equating the excesses of a few should not be allowed to mar a discussion of a principle, Amit. The Spanish court was horrified by the violence, although I agree that their dismay did not stretch to returning the looted gold and silver treasures.' Now there was a heat behind Amit's eyes that had so far remained hidden during their previous conversations.

'Point taken, Alan. But even in my country, you British used the same excuse of the civilising influences of Christianity for looting precious stones from the rulers of the states of India.'

And there they were. Alan examined Amit carefully; how he furrowed his eyebrows as he spoke and how his voice dropped slightly when he said 'you British', but also how he didn't automatically associate himself with the wronged rulers of the states of India.

'I remain unconvinced,' Alan replied, 'once more that the actions of the few – in this case the managers of the East India Company – should outweigh the action of

133

thousands of well-meaning missionaries and other administrators who brought the advantages of the law, of medicine and of good governance generally to the continent.' Alan hoped the words sounded convincing enough to coax out anything Amit might be holding back.

'And I agree totally, Alan. The old India of revenge, superstition, crime and of course caste, held us back. And for me personally, the advent of the British civilisation was of great benefit. I have studied in Germany. My father and family are treated with the utmost respect.' Amit hesitated, 'but....'

'But...' Alan encouraged, and Amit sighed.

'But as a human being, I believe the concept of civilisation is a philosophy that damages the human soul. If we are trying to be closer to whatever God we believe in, then interfering with the lives of others by harsh actions must be destructive. Only by living the pure life of God and by trying to be as close to a perfect person as we can, can we show by our actions the way forward to our fellow man. Your Thomas à Kempis would have us live the best life possible in truth by imitating the life of Christ, would he not?'

'He would. A hard man was our Thomas. His demand for our perfection ensures that we fail a great deal.'

There was a long silence after that. As usual Alan watched the activity in the harbour but could not help glancing at Amit from time to time, who was examining his teacake with great interest. Eventually he picked it up with extraordinary care and slowly inserted into his mouth, which widened remarkably such that he could take in the whole cake in one mouthful. Alan was reminded of a cobra, gradually dislocating its jaw to ingest a vast object of food. Once the teacake had disappeared, Amit returned to sipping the cup of hot tea with equal care, clasping it tenderly in both hands as the steam rose wispily up into his face. Alan had had enough philosophy for one day.

'Amit, my friend, we need to return to the world of men and their deeds. Your task at the moment is to keep as close an eye on Carl and the Ambassador as you can within the embassy. We will watch him outside. If he's going to make any journeys outside the Cape, give us as much notice as possible. Also, any cables from Germany are important.'

Amit looked up from his teacup, almost wearily, and Alan felt a shift in their relationship. Philosophy was taxing, especially when the lines between friendship and colleague, enemy and ally, and the truth and the lie, were blurred.

'And what am I looking for?'

'Diamonds, Amit, diamonds. We need to know about the diamonds.' They finished their tea and Alan remembered the main reason he had come to see Amit today. Before they departed, Alan laughingly told Amit the story of the P.M. and his 'affair', feeling slightly guilty as he watched Amit consider this tale.

'And this would damage the Prime Minister? But surely, he is not married. In my country this would be nothing.'

Alan kept a smile plastered on his face and jokingly replied,

'Ah this is England, Amit. We are a race of hypocrites. And of course we still seem to hold on to the fear of those Catholics.' They both laughed.

'Is it not time, Alan, that the British Protestants forgot Mary, Queen of Scots?' They laughed again and parted ways, but when Alan returned to the High Commission, he slumped himself into a chair in Gloria's office.

'He cannot be deceiving us. He quotes Thomas à Kempis.' He told her. But Alan told himself that he wanted to be right about Amit for the sake of the mission and for him, lying to a man who could discuss literature and history so intelligently didn't sit well. He pushed the feeling aside. It was just a job. But then what did that justification mean for his and Gloria's relationship? Was it all a matter of being caught up in the job? As Alan mulled over everything that had happened so far in the Cape, he realised that Gloria was looking at him as if he has emerged from a distant planet.

'Just explain to me, Mr. Drayson, how it can be that you stride into my office, sink into my favourite chair without even a merry 'Good afternoon' to lighten the drudgery of my current task, and come up with the non-sequitur to end non-sequiturs about Thomas à Kempis? And it being nearly cocktail hour, you have also totally failed in your appointed manly task of asking me if I would like to adjourn to Charlie's bar by the waterfront.'

The shortness of her tone made Alan sit upright and cast aside his thoughts of the probity of one, or for that matter, any Asian chefs. Alan looked more attentively at Gloria, whose sharp tone was softened by the small smile playing on her lips.

'I say, Gloria, you seem pretty dressed-up.' She was of course pleased that he had noticed.

'Since we've been back from Kimberley for a few days, you've not offered to take me out at all, Alan, so I was hinting in the least subtle way, short of asking you. And now that you have emerged from your moderately self-absorbed cocoon, I would be delighted to accompany you to Charlie's bar which, since it is nearly 6p.m., is just opening. Shall we?' and she stands up.

'And when we have a nice cocktail in front of each of us, you can explain why a man who reads An Imitation of Christ cannot possibly be a double spy. Is that a bargain?' she asked laughing at him and offered him her arm.

'A first-rate bargain.' He agreed – and they strolled out of the looming embassy building into the busy street, filled with chatter and noisy vehicles.

Alan saw him immediately, the tall one.

After turning downhill towards the water, Gloria leaned close to Alan and spoke quietly,

'Did you notice our tail, Alan?'

'I did. What shall we do about him?'

'Three options – burn him, bruise him or leave him.'

Alan almost came to a halt and turned towards Gloria, who was looking ahead, smirking.

'What?' he said.

'Alan, surely you remember the lecture by Peter Fawcett entitled *How to shake a tail feather*, where that funny man with the red face taught us about what to do if we were followed. We burn him; that is, we get rid of him; we bruise him; that is we accost him and find out what he is doing and who he works for; and finally we let him follow us.'

'Which would you prefer?'

'Well you were followed before. Frankly I think that we need to know who he is working for.' Alan nodded.

'Agreed. He's almost certainly following me so I'll stroll on. You disappear into a store and I'll walk slowly so that you can come up behind him. Then we can walk him into a side street for a little chat. Maybe that one?'

'Yes.'

'Are you carrying?'

'Certainly. In my handbag. Just a pretty little lady's Colt. But it should scare him enough.' They parted in the classic manoeuvre. Col. Fawcett would have been proud of them. Gloria walked suddenly into a lady's clothing store, knowing that the tall man could not follow her, and ducked down behind a rack of dresses, keeping her eyes fixed on the shop window. Sure enough he stopped, looking uncertain, and then walked on, seemingly intent on Alan. He walked on, and she was immediately out of the store and closing in on him rapidly. Alan stopped suddenly, turned and came up to him with impeccable timing such that they arrived at him at the same moment.

'Stand quite still.' Alan said, watching the man's hands. Gloria let him see the pistol, shielding it from others behind her bag.

'Very slowly put your hands where I can see them, in front of you.' The man, looking petrified as he watched the gun in her hand, did as requested.

'Now walk forward and turn left at the next side-street. Hands at all times away from your sides' He did as requested. They walked forward.

138

'Here. Turn here.' It was a small alley, with only the occasional person walking past.

'Stop, right here.' Alan chose a doorway set back from the alley. There was no sign of life behind the door.

'Now we need to have a discussion.' Alan slipped a knuckle-duster onto the fingers of his right hand, showing the man what he was doing. 'If I don't like any of your answers, I'll hit you. Do you understand?' The man nodded.

'What is your name?'

'Bounteous Siliwele.'

'Who told you to follow me?'

'My boss.'

'Who is your boss?'

The man paused and Alan held up the knuckle duster, letting the sun glint off of the metal.

'Cornelius van der Linde.' Alan and Gloria looked at each other. Gloria shrugged.

'Who is this Cornelius?'

'He runs the company. It's called Cape Containment.'
Alan frowned.

'And what does this company do exactly?'

The man shook his head.

'I don't know, bwana. We mostly follow people and tell him where they go and what they do.'

'We? How many are there of you?'

'We are many.'

Gloria peered down the alley, checking for any lingering shadows that might be watching, or waiting, but there were none, and Alan continued.

'Where would I find this Cornelius?'

The man hesitated, glancing at Alan and Gloria, and then at the knuckle duster glinting in the slither of sun cast into the doorway.

'I report to him in an office upstairs in 16, Longmarket Street. Please don't tell him that you have learned this from me. He is a dangerous man. He would send someone to kill me and my wife.'

Alan looked again at Gloria. She looked away.

'Get out of here.' The man ran. They returned to the main street, chose a small café and sat at the table. He ordered two cups of tea and they slowly regained their momentum.

'Well, that was rather exciting,' Gloria said.

'Indeed. We need to talk through what we are going to do about this.'

'Well, one option would be to do nothing. And maybe let ourselves be followed. They are really not very good at it, and it seems that we can give them the slip if we need.' A wisp of cigarette smoke curled over them from a nearby table and Alan found himself once again staring out of a window in the Cape, this time at the passing pedestrian traffic.

'True, but surely we must know who is so interested in our movements. Or maybe it's just in *my* movements.'

Gloria nodded, taking a sip of her tea.

'Yes, I agree that, without knowing who is following us, we won't be able to deal with it.'

'So, are we going to pay a visit to Cornelius van der Linde?'

'Maybe not to talk to him directly. But it would do no harm to have a look at these offices of his. He'll probably have a file marked 'Drayson' or 'British embassy' or something. If we could gain access....'

'You mean *break in*,' she interpreted. He laughed but Gloria had noticed the slightly nervous undertone.

'Alan, we need to have a short discussion here, centred on things like Wisdom, Risk, Careers, the discomfort of life in prison and other minor matters.' He looked directly at her eyes and saw that behind her playful tone, there was a serious discussion to be had.

'The risk to our careers could be huge,' she reminded him.

'My boss warned me before coming down here that he might not be able to protect me if I got into trouble. His exact words were – 'Try not to get caught doing anything too bad. I couldn't promise to rescue you in a crisis.' '

'Exactly my point.'

'But,' Alan continued, 'if we take no risks in our lives, we miss the opportunities that may present themselves.' They were both silent as they finished their tea, and Alan was reminded that it was only a short while ago that he and Amit found themselves in a similar silence – heavy and stifling, with big questions looming in the air. When they had finished the tea, she took a deep breath, gave him her broadest smile, and said

'Why don't we take a stroll?' They left the café and walked the short distance to Longmarket Street. Longmarket was indeed a long nondescript street with terraced undistinguished houses, most of which had shops on the ground floor. They strolled slowly but nonchalantly towards Number 16. There was a shoe shop on the ground floor with a door on its left. The sign above the door stated 'Cape Containment' in large gold capitals with no other information below. The windows on the upper floors were barred and there were no signs of life. A bare light bulb could be seen hanging in one window, rather paradoxically turned on despite the brightness of the day. They continued to walk past without stopping and paused when they got to the end of the street.

'Did you see the bars on the windows,' he asked.

'Yes, no easy way in there. We need to inspect the rear.' There was a narrow alley leading towards the back of the houses and they walked down it. The alley way had rubbish dumped in it but they managed to walk along until they were opposite the rear of the house. They knew that they were there as it was the only house whose windows were also barred on all the floors. There was a small yard full of boxes and general junk, and two steps led up to a heavily secured back door.

'So, the only way in would be through the front door. Not easy on a busy public street, unless one had a key. No question of breaking and entering,' he muttered.

'Or the skylight.' He looked up and found himself glad that they were doing this together, despite the risks.

'And they all have skylights,' she said, pointing to the other roofs. And it was so. As they looked up at them, Alan noticed that the skylight of Number 16 was ajar. Gloria had obviously seen this too and continued, 'so one could climb out of one, across the roof and into Number 16.'

'One might, one might,' he gently mocked her use of the impersonal pronoun. She blushed, rolling her eyes, and they both continued to stare at the roofs. The roofs looked steep to him. Some of the houses had metal fire escapes at the back, most of them very rusted-looking and a few had missing steps. Number 14, one house down had a fire escape from the ground up to a door on the top floor, but with no obvious missing steps. He felt that it would not be too difficult an entry. The problem might be the access from inside the door to the skylight. There would be no knowing. Of course at the end, there would be no reason why he could not simply walk out of the front door when he was finished inspecting the files.

They walked back into the street and returned to the Embassy. After dinner, he donned a dark sweater, trousers, some tennis shoes and a hat to provide some anonymity and took a torch and a jemmy with him. They returned to the alley. There were no lights in Number 16 but there was a light in a first-floor window in Number 12. The skylight of Number 14 was still ajar.

'Good luck,' she whispered. 'I'll stay here but then go around to the front, after I see that you gain access to Number 16,' and she kissed his cheek. 'Oh and when you are in the office, if you see a list of employees, and hopefully their addresses, please could you copy it or take it.'

He went silently into the back yard of Number 14 and started his climb. His foot slipped noisily on a rung of the fire escape when he was at the level of the second floor. He froze as a figure appeared at the first-floor window. The figure tried to lift the sash window but was apparently unable to move it. After a minute, the figure disappeared. Alan continued his climb and reached the door. He tried the door handle without success so he produced his flat metal lever, and inserted it into the door at the level of the lock. There was a sound of gently splintering wood. The door was open and he went inside listening for noises on the stairs. Sounds of music were coming from below but he couldn't hear any footsteps on the stairs and so he pushed gently on the half open door to his left, which opened into a darkened room with a low ceiling. It was dark with the exception of some light which came from the skylight. A single ladder with two hooks was attached to the wall. He removed it carefully and fixed it on the bar at the left side of the skylight. The leg of the ladder reached the floor at an angle so he was able to climb and, when he pushed, was able to raise the skylight and emerge onto the roof.

The angle of the roof looked even steeper than it did from below and Alan felt his stomach turn. Taking a deep breath, he inched his way across the roof and onto the adjoining house's tiles. At one point, his foot dislodged a tile but he kept his balance, although unnerved. The tile went crashing to the courtyard below and he froze waiting for any voices. A dog barked.

'Bly stil,' a voice shouted. The dog was quiet.

Eventually he arrived at the open skylight of Number 16 and slipped through. He could see the room inside with a relatively short drop onto an apparently carpeted floor with no furniture visible on which he might impale himself. He hung by his fingers and fell, with knees bent, into the room.

His fall made what seemed to him a great sound. He lay quite still and listened. There was no sound from below. His left ankle, which he had fallen onto, felt sore but he could stand. He tested it gingerly; some pain but he could walk on it. He was in a simply decorated room with a bed and cupboard, but no other furniture. He opened the door carefully and walked out onto the landing, hearing nothing. His torch illuminated the stairs straight ahead of him and he trod as lightly as possible down to the next flight below. There were three doors on this floor but he decided to go on down to the first floor assuming that the main offices would be there. He descended and entered the door ahead of him. His torch showed an office with two desks and two large filing cabinets. There were two trays, one with unwashed tea cups and one with two tumblers with what smelled like the remains of whisky. The windows looked out onto the street and he could see Gloria across the street, walking up and down keeping a surreptitious eye on the door of the building.

The desks were covered with invoices and letters but he could see nothing that referred to himself or the embassy. There was however an Invoice addressed to the German embassy with a sum for Personnel services. The invoice was for fifteen pounds.

The first filing cabinet was locked. He did not want to use the jemmy so looked around for the key. A ring of keys was on a hook behind the door and he found the relevant key without trouble. The filing cabinet was tidy and the files were in alphabetical order. He saw his name and extracted the file.

There was nothing from either embassy but a letter from Cape Connections Ltd. dated the previous week and 'confirming your instruction to provide information with regard to Mr. A. Drayson of the British Embassy, and that invoices would be sent weekly at the agreed rate.' There was a detailed list of his movements from four days before, when he had not spotted the tail. There was also a record of his movements which ended with 'subject performed evasive manoeuvre and was lost.' Another sheet recorded the fact that he had 'departed from the airport with Miss Gloria Simpson of the British Embassy – destination probably De Beers'. Another recorded his late evening return to the railway station.

He was returning the file to its place and was about to close the drawer of the filing cabinet when he noticed a file headed 'Diamonds.' He took it out, placed it on the desk and shone his torch on the paperwork inside. There was one sheet of paper inside. It told of a visit, dated the day before, by Mr Carl von Wasserburg of the German Embassy requesting security for the transfer of diamonds on a number of occasions, as yet unspecified, from the offices of De Beers in Kimberley to the German Embassy in Cape Town. The transfer to be made by car or rail. And from the Embassy either to the airport or to the harbour, to be agreed. And just the one sheet of paper. He returned the file and riffled through the titles of the other files but there was nothing that seemed relevant. He shut the cabinet, locked it, and returned the keys to the hook behind the door.

He was just closing the door to the office when there was

a noise from the bottom of the stairwell. He froze. The noise was repeated. He shone his torch in time to see a large rat disappearing into a tiny hole in a skirting board. He crept downstairs to the front door which was unmoveable, locked in two places by large bolts. He went back and collected the keys from the office and returned. None fitted. He returned the keys and stood on the landing considering his options when suddenly there was the sound of a key being turned in the front door. He ran up the stairs and paused at the top and looked down the gap in the stairwell. Below him he could make out the outline of a large white man, just starting to walk up the stairs.

He entered the room that he had dropped into earlier and saw that there was an equivalent ladder to the previous skylight attached to the wall. He gently unlatched it and set it up with the feet on the ground and climbed it quickly, reaching the cool night air. He sat wondering what to do about the ladder. He could not put it back on the wall, and he could not drop it back into the room. The only option seemed to be to take it with him, but could he carry it across the roof? And would they notice that it was missing? Probably not for a few days. The upstairs room was obviously a bedroom but did not appear to be used often. It would probably be days or maybe weeks before the ladder was noted as being missing. Maybe no-one would notice at all. The ladder was not heavy but it would add to the danger of the climb back across the tiles, but there did not appear to be any other solution so he climbed out, holding the ladder tightly in his right hand. He closed the skylight behind him.

He stepped gingerly down the tiles to the gutter between the two roofs, and started his climb toward the skylight of the other house. He arrived and manoeuvred the ladder through the skylight, slowly descended the steps and stopped. The building was still. He detached the ladder from the skylight and replaced it back into its attachment on the wall. But he decided that he must take the ladder from Number 16 away and out of the building. Carrying the ladder he left the room and opened the door onto the fire-escape, and was pleased to see that the damage that he had done to it was hardly visible from inside. He closed the door gently behind him, carrying the ladder carefully so that it would not bang on the metal rungs of the fire escape. The ladder helped his climb over the back wall and he propped it on the other side and descended into the alley. He left the ladder flat on its side in the alley, putting some bits of rubbish on top so that it was partly concealed. He looked out into the street and could see no pedestrians, cyclists or cars. He walked up the street and Gloria appeared beside him. The light shone in her eyes and he kissed her so gently on the lips. She took his arm and they strolled back through the deserted streets to the embassy.

'Tell me,' she said when they were seated in the comfortable reception room where important visitors waited for the ambassador. It was a room of large windows, velvet curtains, comfortable armchairs and a fireplace which was not much used. He told her without missing anything. Even down to the rat.

'So, we've learned a great deal,' she said. 'They are the ones who are following you, but it may be simply because they don't know what you are up to.'

'Probably,' he agreed.

'And they are planning to bring a number of consign-ments of diamonds back to their embassy, but we don't know how many nor how often. Maybe because they don't know themselves.'

'Yes, I think that that is the most likely explanation.' He looked at the carpet, distracted slightly by the curious weave of the threads.

'Nor do we know what happens after they arrive at the embassy. Maybe again because they don't know themselves. Their problem is going to be getting them out of the coun-try.'

'And that is going to be when their plot will be at its most vulnerable. Even if they have a courier of some sort, they will have to disguise the diamonds in some way. And if the disguise is good, they might get past our eyes and back to Germany. How are they going to do that?' he asked.

'We'll need to think of likely ways,' she said, 'but not now, I think. Personally I'm so tired, I might fall asleep here and now.' And she stood and came over and curled up in his lap. He stroked her hair and she looked up at him and pulled his face down to kiss her.

'Sleep well,' she said and rose to her feet.

'Oh, by the way, I met Amit this morning, and fed him the story about the P.M. We'll have to see whether it emerges when you meet Carl.'

'Marvellous. Well done. I'll set up my date.' she said. He grimaced. They went to their rooms and were asleep in minutes, although Alan did for a moment visualise himself on the rooftops again.

Chapter Fourteen

A Riot and a Question

It was quite unclear what started it all. It had seemed to be a normal Cape Tuesday. The sun had shone, the traffic was horrendous, and a gentle breeze blew in from the ocean. A small cloud hung over Table Mountain, a common enough sight at this time of year.

Alan had taken a taxi up into the area behind the mountain and emerged into Constantia and strolled around, admiring its mansions and the views across the neighbouring vineyards. He returned from his trip with a bottle of wine under his arm, bought from a vineyard shop, which he had intended to share with Gloria. As his taxi approached the embassy, suddenly there were police everywhere. 'Where are you going, man?' An enormous police officer asked Alan, stopping him and the taxi driver from going any further.

'The British High Commission.'

'Unlikely,' was the caustic response. 'We have a full-blown riot there. Blecks everywhere.' Alan squirmed at the police officer's choice of words and cast a quick glance at

151

the taxi driver, who kept his eyes firmly on the road.

'What's going on?' Alan asked.

'Yes good question. One minute there was a peaceful protest about pay in the docks and then suddenly people started breaking windows and stealing goods and attacking everyone. So I regret that you can't go further at this moment by car. Are you working at the Embassy?'

'Yes.'

'O.K. Hop out and I will see what I can do about getting you there.' Alan got out of the taxi and immediately saw smoke billowing upwards and tasted an acrid sensation in his mouth. The officer summoned what appeared to be a deputy. 'Take half a dozen men and get this man to the British High Commission, as long as it's safe. If his head is broken, I will personally do the same to you. Now go.'

'Come with us, sir,' the deputy beckoned. His squad formed a protective ring with two in front of Alan, two alongside and two behind, rifles ready with bayonets attached. The small platoon moved forward along Adderley Street and rounded into Riebeek Street where all was chaos. Windows were being smashed and police were beating heads with truncheons. Anti-British slogans were everywhere, and stones were being thrown at police guarding the front entrance of the embassy. Billows of smoke wafted along the street. His eyes stung. They moved down a side street.

'We are going to try approaching from the back of the building, sir. Keep safe in the centre of us and keep your head low.' They were jogging now with the front pair of soldiers pointing their bayonets ahead. He felt they were like a human armoured vehicle of some sort. Rioters took one look at the approaching posse and moved away rapidly.

At the rear of the High Commission, it was relatively quiet. The guards at the back gate allowed him to slip between them and Alan thanked the platoon leader as he ran into the safety of the rear courtyard, and through a back door into the building. Most of the staff were watching the street chaos from upstairs windows and he found Gloria with the High Commissioner.

'Ah, there you are, Drayson. Did you start this?' He thought that Sir Robert must be joking. Apparently not.

'Not that I am aware of, Sir Robert.'

'Well we have never had this sort of trouble before. You arrive and within a few days we have this. Seems likely the two events are connected.' And the High Commissioner turned on his heel and went back down stairs.

'Perhaps they heard that you were a trouble-maker.' Gloria was grinning at him, rather inanely he felt. Looking at her, it was possible he supposed that maybe she was a bit frightened. But the local police, having formed a cordon around the front of the High Commission were wielding their truncheons aggressively and doing a good job keeping the rioters away. Although maybe a 'good job' was not the best way to describe it. Anyone coming within reach was getting his skull busted and falling to the ground in a sickening way, and left there.

'But, of course, HH has a point about this not happening before, Alan. It all seems very strange. It was a simple march about pay for the labourers in the docks, and then suddenly it was a riot. We have these occasional protests which are normally rather good-humoured affairs, often with the men singing traditional songs. And they were singing this time. I rather like the harmonies myself; they seem to have a natural ability to sing in beautiful harmony so I often stop to listen. And I was listening this time and I heard the songs turn to a Zulu war song, a very threatening sound, with the men's feet starting to thump in time. And then the war cries began and a full-scale riot emerged out of nowhere.' She definitely was frightened.

But by now the sounds were slowly receding and when he looked out again, the rioters, and most of the police, had disappeared from the front of the building with the men retreating back down the street in the direction of the docks. There was still the smell of the smoke seeping into the High Commission building and a slight haze out in the street. And there was broken glass everywhere, all over the pavements and sparkling in the sun shining on the street.

The following day the local newspapers were full of it all. Plenty of editorial speculation as to the sources of the discontent and the anger, but no real hard evidence. The ambassador had called a staff meeting and talked about security and personal safety. He told them that he intended to double the High Commission's small security staff detail and they rehearsed procedures for burning important papers in the event of rioters gaining entry to the building. Gloria and Alan wandered away at the end and walked down towards the harbour. Many shops had boarded up windows with staff sweeping up glass and other debris. They settled at a café near the water and sipped on iced lemonade. Somehow the previous day's events seemed unreal. Everyone milled around with no signs of obvious hostility between races, but there was tension in the air. There were fewer smiles on the faces than normal and the locals made somewhat bigger detours when whites approached.

'What I fail to understand is what that was all about,' said Gloria. 'It cannot have been at the origins of the march which was truly supposed to be about a very small amount of money.'

'Someone stirring them up?' wondered Alan.

'Maybe but why now? Nothing here has changed and employment's much better than it was a couple of years ago when America and England were sunk in the Depression and no-one wanted the gold or diamonds. Things are so much better. Buildings are going up everywhere, the harbour can hardly cope with the numbers of ships any-more.' They gazed down at the never-ending fascination of a major port with small vessels bustling to and fro servicing the large ships resting on their way to India and the Far East, or loading goods on the long trip back to European ports. Two of the White Star liners were in port showing their sleek modern shapes to the world. Small boats full of tourists were travelling in and out.

Alan thought about Amit and his cooking. He wondered vaguely what the German reaction was to the events of the previous day.

'When we go back, let's walk past the drop site. I want to see whether there has been any communication from the chef.' She looked enthusiastic and Alan thought that she needed to have her mind back onto the world of secrets and away from destruction and violence. She rewarded him with a surreptitious hand squeeze under the table.

'I wonder what the tourists thought,' she said.

'Maybe excited. Something to tell the folks back home. They would be able to portray the scenes of unrest. So different from their nice lives back in the Home Counties. Not many riots in Surbiton, I guess.' Alan watched a street sweeper working his way along the street. The man seemed weary, moving slowly brushing glass and debris into his cart.

'Probably as frightened as I was,' said Gloria, sipping contemplatively 'Maybe it will never happen again or we will be gone back to leafy Britain before we have another occurrence.' As it turned out, she didn't quite get that right.

They walked past the building with the pipe and Alan thought that he could just see the edge of a piece of paper. He looked up and down the street. No-one seemed at all interested. He crossed the street and retrieved a small envelope which he put into his trouser pocket and crossed back to Gloria's side.

'There's a note,' he whispered, putting his mouth close to the side of her head. She moved her neck close to him and he was unable to resist the smell of her perfume and gave her a gentle kiss just at the point where the neck was emerging from the collar of her dress. She pretended to pull away, and he laughed, before she squeezed his hand tightly and moved them both towards a wall, slightly tucked away from the main path. To an outside observer, they looked simply like a new couple in love, which was not entirely untrue, but it was here that Gloria positioned Alan in front of herself so that they could read the note quickly and discreetly.

We must meet. I have interesting news. A.

'What do you suppose it's about?' Gloria whispered, her hand against Alan's cheek, but her gaze focused firmly on the words of the note.

'I'm not sure.' He scribbled a reply suggesting a different café for the next morning and the two of them checked that no-one had been lingering near them for too long, watching for their next moves, before leaving Alan's own note at the drop off point.

At 11a.m. the following morning Alan found himself seated quietly near the back of the cafe sipping his tea, when Amit walked in and immediately walked out again. Alan rose to his feet automatically preparing to leave but then hesitated. They'd met many times, but never had their meetings started like this. Alan frowned. He had no idea what Amit might need to tell him, but he couldn't decide whether that was a good thing; was it a trap, or was this the start of a huge breakthrough? Walking slowly to the door Alan watched Amit as he strolled up the street. His gait was slower and more intentional than normal, and he made no obvious attempts to watch his back, but Alan was doing it for him, immediately noticing the tail. Alan was about to leave when he saw another operating on the other side of the street just about to pass the café. He quickly ducked behind an elderly couple who were slowly leaving the café and arguing rather noisily, then left immediately behind them using them as a screen. The couple walked up the street in the direction that Amit had left and he was able to use them as cover for a while, when suddenly Amit was gone.

He stopped immediately but the two tails were also in a state of alarm. They were conferring on the pavement before one ran on, while the other walked back towards the café. Alan vanished into an alley way and watched the returning tail pass him and continue down the street. He looked up and down the street and returned to the point where Amit had disappeared. There was a street off to the left and Alan ran down it and turned left again. He had a feeling he knew exactly what Amit had done, but still his heart was racing and he hoped that the tails were none the wiser. Alan hurried down the new street when a small click made him look left. Amit was tucked into a doorway and quickly emerged racing on down the street, allowing Alan to follow him. They turned left yet again and finally Amit slowed until Alan caught him up.

'Down to the harbour, I think.'

'O.K. I will cover your back.' Alan dropped back keeping a careful watch behind but they appeared to have lost their tails. Eventually they ended up on a street just close to the harbour walls with a small park on the side away from the water. Amit sat on a bench and Alan joined him, both men looking nervously around.

'Let's make it quick, Alan. I was followed right from the Embassy doors.'

'I got your note, what is it that you wanted to tell me?'

'The riot. I heard the ambassador discussing it with Carl. They were laughing. The ambassador congratulated him.

'Just the right level, Carl', were his words. 'Enough to cause outrage, but no deaths.' And then Carl said 'Next time a few deaths, I think.' The ambassador had sounded concerned, and then I could not hear any more words. I thought that you should know.'

'Good gracious. You were absolutely right to tell me. So you think that they had something to do with creating the riot?'

'It sounded like it.'

Alan could see the concern etched across Amit's face, and had to remind himself that despite all his help and his clever deception when tailed, Amit was still new to all this.

'You don't think that Carl was just boasting?'

'Well, I could not be certain, but it didn't sound like it.'

Alan thought carefully but could not understand it. He looked around.

'We must go, Amit. I need to think this through and talk to my boss here about it. But why should they want to create a riot. It just makes no sense. I'll contact you, but you watch your back. We'll need to be especially careful about meeting next time. Now go, quickly.' Amit nodded and hastily left, and Alan stayed for a few minutes before leaving in a different direction.

As expected, Gloria was in her office working when he burst in.

'Where on Earth happened, Alan?'

He related the events as he paced around the room.

'What I don't seem to understand is why the Germans were involved in causing a riot? It doesn't make any sense. And why were they having Amit followed? Do you think they know he's working with us? Or was it all a ploy to make us think that he's with us when really he's working for them? I have so many questions, Gloria, and no answers!'

Gloria thought for a moment, surprised by Alan's outburst. She hadn't seen him this worked up before and it worried her, but she was determined not to let that show.

'Cocktail time, Alan. We need something stiff to calm our rather shocked nerves, I think. I feel that this is getting away from us. And there is yet another question to be resolved.'

'There is?' Alan asked anxiously, 'I don't know about you but I suspect that two impossible questions are probably enough for one day.'

Gloria sighed. He wasn't wrong.

'The final question has to be 'What an earth has all this to do with diamonds?' '

Somewhat glumly, Alan could only agree. They ventured out into the gloom of the early evening and entered the bar around the corner. A lone saxophone player was improvising on 'We're in the Money.'

'I never liked that Dick Powell,' Alan ventured. The notes were drifting through the bar, half empty due to the early hour. He ordered two gin and tonics. They sat mournfully both trying to think through the situation. The sax player moved on to 'Sophisticated Lady'.

'He saw you come in,' opined Alan mischievously, trying to lighten the mood.

'Sweet, but inappropriate.'

'Are we having our first argument?'

'If you wish.'

'Oh no I'm a peace lover.' He wasn't going to disturb the mood, and he wanted to delay those impossible questions.

'Same again?' he asked, noticing that her glass was already empty.

'Seventy-five, please.' He ordered two. The bar began to fill up and the sax player had been joined by a couple of colleagues. They launched into a slow understated version of Night and Day.

'Shall we?' he asked and they strolled to the small dance floor in front of the band. She nestled into his shoulder and he held her close, his hand just touching her spine The sax player slurred his notes in the way that only truly talented musicians can, as Alan and Gloria danced slowly, letting the warmth of the atmosphere lull them into a dreamy cocoon.

Eventually they gave up and emerged into a sullen Cape evening, with a noticeable increase in humidity.

'Rain coming?' He asked.

'Unlikely at this time of year,' and she looked gently at him, holding his eyes in her gaze. He kissed her lips, just letting his tongue brush them softly. They walked hand-in-hand back to the Embassy and nearly ran up the back stairs to her small room under the eaves. Their clothes fell in two piles onto the floor.

The next morning, as Gloria's head lay on Alan's chest, she said,

'I think that the High Commissioner needs to know.'

'About us? But why?'

Gloria laughed and looked up at him, swatting his arm.

'Don't be silly, Alan, about the Germans and the riots.'

The morning was a little cloudy for once with white Christmas baubles of high cirrus clouds spreading in from the west, as Gloria and Alan descended to breakfast. Last night's haze had vanished and they were now faced with the harsh reality of what Amit had told Alan on the park bench. Gloria picked up her knife and fork, and began to cut through some eggs and bacon. Alan had been unusually quiet since she brought up the Germans, but nonetheless she brought it up again.

'This is too important for him not to know.'

'Yes, I agree but we have to be careful about the integrity of Amit.'

'Hmmm.' A tiny drop of yolk fell onto his much loved university tie. He carefully removed it. She watched him with a smirk.

'It does sort of prove that Amit is on the side of the angels, doesn't it?'

'Yes.' He paused. 'Unless of course they fed that to him because they wanted us to know.'

'Why would they want us to know?'

'Not a clue.' They finished and walked to Sir Robert's office. His secretary sat them in the waiting area and poked her head around his door.

'Gloria and Alan would like to see you, sir.' They heard a groan.

'He will see you now,' she remarked rather cheekily, clearly within the ambassador's hearing. She grinned at Alan, making eye contact with him. Gloria was not amused. They both rose and entered the room to find the High Commissioner seated behind his desk, a copy of the

London Times before him. The paper was open at the crossword. 'Good morning, sir. My boss in London does the crossword every morning.'

'Does he indeed? Well, are you any good?'

'You could try me on a clue, sir.' Gloria watched the two men amusedly, trying desperately not to laugh. The High Commissioner regarded Alan with some thought.

'Maybe not just now as I am sure that you are here over other business.'

'We are, sir. A matter of some delicacy.' Gloria had chosen her words. Suddenly she had the High Commissioner's full attention. She spelled out the situation. He listened in silence. When she had finished, he asked,

'And this Amit. Is he trustworthy?'

'We cannot be sure, sir.' And Alan spelled out the history of Amit's recruitment. There was a long silence.

'So what on earth are the Germans up to?' Sir Robert asked.

'We rather hoped that you might have an idea, sir.' He looked at Alan.

'Must be related to their new Chancellor. Perhaps they want to de-stabilise us down here. Strategically this could be an important place in the event of a European conflict. Just a couple of our warships in port here combined with our troops at the Suez Canal, could dominate the whole trade route to the East. Suppose war with Germany broke out again, this would be an important factor.'

Alan and Gloria exchanged glances. 'Yes, but why now?' asked Alan.

'Good question, young man. Maybe it has something to

do with whatever it is that you are doing down here?' Alan looked at his feet considering the situation and decided that this was too important not to inform the High Commissioner of his mission. He spelled out the details.

'And the question that Miss Simpson and I failed to be able to answer was what the business with the diamonds has to do with the riot?'

'Yes, I see the dilemma. I'd better think about this, and maybe have a chat with London. They will be on the blower soon anyway to know about the riot. I think I need to send a confidential telegram to the Foreign Secretary.'

'It would be very important for Amit's safety that no-one in London should know about us having a man in their embassy sir.' The ambassador looked at him with a sneer.

'No-one in London except you S.I.S. wallahs, huh?' Alan was embarrassed.

'Or is it that Sir John Simon, the Foreign Secretary of the United Kingdom cannot be trusted with confidential information? Is that it?' Sir Robert was visibly reddening. 'Get out of my office, both of you.' They got up and walked to the door, and as they were leaving,

'But I understand the points that you have raised and will exercise caution. Let me contact Sir John. I will call you when he and I have discussed both the riot and the diamonds.' They left and strolled away down the corridor.

'Sorry.' Said Alan.

'Well hard to know how else to make the point, I suppose. You need to let Shuttleworth know about all this. He will not be amused by a call from the Foreign Secretary.'

'Oh Lord, hadn't thought of that. You're right.

Chapter Fifteen

A Holiday in Oudtshoorn

She is looking at him but says not a word. In turn, he watches her nervously. She has a gleam in her eye and he feels that she is plotting, but he is quite unable to think what she might be planning. Her silence compounds his anxiety. Eventually he gives in and speaks.

'I surrender. I have a feeling that a plot is afoot. In fact I feel somewhat like Watson when Holmes is about to reveal all but he has no concept of Holmes' dastardly strategy to get the villain off guard.' She laughs.

'I was wondering whether it would be good for your soul to get out of this town for a few days.'

'My soul, my soul. My soul is in need of many things. A good Christian overhaul would be one plan. Whether leaving Cape Town would help is a matter of opinion. In any case an enforced absence from you would make me sad and unable to focus on my so-called soul – whatever that is. Is my soul in need of salving? When I was younger, I read Thomas à Kempis to try to save my immature teenage soul. It plunged me into a crisis of guilt and depression with its high ideals and unassailable peaks of virtue to climb. My sins were exposed; I knew that I was a total failure. Since then I have not examined my soul in great depth.' She regarded him.

'Thanks for that monologue of self-indulgence. Frankly the state of your soul is not really of much concern to me.' He looked at her.

'Gloria, I am a bit tense after the last couple of days. I can feel all around me that bad things are being concocted. I can also sense that the political pressure around here is going to become very tense, and I am not use to dealing with politics. I can do the clever S.I.S. stuff but politics makes me anxious.'

'I can totally understand that. So let the boss, and to a lesser extent me, help with all that. It would be good for you to have a trip out of town, as I said. But this is not going to be totally a holiday. We are going partly to de-stress you but also partly to see a friend of mine. He lives out in the country and it will be a marvellous drive to visit him.'

'But I thought you said that…'

'I know what you thought,' she interrupted. 'In fact you seem to have completely the wrong end of whatever stick you were munching on.'

'Munching on, munching on…? Aren't you mixing some very weird metaphors?'

'So smart. Returning to the point. You will not be alone on your trip. I will be accompanying you on your soul's, and I hope, your body's pilgrimage. I thought that we might take these few days holiday together, you and me.'

'Well that's a lovely idea. Did you have a plan as to where we might go?'

'Indeed. Let's drive to Port Elizabeth along the coast and take in a few landmarks. How does that sound?'

'Marvellous. Shall I hire a car?'

'Oh I expect that we can take one of the High Commission's cars. Sir Robert won't mind. But I am sure that he wouldn't want us to take the Rolls.' And they laughed.

They set out the next morning in a Chevrolet Sedan, driving east. The road passed through the hills at the start and eventually joined the coast road later in the afternoon. She chattered on about this and that, keeping well away from any work topic and he fell into the mood. Eventually they found a large hotel high on a hill looking down towards the Indian Ocean. The hotel seemingly had plenty of rooms and they took one with a large balcony and ordered a bottle of champagne. They sat looking out over the vast expanse of ocean, each with a glass in their hands.

'My father would have loved this,' he said. 'I think that he had a real eye for beauty. He used to paint a little and always told me to 'value the beauty' when I looked at something. He used to talk about the difference between seeing and looking. When you look, you are not only taking things in but you are thinking about them. It's an active process.'

'Would I have liked your father?' she wondered.

'Oh yes – mostly.' She looked up. 'He had a weakness. But he had so many lovely features. You would have adored him. Most women did.'

'I have no desire to be categorised with 'most women'.'

Figure One: On the Coast road to Port Elizabeth

'Yes, I can understand that. Perhaps what I meant to tell you was that he was very handsome, and very charming. He was an excellent conversationalist with a particularly wide knowledge of nature. When I went on walks with him, he could name every tree, and knew interesting things about them which he would try to teach me. Sadly I had no interest in that sort of thing when I was younger – and he is dead now. We lived in a small country town in North Norfolk called Holt. He was a local doctor in the town, and much in demand. Sometimes we hardly saw him throughout the day. As I got older, I was allowed in school holidays to go out with him on his visits to his sick patients,' and he paused.

'Keep talking. I am enjoying the story.'

'I would sit in the car with my book and he would walk

up the path, and knock on the door. The door would open and he would vanish. I remember my excitement when at last the door would open and he was saying goodbye on the doorstep, and then walking back down the path. He would climb into the car, and often would tell me about the patient's illness. So I got to hear about tuberculosis and pneumonia and measles and other common illnesses. The stories were far more exciting than anything in my book. And off we would go to the next visit. Sometimes he would go to the house of one of my friends, and then I could get out and play. And sometimes the mother would give me a cup of Horlicks. I loved Horlicks. I remember that Mr Amundsen took it with him to the North Pole.' She laughed.

'How old were you then?'

'I don't know. Maybe seven or eight. It was well before the war.'

'And what was the weakness?'

'Morphine. He had started when he was a medical student at Guys. He had easy access of course. And gradually it took over his life. And he started to make mistakes. And then he made a big one and a pregnant woman died. Her husband complained and it all came out. By that time, he had contracted tuberculosis from one of his patients and he was dead within 6 months.' He gazed out across the ocean. 'But he would have loved the trees and shrubs here.' His sadness touched her. She put her hand in his. The sun had set and lights twinkled below on the beach. A boat out at sea moved slowly on the horizon.

'And your mother?'

'Yes, she is still alive and well, living in Holt still. It's a fine country town, economically made by the school. I went there of course – to Gresham's. All the rich parents of the boys come to the town visiting their boarding children and contributing to the wealth of the town.'

'Did you like the school?'

'Oh yes. I was taught well – and of course I was a day boy so I saw my parents too. Some of my friends hated it, missing their parents. We were pretty young when we started. My friends came to see me at the weekends and some stayed overnight. They cried for their mums in the first year and my mum would give them a cuddle and occasionally, if they stayed with us for the night, tuck them in to bed at night. It was harsh, but by the second year everyone had settled down.'

And then he remembered the lads, especially Bill. Red haired and freckled and better than them all at maths. And sometimes Bill had been sad and lost, feeling that he had done something wicked for his parents to send him to this miserably cold place where the wind whipped off the North Sea and there was often ice on the insides of the windows in their dormitory. Later the boys had discovered the crabs in the harbour at Blakeney and lowered their lines off the quayside. They had pulled up scores of the crabs and placed them decorously in their buckets full of cold salty Blakeney sea water. And they watched the crabs' attempts to climb out, which they occasionally achieved. The lads would chase them but the crabs were fast and often outran the boys, tumbling over the quayside and plopping back into the water.

And eventually they had learned to appreciate the salt marshes with their miles of flat coastline and flocks of birds nibbling at insects amongst the tall reeds and bulrushes. They had made cycle trips to the big Hall at Bayfield and walked the path along the trickling river Glaven, meandering its way through the valley. He had shown them how to sit quite still by the river banks and watch the water voles run from the cover of the old hedge and perform wondrous belly flops into the river with their legs all spread. The river was covered in water cress much of its way, dragon flies hovering over its surface. He remembered it all so clearly.

And then they would cross the old stone bridge where the river widened at the pond before the mill at Glandford. And they would knock at the door of the cottage, where the cheery housewife would let them into Jodrell's Shell Museum and they would wander around, looking at the shells that Jodrell had collected from all over the world. And on the hour, from the old grey stone Norfolk church, set above the Museum, bells would sound in the form of a verse of a hymn tune.

They would enter the church and if no-one else was there and they were feeling brave, they would take out hymnals, sit in the pews and sing the verses of All things bright and Beautiful. And one of them would be up in the pulpit conducting gravely. Mrs Alexander would probably not have approved of the way that they had roared out her lovely words but they had been boys, young and energetic. And as they left they would all stroke the little wooden mouse carved delicately in the wood onto the side of one of the pews, and Jodrell's dog carved onto his pew in his master's sadness after his death.

And somehow the mixture of the old church, the Museum and the old Mill and the voles gave them an understanding of continuity and calm, distracting from the ardours of Latin Grammar and other lost families. Alan was still remembering the time when he had taken his violin to the church and played the tune of All Things Bright and Beautiful which had seemed so appropriate for the beauty of the little church and the nature in the fields all around.

Eventually Gloria gently broke the silence. She coughed, and he realised that he had drifted off.

'Lost you there,' she told him.

'Dreaming of Norfolk, where I created myself.'

'And was the creative process gentle and kind to you?' He considered the question.

'Indeed, it was.' The gong sounded.

'Dinner?' she asked.

'I suppose so,' and he rose to his feet, taking a last look at the dark ocean below, sparkling with its beauteous lights. They walked into the dining room and he noticed that they attracted looks, maybe of curiosity, maybe of envy. Her shimmering grey silk dress undoubtedly suited her, and he enjoyed the simple oval shape of her Modigliani face. He studied the menu.

'What's Snoek?' he asked.

'It's one of the local fish. It has an especially gamey sort of taste. Quite delicious. But often you have to navigate around a lot of bones. Definitely worth the fight. It has teeth like razors – only a problem for the fishermen, though,' she grinned.

He braved the Snoek and she had a fish stew. They talked of England and South Africa and he watched her. He understood deep in himself that he did not normally 'watch' a woman. In his work, he watched people, he watched crowds, he followed an individual but did he truly watch one of *his* women. In the end the feeling of watching unnerved him; he felt it disturbing his other senses. He could smell the fish but he knew that the smell was blunted. He could hear her conversation but the meaning was flattened somehow. He could see the other guests at the surrounding tables but they blurred in his mind.

She watched him watching her and wondered what was underneath. He had talked so openly about his childhood and she had felt the privilege of the openness. She was flattered and almost overwhelmed by his attention. Deep in her heart she knew that a bond was forming and that she was being sucked into the vortex of his charm.

They drank a bottle of local white wine, had coffee and walked slowly up the stairs, holding hands. He turned the lock on their door and she went and sat on the bed. Very gently he sat beside her and kissed her first just behind the ear and then with the utmost care, on her lips. They made love and slept like new born lambs.

The next day they woke rather late and it was almost midday before they were on the road again. After an hour of driving,

'Turn left here' she had said. The signpost said 'Oudtshoorn'. It meant nothing to him. He asked but she just grinned. They turned off the sea route and headed into the hills, with the occasional farm surrounded by fields towards their destination of the town of Oudtshoorn. They arrived at the top of the Pass through the Attikwas Mountains with the sun headed for the horizon. A sign announced The Eight Bells Hotel. A vast oak tree spread its branches across the hotel's porch.

'Welcome, travellers from afar,' came a voice apparently connected to a large white man who emerged from a doorway.

'Nice car,' he said, 'and because of that, and despite your Englishness, you are welcome to my household,' and the large extended paw crushed down on Alan's hand. 'Forgive my vicious Afrikaaner handshake. My family always used to believe that only a bone-crunching shake was acceptable Dutch behaviour.' And he grinned, surprisingly sheepishly,

'May we stay the night?' asked a mildly intimidated Alan.

'Of course you may. I am Johannes van der Blank and this is my oasis of calm and peace. You may or may not be delighted to hear that the place is crawling with you British. There are a number of officers from the Royal Navy ships docked at the base in Mossel Bay.' He gestured vaguely towards a group of men in naval uniform standing admiring the view of the mountains losing their colour, outlined by the flame-red of the setting sun.

'Our hotel used to be called the Bosun's Whistle, but when I took the place over from my dad, who died a few years back, I modernised it and changed it from a simple farm with a few rooms to a farm with a hotel alongside. So we gave it the new name – 'Eight Bells' – of course being the end of the watch.' They both clearly looked blank. 'At sea, the bell is rung for each half hour of a four hour watch. So our name demonstrates that we wish to provide a haven of rest for the officers.'

'Of course we have a few air force types as well, as there is quite a large base now at Oudtshoorn. They fly around there as the Little Karoo is rather desert-like in parts and so you Brits thought it to be great training for any battle to be fought in North Africa.' Alan nodded in agreement, having known of the thinking behind this, when working in Morocco. They were taken to their rooms and had a walk in the warmth of the evening in the hills. Food and passion passed the stay.

The next day they were back earlier in the car.

'To Oudtshoorn, driver.'

'And why are we going to this Outdshoorn place?' He wondered.

'Ostriches, mainly.' He looked at her in amazement.

'Get your eyes back on the road, bad driver.' He returned his eyes just in time to miss some large animal, that he failed to recognise, running across the road.

'What was that?'

'Looked like an Okapi to me.'

'An Okapi. Can't be. Surely they aren't as far south as here?'

'Well if you know so much, why ask me?' Even a man as insensitive as Alan could tell a sulk when he saw one.

'Sorry,' he said and gave her his best smile. She laughed.

'Anyway we are off to see an ostrich.'

'What on earth for?'

'You'll see – and stop looking at me.'

'I can't help it. You are so lovely.' She sniggered. And after a while they came to a sign saying 'Oudtshoorn – Home of the Ostrich.' Oudtshoorn, at first glance was a prosperous-looking town in a valley dipping downwards surrounded by hills and fields with a crop that Alan didn't recognise.

'All built on feathers,' she said enigmatically.

'On feathers?'

'The farmers around here in the 19th century built up farms of ostriches, the feathers of which were all the rage for the fashionable woman at the end of the century. And for a while the lovely plumes of the ostrich were so much sought after that the value of ostrich plumes by weight nearly equalled the value of diamonds.

'Good gracious.'

'Indeed. The white feathers, most treasured, were named 'white gold, and the farmers of the region, realising that ostriches were far more profitable than any other activity, ripped out their other crops and planted Lucerne, which was used as feed for the ostriches.'

'Lucerne?' he asked.

'Oh, you probably know it as Alf-alfa. That's what all this is,' and she gesticulated vaguely at the passing fields. 'Anyway, the problem was that by the start of the war, groups of bird protection organisations began a series of campaigns aimed at preventing wild-bird plumage from entering the London and New York markets. This was all because in the United Kingdom the Victorians had started having fun shooting birds. The train companies had even arranged special trains to take men to the Welsh coasts and Lundy for a weekend of slaughtering innocent creatures. So, a social stigma arose associated with the wearing of feathers, although to be honest no-one campaigned specifically against ostrich plumes.'

'Also of course that Mr. Ford over in America started building open-top cars, so a lady travelling in one would lose the feathers from her hat. So what with both those things, the market for Ostrich plumes crashed and many of the farmers of this town were ruined. Nowadays there are only two ostrich farms left and we are going to visit one.'

'Oh my goodness. Will I enjoy it?' She looked at him with some care.

'Maybe,' and she grinned.

'You are plotting.' And she grinned even more. He groaned.

'I suppose you are not going to tell me.'

' 'Fraid not.' There was a pause while he thought.

'I just remembered something you said earlier. When I asked you why we are going to see this place, you said 'Ostriches, mainly'. What is the bit that is not ostriches?'

'Mmmm, so you were listening then.'

'Of course. And....'

'For later, daaaarling,' she slurred, putting on her best Jean Harlow sexy smile. He was not deceived but decided on balance that he would not press the matter. They drove into town and he looked with amazement around him. They passed a vast building, apparently a boys' school, with a tower that must have been over a hundred foot tall, followed by street after street of enormous palatial seemingly private dwellings.

'Ostrich money,' she said. 'All built before the war. Many are uninhabited now after the collapse of the market.' And indeed when he looked a little more closely at the buildings, some of the buildings were looking dilapidated with roof tiles missing, paint peeling etc.

Figure Two: Oudtshoorn ostrich farmer's house

They turned left and drove out of town until they came to a sign saying Safari Ostrich farm, and drove in. The first thing that they noticed was the smell, presumably the odour of the ostrich, an unforgettable vaguely foetid sensation. They were met by a middle-aged woman, who introduced herself as the owner's wife. They walked around the farm and he stared in wonder at the large numbers of the vast beasts, some of which were pure white in colour.

'The white ones are the most valuable', she said, 'because we can sell the feathers as pure white, or dye them green or red or whatever colour becomes fashionable.'

'And now for the highlight of your tour. I will demonstrate first.' They were led to an enclosure in the middle of which was a small flight of wooden steps, where an ostrich was being held in a triangular pen. 'First you climb up, then you sit on the beast, then you hold it by its neck and put your left leg over so that you are sitting on its back – like this.' And he caught her picture with his Kodak.

With much trepidation he followed. The ostrich's neck

Figure Three:
Mounting the ostrich

was soft and pliable and seemed to collapse in his grip. He was terrified but after a few gentle walks around the paddock, he managed to relax a little. The animal seemed quite placid and eventually the ride came to an end and he noted with some pleasure that he had survived.

'Well done, Alan. I was scared my first time on too.' And she laughed. They left the animals and were directed to the farm shop. It appeared that there were rather a large number of products for man and woman produced by the ostrich. He bought her a single green feather which matched her silk dress. She bought him tinned ostrich steak. He bought a map of the surroundings printed onto ostrich hide for his colleagues at home in the S.I.S. They drove off, laughing at their presents and found a small hotel near the centre of town and sat in the bar drinking Gins and tonics, enjoying a reminiscence over the afternoon's slightly bizarre events.

Somewhat to his surprise the barman was called David Steiner, his name badge announcing that he was 'The Best Jewish Barman in the Southern Cape.' He mixed their cocktails with gusto and chatted amicably to them. Apparently the town was full of Afrikaaners and Jews. The Afrikaaners had arrived first, and then an influx of Jews after the European war. He told them that the two races got on very well and respected each other's customs; both races being hard-working, good at making money with the Jews often contributing to Afrikaaner charities, and vice-versa. They retreated to a table in the back of the room and the room started to fill, and indeed Afrikaaner farmers in dungarees and hats arrived in conversation with orthodox

180

Jewish men with dreadlocks and yarmulkes. They were stared at by the men of both racial groups.

'Time for a walk,' she suddenly announced, 'and then we can enjoy a small repast. I thought that you might like to meet a friend.'

'What friend?' He asked suspiciously. 'Oh, yes you did mention a friend when we started out.'

'Well – perhaps 'friend' is not quite the right word. A 'friend of our country' might be more accurate.'

'Does he have a name?'

'Indeed. His name is Dieter Furtwangler. I believe that his uncle is a famous music conductor.' Alan was stopped in his tracks, looking at her.

'If his uncle is Wilhelm Furtwangler, he is the conductor of the Berlin Philharmonic, and probably the most famous conductor in the world.'

It was her turn to look surprised. 'That famous?'

'Oh yes. He has a rare and great gift of going beyond the printed score and showing us what music really is. He has a subtlety of tone colour that is rare. His sound is beautifully rounded and incomparably more interesting than that of the other great German conductors.' He stopped, looking slightly embarrassed, realising that he had been giving a lecture. . She was looking at him in wonder.

'I did not know that you were an expert in classical music.'

'Oh I am no expert, but I do play the violin. Some of that short speech was from the mouth of my uncle, who is a conductor of an English orchestra. He tells me that there has been nothing like Furtwangler – ever. He took me to a

Furtwangler concert last year in London, when Furtwangler came over and conducted Brahms.'

'Thank you for telling me all that, she said. 'Anyway, I met this young man last year when I was looking for contacts here and he was recommended to me by a friend at the Embassy. Dieter had just left Germany and had met her at a concert in Cape Town. They had got chatting and my friend realised that he might be a useful ally, at the time when I was just starting to build up a group of contacts.'

'You have a team?"

She turned to him. 'Well I am a member of S.I.S., Alan. What do you expect me to do? Sit around all day, polishing my nails?'

He was suitably chastened. They had arrived at a small house on the edge of town. She knocked and the door was opened by a tall slim, fair-haired man in a grey suit.

'Gloria! You are so welcome.' And he gave her a rather formal kiss on her cheek.

'Dieter, this is my colleague, Alan Drayson. I told you of him last week.'

'Yes indeed. Welcome to Oudtshoorn, Mr. Drayson. Do come in.' They sat in the parlour, a room of precision and yet warmth. The deep red and golden hue of the seat colourings contrasted well with the almost olive green of the carpet and curtains. They were served tea in slightly distasteful ochre-coloured Delftware cups. Dieter lit a cigarette and made a vague gesture of offering one to them, but in a strangely secretive manner. The conversation flowed with a rather banal awkwardness, as if he was uncertain of the tools available for discourse. A propos of nothing, he suddenly blurted out –

'He was here, you know. That Carl.' A silence filled the gap.

'Carl from the Embassy?' she asked.

'Yes, the one with the name of the town in Alsace. The blond one.'

'Carl von Wasserburg.' She was watching him.

'I keep forgetting the surname. He wanted me to do something. He thinks that because I am German that I owe some sort of allegiance to them. How can they not understand that I have left because I hate my country, and what it is becoming? This degradation of the soul, this demeaning of our culture by the thugs, the thugs.' She waited for the rant to finish. It didn't.

'But my uncle is brave and stands up to them. I can't. I am a coward.' And for an alarming moment Alan thought that he would cry.

'He has written a public letter to Goebbels about music, art and the Jews in our country. He has sent me a copy. I will read to you,' and he walked to the mahogany bureau and picked up a sheet of paper from the desktop. He read,

'Ultimately there is only one dividing line I recognize: that between good and bad art. However, while the dividing line between Jews and non-Jews is being drawn with a downright merciless theoretical precision, that other dividing line, the one which in the long run is so important for our music life, yes, the decisive dividing line between good and bad, seems to have far too little significance attributed to it. If concerts offer nothing then people will not attend;

that is why the QUALITY is not just an idea; it is of vital importance. Men such as Walter, Klemperer, Reinhardt etc. must be allowed to exercise their talents in Germany in the future as well. We Germans should bear in mind that in the past we had Joseph Joachim, one of the greatest violinists and teachers in the German classical tradition, and in Mendelssohn even a great German composer – for Mendelssohn is a part of Germany's musical history'.

'Last year he wrote to me in a letter discussing whether he should stay or flee like myself, that "Hitler is a hissing street pedlar who will never get anywhere in Germany." How wrong he was, how wrong,' and he held his head in his hands. We sat carefully still, waiting, but it appeared that some sort of catharsis had occurred, and a bleak cheerfulness even an eagerness, returned to his demeanour.

'I have exciting news for you Gloria,' and he turned to her, looking at her with slightly more adoration in his eyes than Alan would have personally liked. 'I can help your excellent country, your land of Edward Elgar, my favourite composer,' and he paused. 'Well – after the great German composers, Bach, Mozart and Beethoven of course. Promise me never to speak of that barbarian Ricard Wagner and his medieval so-called "German culture." Music of the Dark Ages if you ask me.'

'Wasn't Mozart Austrian?' Alan asked. He was regarded with such scorn that he felt myself visibly shrink.

'I can help your nation. Carl has inveigled me into his plot to smuggle diamonds out of the country. And I expect that you want to know how they are going to do it?' Alan watched Gloria holding her breath and sitting forward on her seat. And then noticed that he too had stopped breathing momentarily.

'Well you must wait a moment as I have forgotten to bring in my Lebkuchen for you. What a host,' and he sprang to his feet and disappeared presumably to the kitchen.

'He is toying with us,' Alan said.

'I doubt it. He's not like that,' she replied.

'Anyway, what are Lebkuchen?'

'Lebkuchen are...' and he was back with them

'... delicious spicy ginger biscuits.' He finished her sentence, and passed the plate around, handing them each a tiny platter to put them on. Alan bit cautiously and was delighted by the mixture of sweetness and spice.

'Here, have a glazed one. It's just a sugar glaze. It's my grandmother's recipe. She was a simple country girl from the hillsides near Oberau – near Garmisch-Partenkirchen if that helps.'

'Not much,' muttered Alan.

'Southern Germany, foothills of the Alps, close to Austria,' Gloria educated him.

'Anyway I was about to tell you about Carl's plan. Actually it's very smart. He knows that I work here for the organisation that markets and exports ostrich feathers around the world. When I first arrived here two years ago and was newly arrived at Cape Town, I heard of a job in this town from Carl. A friend of his manages the company, I needed to work and was happy to accept any job even if it was here in the Karoo, packing feathers. In fact, this isn't any old town. Everyone gets on well, and because there is a big Jewish community, we have plenty of music performed.'

'But I am deviating. My job is to pack the feathers into boxes and crates. Then we transport them by lorry to Port Elizabeth. From there they go all over the world. Now the devilish thing is that when I started, I explained my job in some detail to Carl, and he remembered a small detail that I told him.'

'The feathers need to be kept very dry during their long journey. Sometimes there is a lot of moisture in a ship's hold. So when we pack the feathers, we mix with them some packets of pieces of silica. Have you ever seen a packet of silica?' We shook our heads. He leaped to his feet and opened a drawer of the bureau.

'By an amazing coincidence I liberated a pack from the company yesterday knowing that I was going to be telling you this story,' and he produced a small white sachet and, with a pair of scissors opened it, and tipped the contents onto the table.

'Do they remind you of anything?' He grinned proudly.

'Oh, yes. Oh yes indeed. Small uncut and unpolished diamonds.' She said excitedly.

'And you...'

'Indeed.' Conversation had become a touch cryptic, Alan felt.

'So, Carl's proposal is that we should open the sachets, get rid of the silica, fill them with diamonds and sow them up again. We would then add the diamond-filled sachets to other genuine silica sachets in a crate of feathers destined

186

for Germany. Once there…'

'Carl is even going to send me a secretary from the embassy when the diamonds are delivered to me, to sew the sachets up carefully so that they don't look any different from the silica sachets. All I have to do is make sure that I get the diamonds into the correct crate and give him the identity details so that they can be intercepted at the port of arrival, probably Hamburg.' They were bemused. The scheme was remarkably neat, and it seemed most unlikely that even the most pedantic Custom Officer would take a second glance at the silica packets scattered amongst ostrich feathers.

'And did he mention when this was all to start?' she asked

'Oh, yes. The first delivery would be next week.'

'Next week,' repeated Alan. 'We need to get a move on. And on a separate topic, are they paying you?'

'Handsomely.'

'We would like also to give you some reward for the information.'

'Very generous, but I will accept no monetary reward. But I do have a favour to ask?'

'Of course,' said Alan. Dieter looked at the floor.

'Should my uncle wish to leave Germany, he has written to me that he would want to go to England. Would that be possible?'

'Possible, of course it would be possible. England would be honoured to have him. I am sure that the Foreign Office would not only welcome him, but that the government would find him a prestigious and well-paid job conducting one of our leading orchestras. Maybe we would pay him a salary and he could be 'Guest Conductor' to whichever orchestra he wanted. I am sure that they would vie with each other to obtain his services.'

'But surely the other conductors would be jealous of their jobs?' Dieter wondered.

'The London Symphony Orchestra will be his for the conducting. Sir Hamilton Harty is presently in charge and I am sure that he would welcome him. I could ask my boss in London to set up preliminary arrangements with the cooperation of the S.I.S., so that we could assist with his departure from Germany at the shortest notice if need be. I will be back to you in a few days, so that you can communicate with your uncle and we can set everything up, to be activated at his request.'

'Wunderbar, wunderbar.'

Before they left, they sorted out a secure communication method for Dieter. There seemed little choice but that he should telephone Alan at the High Commission, even though the telephone might be bugged. But they set up a series of codewords for him to use. As they were leaving, he said to them,

'Oh by the way, Carl did mention that they were going to set up an alternate way of smuggling the diamonds in case this one was intercepted.'

'And did he mention what that was?'

'Not at all, but he did say something unusual at the time. He said that he was 'going to cook something up' and he roared with laughter as if he had said something enormously witty. I have no idea what the joke was – and maybe it is not relevant. Who knows?' And he shrugged his shoulders. They wandered back to their hotel.

Chapter Sixteen

Another riot disturbs the romance

Gloria had her date. Alan hated it but managed to occupy himself until she returned. That afternoon he had bought himself a second hand violin from a surprisingly well-stocked music store in town, and spent the evening practising the opening two movements of Mozart's 3rd violin concerto. He was playing when she opened the door of his bedroom and did not hear her enter.

'That is the most beautiful music even for me, a total ignoramus.' Alan turned towards her and smiled, relieved to find that nothing about her seemed to have changed over the past few hours whilst she was out on her date.

'Sit down, let me play this to you.' Gloria closed the door and sat on his bed, and he played the singing opening solo of the second movement. He played it slowly and as lyrically as he was able. Tears fell from her eyes as the beauty of the notes entered her soul. He watched her closely as he played, seeing her overwhelmed by the deep innermost feelings elucidated by the composer's command of the violin.

At last he stopped, put down the instrument and sat on

the bed next to her. He held her hand, leant across and allowed his lips to brush hers as gently as he could. Somewhat to his alarm, she went deathly white and fainted.

When she stirred a few minutes later, she wrapped her hands in his. They lay there.

The next morning he awoke to feel her, tightly wrapped around him. Her eyes opened.

'Play me that beautiful music for ever and ever,' she demanded. He smiled.

'Orange Juice? And tell me whether Carl mentioned anything from our trap that he might have been fed by Amit?'

'No, not a word.'

'Good. I hope that that means that we can trust Amit.'

'I suspect so.'

The day was long and filled with work for them both. Towards the end of the afternoon, there was a knock on Gloria's door.

'Excuse me, Miss, but there is a man waiting for you in reception.'

Gloria frowned and noticed the receptionist's eyes darting around her office. She moved some papers to the side.

'And did he say who he is?'

The receptionist refocused his eyes on Gloria and nodded nervously.

'Said his name was Amos. He said that you would know him.'

Then he hesitated for a moment, trying to gauge Gloria's reaction.

'Anything else?'

'It's just that he didn't come in through the front door. In fact, I don't know how he got in. He just sort of, appeared.'

Gloria rested her arms on the desk, in a way which she hoped looked relaxed and nonchalant. It was a move she had noticed some of her superiors do, alongside other flippant gestures like lightly shrugging their shoulders or flashing her a well-rehearsed casual smile.

'I'll be down in a minute.'

After the receptionist left, Gloria stood up and made her way downstairs deliberately – not so fast as to arouse suspicion to anyone that could be watching her, but quick enough to show she meant business. She was getting quite good at this, she thought, although if Amos was here, it could mean real trouble. Her stomach flipped and she walked a little faster.

Gloria spotted him sitting under the watching eye of one of the embassy's guards and she joined him.

'Sorry, miss, I know that you said never to come here but I think that this is an emergency.'

'Better be good, Amos.'

'My brother's niece talked to her uncle just now. Told him that there was going to be trouble tomorrow. Maybe big trouble.'

Gloria watched him carefully, his leg jittering and his eye's darting about as he spoke.

'Did she, indeed? Well thank you Amos.' She summoned the guard.

'Please escort this man out through the back. Get him

onto the street through the rear passage.'

'Way I got in, Miss' and Amos grinned. She looked at him until he had vanished with the guard, and then got up and went back upstairs to get Alan. After she relayed the information Amos had provided, the two of them agreed they needed to talk to Sir Robert together and arrived outside his office within a couple of minutes.

'We need to talk to the boss.' They sat waiting outside until the secretary let them in and Gloria hurriedly explained what she knew.

'It seems likely that there will be a riot tomorrow.'

'Is that so? And may I ask how you know?'

Gloria nodded and replied, 'a source, sir, a source.' Alan and she both looked at each other. He slowly turned towards Alan.

'Have you anything to add, young man?'

'No, sir.'

'How about 'when' and 'where', Miss Simpson.'

'I'm afraid I don't know that either, sir.'

'Alright. I will call the Police Chief. Miss Simpson, tell my secretary to call a staff meeting for 6p.m. No excuses. And make sure that the Captain of the Guards is included. Goodbye,' and they both rose quickly.

'And try not to get in the way, Drayson.'

At 6p.m. the main embassy room was crowded and full of chatter, which ceased immediately when the High Commissioner entered. Rumours and expectation weighed heavy in the air.

'My resident spooks tell me that there is going to be a spot of bother tomorrow. No-one leaves the building from midnight tonight until midnight tomorrow. Those not resident may camp out here, if they wish. My secretary will arrange. Bring your families if you wish but the doors will be locked and barred, and in any case your families may be safer away from here. Also it may be scary for children. Captain Richardson – No shooting unless anyone gains entry. Otherwise all read embassy Order 916/32, last year's instructions from London entitled 'In the event of extreme danger to Embassy Personnel.' If you don't have a copy, ask my secretary. Weapons will be issued to some chosen members of staff by Captain Richardson. Any questions?' There was a noticeable change in the air; from gossip and expectation, to the reality of the danger that they, and their families, may be in. For a few moments, no-one seemed to move.

'Goodbye,' and Sir Robert was gone.

By morning the building was surrounded by police standing around in pairs chatting and watching, with batons drawn. The ends of the street were blocked with police and soldiers intermingling. A senior officer was standing with two others watching and waiting. All was quiet, unusually quiet. Then just a little sound drifting in from the direction of the port, just a murmuring, like the patter of footsteps on a hall carpet.

And then slowly, slowly over the gentle breeze came the stomping and the chanting, the beat demanding attention. The smell of burning was next, carried into the hallways of the High Commission by the same gentle breeze. Finally the crash of glass falling, and the screams, the shattering screams. They watched from the upstairs window as the police started the beatings but despite that, they had to slowly withdraw until they formed a tight semi-circle around the front of the building. Smoke was now billowing around the street, police and rioters coughing. Some of the rioters had stones and suddenly, in unison, a volley was aimed, clearly at the embassy, glass breaking everywhere from the front windows.

A cry from downstairs. A blood-stained body on the floor. Three guards there fast and two nurses with bandages. An ambulance getting through with the police forming a cordon, hitting and beating. Bodies being pulled away by their fellows. The doors open, the men through with their stretcher, and out rapidly putting the body into the back of the ambulance. Outside again, police pummelling and pounding.

And then it was gone. The staff were all shocked by the danger, the blood on the floor, and a colleague damaged. The colleague turned out to be Sir Robert's secretary, Gladys, who had been standing behind a downstairs window. A stone had caught her on the side of the head, and glass shards had shattered over her head and neck. Alan bumped into a highly distressed man.

'Oh Gladys, Gladys. This is so ghastly, so ghastly. I am so fond of her, Alan, you see.' Sir Robert gradually sat down on the floor and for a moment Alan thought that he was going to cry. Alan held his head in his hands, and sat down next to him putting a hand gently on his arm. Gradually the head came up.

'Sorry, sorry' he said. 'Just lost it there for a moment. Hope to God she's going to be OK. A wonderful woman, you see, Alan. And a bloody fine secretary. Sort of thing a man needs when he is over here. Tower of strength for me. Lost without her, lost without her.' And then he got up and walked away. Alan stood and Gloria was there. He told the story to Gloria, who had been calming a hysterical attache's wife. And at the end, he told her the Sir Robert's words and said

'And he called me 'Alan' – twice.'

'Wonderful. There's a real human being in there. The story about the pin-stripe is untrue.'

'What?'

'When I first arrived I met a pathologist when I was taken on a tour of the local hospital. The conversation had drifted around to Sir Robert. The pathologist, who had met him, had said 'if I transected his body, I am sure that I would find pin-stripe all the way through' and I had laughed. My error of judgement.'

Two hours later, they were summoned to Sir Robert's office. When they arrived, all the senior attaches were already there seated in a semi-circle around his desk. Tumblers of Scotch whisky or local wine were being dispensed. The High Commissioner began.

'I have heard from the Chief of our Cape Town hospital. She is unconscious but the doctors think that she will live. The Prime Minister, Mr. Hertzog, has just telephoned me to express his hopes for her survival. I have just sent a telegram to the Foreign Secretary. Miss Simpson, the stakes in this game have been raised considerably by the injury to a member of High Commission staff. Do we have any evidence of outside influence causing these riots?'

'Sir Robert, gentlemen. Perhaps I should explain that I am Head of S.I.S for southern Africa.' Several members of staff, clearly not aware of Gloria's work, looked at her in astonishment. 'I received notification from a member of my network yesterday that this riot was being arranged. It is possible that it was encouraged by the Mission of another country. I can give you no more information at the moment but I will be keeping Sir Robert up-to-date as soon as I get reliable information.' She finished and there was a buzz of conversation as the meeting broke up. Alan walked with her back to her office.

'How did you know all that?' He asked.

'Doubtless you remember your break-in at the offices of Cape Connections? You brought out for me a list of employees, one of whom turned out to be the niece of the brother of one of my network. He has been keeping close tabs on her through the family. She dropped a hint to the family to keep away from the downtown area. The brother told my man, who came to me.'

'And is it the Germans who are behind this?

'We don't know. But as they use this company for their diamond games, whatever they turn out to be, it must be possible that they are using the company to stir all these riots up. Remember we have never had anything like this before. And there definitely seems to be an anti-British element.'

'Maybe it's just because we British are in charge?'

'Maybe. I am going to find out. I am going to set a tail on this van der Linde and let's see who he meets. And I am going to have a little chat with the little girl who works in the office and see what she can tell us.'

'Careful now, Gloria. This might get a tad unpleasant.'

'Yes well you can be my hero, riding in on a silver charger.' He was unamused.

He strolled back upstairs and met Sir Robert as he was emerging from his office.

'Come in, Alan. Have a glass of something. We need our nerves steadying, I suspect.' They sat in his office companionably. Sir Robert looked out of the window.

'Very shocking to the system all this. Not quite what I was brought up to.'

'Where was your home, Sir Robert?' He asked.

'Oh my childhood, my childhood,' and he sank into a reverie. After a pause, he looked up at Alan clearly having made a decision that he would talk. 'I was raised in Margate on the Kent coast, along with my older brother John where we lived in a small house close to the sea-front. My father was manager of the local Barclays.' He paused, clearly thinking his story through.

'My parents were deeply religious with a definitely puritanical bent. There were no games on Sundays, no book was to be placed on top of the bible. The home was appropriately gloomy with thick velvet curtains everywhere and no pictures on the walls, but there were books, rather a lot of books apparently and I had devoured them.' 'A substitute for the deep dark homestead,' Alan guessed.

My father decided to send us boys to a small private school, St Lawrence College, down the road in Ramsgate where I excelled in Mathematics and Latin. Both I and John were also pretty good at both hockey and chess. At home John and I shared a bedroom close to the sea-front in Margate. In the Lancaster homestead, even for young men about to go to University, there was the institution of 'bedtime'. After we were in bed, and of course, after kneeling at the foot of our beds to say prayers, the lights were turned off by our unbending papa.

'Our energies, having not been expended during the day, we lay in the darkness playing blind chess, calling out moves until one or other of us fell asleep. I recall once, as teenagers, we had been taken by our father to Hastings a little way down the coast, to watch the eminent players in the famed British National chess tournament. We had watched in amazement as a small insignificant man named Fred Yates had crushed the field.' He laughed at the memory.

There was a pause. 'And after that?' Alan had asked, desperate that the opening up should not falter.

'After that, after that. Oh yes. Well I got into Oxford, read politics and been accepted into the Civil Service after graduating. Then I had various postings to the Diplomatic Corps, but apparently there were 'occasional slips' in my career, one of which occurred shortly after my knighthood.' Alan had looked quizzically but there had been no response

'So it looks as if this appointment to the Dominion is as far as my career is going to progress, and that I am not going to be awarded one of the big ambassadorial appointments to Washington, Paris or Berlin,' and he shrugged his shoulders.

His obvious sadness at the lack of ultimate success in his

career, as he clearly saw it, was clear to Alan, who in his turn felt both a surge of affection for the old man and a feeling of privilege that he had been permitted to share his emotion. The moment had passed quite quickly but the curtains had been withdrawn a little and Alan glimpsed the reality lurking inside his room.

After they parted, Alan walked around the streets, seeing once again debris-littered signs of destruction, causing him to ponder the causes for all this anger. He wondered 'whether deep down the blacks simply hated the whites, or was that too facile an explanation? Perhaps it wasn't so much a skin-colour problem or maybe it was about money? Maybe the divide is too great, maybe the communists have a point when they discuss the equal distribution of wealth in a society.' He passed a burnt–out grocery shop, fruit smouldering bizarrely in one corner, fried apples jostling with melting pears in a blackened fruit salad. He passed the coffee shop, seemingly untouched but boarded up, obviously prepared for the trouble. 'Maybe one of the waiters had known, and warned the boss. Perhaps that waiter had served him at his last coffee-visit. What did he know of the lives of the black people living here? Perhaps the resentment was a mixture of things – money, race and perhaps they were paid to create this mess?'

'Good afternoon, Alan.' He had almost collided with a man, so engrossed was he with his thoughts. He looked up. It was Louis du Plessis. 'What a mess.'

In his training, Alan had been taught never to believe in coincidence. So on the face of it, for Louis to appear here at this moment, was eminently suspicious. Alan remained calm and observant.

'Good afternoon. Yes it is a mess. I was just wondering what the motivation behind all this, was? Maybe you have some ideas?'

Louis laughed. 'Oh, indeed I have plenty of ideas. Things like race, skin colour, lack of integration. Matters such as that. I would sum it up under a general heading of 'Failure of fellowship.' And maybe something on top.' Alan looked at him carefully and understood that he might be about to learn something important. They walked in some silence towards the harbour, passing a small park dotted with trees and flowering shrubs. An empty bench appeared on their left and they sat down by mutual agreement.

'You mentioned '…something on top',' Alan said.

'Yes, well, I wondered what it was that triggered these two riots at this particular moment in time. We have never had this sort of problem. In 1922 we had a terrible strike called the Rand Rebellion but that was white miners striking over pay. In the end the army had to shoot many before the miners surrendered. Occasionally we have marches, but never this sort of violence from the Blacks. So I was wondering what had changed.' There was a pause. Eventually Alan asked,

'And what possibilities did you envisage?'

'I wondered whether there was anything or anyone behind it.' Alan decided to try not to seem too interested.

'Anyone in mind?' he asked smilingly, still completely in the dark about what on earth was going on in Louis' mind. He had clearly been picked up by a man known for his racial sympathies for Blacks, but about whom he really knew little, who wanted to discuss an important matter. Was he about to be fed information? And if so, who was behind the need for Alan to know that information?

'Well I did wonder about the coincidence of your own arrival with the timing of this disturbance.' Alan had been ready for much but he was now on his guard.

'How would I be involved?' he asked, trying hard to keep a relaxed smiling attitude.

'Well it seemed to me a possibility that you might know the answer to that,' and Louis smiled gravely. So – it was a fishing operation after all. Neatly turned, he felt, but he was far too experienced to let his guard down.

'Not a clue, old man,' he replied. And Louis saw the light flickering around Alan's head change colour and smiled to himself.

'Well, I had wondered whether some enemy state had read your mission wrongly and made assumptions about your presence here.'

'What enemy state and what assumptions?'

'I had wondered whether your presence related to some other European tensions.' Indeed he did. Rather too spot on for comfort. Alan looked at him seemingly nonchalantly, but in reality wondering on what form of words might extract something concrete from him. He had no idea that he was now covered in a frisson of purples and greys clashing unpleasantly to Louis mind. Clearly Louis knew or maybe had guessed something. If he knew, then the information must have come from the Germans unless... and he was struck with a somewhat worrying thought… Clearly, there were other options.

The first was Amit. They had thought that Amit was in the clear but it was still possible that Amit was playing a double game. If it was not Amit, then who else might know? It seemed unlikely that Gloria was a double agent, but what did he know of her? All he knew was that she was lovely looking, daddy was a Duke, and she presumably had been vetted some time ago by the Service. Maybe the vetting had been a touch light as daddy was a Duke. And then his mind wandered to anyone else at the High Commission. There were many of course that he didn't know. But there was Pringle. 'Pretty Useless Pringle.' But maybe Pretty Useless was playing up the 'pretty useless' tag and was not as feckless as he made out? Maybe a good disguise. Hiding in plain sight. Easy to hide behind everyone thinking of him as feckless when in fact…. He had been asked a question.

'Sorry, dreaming.'

'I wondered whether, supposing it was stirred-up, as to who gained? Mysteries are sometimes unravelled by asking that question.'

'Yes my Latin teacher was fond of it,' Alan replied. 'Cui bono. Well perhaps if we look at it simply, the rioters gain if they are paid. Then the paymasters are paying them to gain from the riot. The riot causes knock-on effects such as maybe a crack-down by the authorities. So maybe the Prime Minister could use it as an excuse to tighten restrictions, flood the streets with troops, enact certain legislation, or some such. You tell me. I have only been here a very short time. You have lived here all your life. What do you think?' Alan paused looking down towards the harbour, the sun warming the back of his neck.

'I doubt somehow that the Government are involved. Especially as the riots were clearly anti-British in nature. Down here at the foot of Africa, we often need to look at the European sector for answers to our local dilemmas, if they are inexplicable in local terms.' And Louis rose to his feet.

'I trust that our conversation has been enlightening, Mr. Drayson. Don't hesitate to have further discussions with me at any time. I am truly a great anglophile and I would hope that I could continue to help you on any local matters that are, shall we say, a little opaque. And of course bring the lovely Miss Simpson, should you wish. Good day to you.' As he walked back away from the park, Alan thought about the conversation and particularly the last sentences. If he had got it correct, du Plessis was offering information. Not only that but he somehow knew that Gloria was closely involved. So how did he know that? Maybe his friend at De Beers had told him. Or maybe he just knew anyway. And then there was what appeared to be the offer of more and regular information about, now how did he put it '…local matters that are a little opaque.' So that was a clear suggestion that he knew either of other things or of more depth to the matter in hand.

He sat with Gloria at the back of the local bar and watched her take in the information. Her gin and tonic sat momentarily untouched while she focussed on his encounter with Louis. She agreed that the contact needed some urgent follow-up.

'Funnily enough, Louis' name cropped up at the cocktail party last week. I was talking to Carl about poetry and Carl had mentioned that Louis was a fine home-grown South African poet and writer.' After a pause for thought, Alan said,

'So Louis seems well-connected. First de Beers and then the German embassy. He has fingers in many pies around here. I just hope that he is not working for someone else. We will certainly need to tread carefully with any more of his snippets. I am going to arrange another visit and perhaps you should come too as anyway he clearly understands that we are working together.'

'Sounds good and sometimes a second pair of ears helps. Anyway, I would be curious to see this garden of his.'

Chapter Seventeen

Louis' past is revealed

There was a message from Amit in the Drop. Alan met him at a new rendezvous on a green bench on Beach Road, looking out towards the ocean. A large P. and O. liner was just leaving harbour, with two others outside waiting to enter the port. A few smaller vessels were steaming around the point heading towards the Indian Ocean.

'Lovely meeting point, Amit. I could sit and watch the water for hours from here.'

'I am glad that you like it here, Alan. I walked here on my first day, having no idea of where I was. It always seems a place of peace and calm.'

'You have some news for me.' Alan was not in the mood for idle chat. Besides which, even though most people were families headed for the beach, it was clearly not at all private.

'Yes, indeed. They were excited last night at dinner.'

'Who was excited?'

'Just the two of them were dining. Carl and Ambassador von Bauer. I made a sea-food curry. The plates were emptied rapidly but they took against my raita.' He looked momentarily saddened at the thought of his yoghurt and cucumber delicacy.

Frankly Alan was appalled at his lack of focus. 'Amit, we are very exposed here. Please leave all thoughts of your dinner and its side-dishes and focus on the information. I need to know what we are doing here and then we need to go our separate ways as speedily as possible.'

'Sorry Sahib. There is about to be a delivery in the next day or two. That is all that I know.'

'Any comments on how it is coming, who is bringing it?'

'Nothing, Alan.' I stood.

'Thank you, Amit. Keep me in touch as soon as you know anything more. In an emergency, get a runner to bring a note to me at the High Commission. Make sure that the runner cannot identify yourself.' Alan walked away rapidly. He saw one man looking vaguely at himself but was certain that he was not followed, as he made a circuitous route back to the High Commission. Gloria was waiting for him at the entrance.

'Where have you been? I have been looking for you everywhere. I have exciting news. Come to my office.' He trailed after her and slumped into the seat after closing the door.

'Dieter Furtwangler has called me from Oudtshoorn. He has been told by Carl to expect a delivery of diamonds 'very soon.' And also to expect the arrival of the promised secretary from the embassy who will help with the sewing up of the silica bags. You will be amused to hear that Dieter was much embarrassed because Carl has told him that he must give her a room to sleep in. Dieter was worried about 'his reputation!"

Later Alan told her of Amit's offering. So they realised that it seemed to be true that the Germans were going to use a dual system for the smuggling. Maybe they were using a first batch to test each route to ensure ease of use, and the safety of the supply lines. They wandered off separately to have lunch and Alan went to his office to think through the scenario and indeed what should be their plan of action. They had established their information lines with great efficiency. Firstly Roderick Patterson at De Beers was going to notify them when a shipment was due. And now he was thinking about it him, he was surprised that he had heard nothing from the Scot, if a delivery was due. He would remember to talk this through with Gloria later. 'Maybe an excuse for an after-work cocktail!'

Next they had the ostrich feather packaging strategy sorted via the great composer's nephew. But the transit through the German embassy was a mystery, as was its' onward transmission to Europe. Maybe the Germans were simply planning to use the Diplomatic Bag. It was of course a safe and tested method of transmission, but if they were using this method, why would they use another? And clearly the answer must be that they were using some other method. Clearly he needed better intelligence from inside – and that meant Amit. And Amit had told him today that he only knew about the delivery and no mention of any trans-shipment. His thoughts went round and round but without any easy answers.

And then there was Louis du Plessis. He clearly knew

more than he had said, and it was also quite unclear what role he was playing. Maybe he was just a freelancer playing with them all? Or possibly one of Carl's agents? Alan decided that a further cup of tea with an Afrikaaner poet might be useful. He picked up the telephone and arranged for a visit.

'Oh yes, and the lovely Miss Simpson would more than double the pleasure of the visit. And this afternoon at 3.30 would be perfect as I have some news for you.'

Alan wondered on the nature of the news. He also wondered if the man's manners were too perfect to be believable but decided that this line of thought was not profitable, and hurried off to find Gloria. They walked to the Du Plessis mansion in the warmth of the afternoon sun. The only thing following them was a sad and hungry looking stray dog.

They sat on the terrace in an almost identical position to Alan's previous visit. Gloria was clearly enchanted by the double borders and the pool in the distance. Louis was at his most urbane.

'I had hoped for a visit. And bringing Miss Simpson enhances it. I feel that you have favoured me, Alan.' Tea was served. There were small biscuits.

'Please have one. They are home-made by myself. The formula is from a neighbour whose mother handed her the secret. She refuses absolutely to divulge it to me – but my servant George has a warm and intimate relationship with her maid, Betsy and has obtained this precious recipe.' and he grinned, vaguely maliciously Alan felt. 'It's going to be in my next cookbook but my neighbour doesn't know yet.

Doubtless there will be hell to pay when she finds out.' The grin remained.

'Please don't tell your Amit, Alan,' he continues. Alan and Gloria both regarded him with surprise.

'My Amit?' Alan queried.

'Just a manner of speech,' he replied. They looked at each other not knowing quite what to say. But he continued quickly. 'Indeed I am pleased that you are here by such good chance. I received a call from my good friend, Roderick Patterson, the Scottish man who I believe has had the privilege of meeting you both. Indeed he tells me that you were both 'utterly charming.' He wanted you to know that the man that you both know is collecting 'a very small packet' from him tomorrow. He also wanted you to know that the German was bringing a woman with him.' Louis looked at them both, clearly wondering why that piece of information was of such importance. And Gloria had looked at Alan, clearly also puzzled. Alan understood the significance immediately but decided not to be too transparent with Louis, who clearly wanted to know.

'And his words were 'a very small packet?' Alan asked mainly to divert the conversation away from the mysterious woman accompanying Carl.

'Yes, his exact words. Roderick made me repeat back the words that I have now relayed to you.'

'Well, thank you for being a courier. I hope that you are content with that role?'

'Do I have a choice? It seems to me that 'the game's afoot', but I am unclear of the nature of the game.'

Alan laughed.

'Aha, I spy another fan of Sherlock Holmes.'

'Not really. In fact the quotation is really from that famous speech of Henry V before Agincourt, that begins 'Once more into the breach, dear friends' and ends… and at this point, their host rose to his feet, assumed a tragic pose with arms outstretched and declaimed –

'I see you stand like greyhounds in the slips,
Straining at the start. The game's afoot
Follow your spirit; and upon this charge
Cry 'God for Harry, England and Saint George!'

'Bravo, bravo.' Applause and laughter could be heard from the English.

'Were you ever on the stage, Louis?' asked Gloria.

'In my youth, kind maiden,' he smiled at her, gracing her with a sweeping bow.

'I am sure that you were marvellous,' she said. He bowed again – as an encore.

'So I am afraid that Mr. Conan Doyle has pilfered the phrase from a king of England. What a nerve the man has! But I have subverted our conversation, I fear.'

'That's not a problem, Louis. Time is no problem for us.'

'We are spared and blessed by time.' And again he was up on his feet declaiming. Alan felt that he was seeking admiration from Gloria, but could not stop himself asking, 'Shakespeare?'

'Actually, your Lord Byron. Childe Harold. There I have wrecked the flow of conversation again. Back to the game. I was trying to press you for the nature of the game.'

'And I was valiantly resisting,' laughed Alan. 'But I value your help with this game and for your statement earlier about being an Anglophile.'

'How can any thinking poet fail to be an anglophile. You and the French have given us so much to be grateful for. Other nations are but bystanders in the race.'

'Even the Russians?'

'Hmm. Pushkin is of course a treasure. Such a mind, such an expander of language. But for the rest, I do not like the moderns. The Lermontovs, the Mandelstams of the new Russian poetry clique.' Alan was admiring, and very aware that this polymath's knowledge was out of his league. Louis turned to him and asked,

'By the way, did you know that there is a Pushkin Diamond?'

'Found here?' and the words were hardly out of his mouth before Alan realised that he had fallen into a large bear trap.

'No, Alan, found in Russia, but I am fascinated to hear of your continuing interest in our mining enterprises. Do elaborate.' Alan could see no way out of the trap that he had allowed himself to fall into. And Louis laughed to himself as Alan's colours changed from their pure greens into a turmoil of rainbow shades as confusion muddled Alan's thinking. Louis watched his colours coalesce as Alan determined a way out of the obvious hole that he had dug. Gloria rescued the hapless rainbow-hued Alan.

'Now Mr. Du Plessis, I am yearning to see your garden borders,' Gloria told him.

'Two things. First, do call me Louis. Second, I am a man

who is unable to resist the yearnings of a beautiful woman,' and he rose to his feet. 'Let us walk.' Alan followed behind, feeling sulky.

Eventually Gloria and Alan strolled home, deviating slightly so that they could drink a cocktail in the courtyard bar of the Hotel Metropole in Long Street. Gloria pointed out a couple of members of parliament at a corner table, and Alan found himself both impressed that she had spotted them, and wondering when it was that she had gotten so observant or whether she had always been this way and he simply hadn't noticed.

A small band played jazz and cigarette smoke wafted across the room. The dance floor was occupied by a few couples moving idly, occasionally in time to the music. Gloria had ordered two 'Sidecars,' and explained to Alan that it was simply a daiquiri with brandy in place of rum. He was not much the wiser for her explanation, but he appreciated that no-one knew their cocktails quite like Gloria did, and he wasn't about to tell her that his knowledge was very much limited to drinking whatever it was that she was having.

'I cannot quite decide what game Louis is playing. He professes to love us as the *fons et origo* of the world of poetry but it is by no means clear to me that this is the simple explanation behind his desire for information. And I wasn't very keen on his attachment to you, either.' She ignored the personal comment.

'You think that he might be working for someone else?' she wondered.

'Well that must be possible, and Germany is a possibility.

213

He did set us up with Patterson at De Beers. But now Patterson seems to be telling us about the first shipment, so on the face of it that looks like helpful information, suggesting that they are batting on our side.'

'Supposing he is just collecting information for use at a later time to bargain against us, or even the Germans.'

'Possible, but it seems like a rather dangerous strategy even for a long game. He would risk one or the other of us getting rather cross with him. I think that something else is going on that we know little of. I am not sure what it is but it feels strange to me, just strange.' They both studied their empty glasses.

'Time for another?' he asked. 'And a dance?' The waiter brought them new drinks and they moved around the floor in a friendly but somehow intimate way. He could feel her breath on his neck and her head laid gently on his shoulder.

When they got back to the High Commission, a note awaited Alan.

'Carl and Maria Weber, one of secretaries, left this afternoon with suitcases. He was driving – Destination unknown. A'

'As Louis would say "The game's afoot." So why the secretary and where have they gone?'

'Well how about they are going for a little R. and R. as the soldiers used to say. Maybe they are having a mad passionate affair?' She giggled.

'Are we having a mad passionate affair?'

'Quite possibly,' and she stroked the sleeve of his jacket. It occurred to him that 'mad and passionate' were historically a combination that didn't end well, but with Gloria's hand against his arm, it was easy to push the thought aside. Now wasn't the time to doubt what they had, professionally and personally, and he dragged himself back to the matter of the two escapees.

'But maybe they are going to Kimberley.'

'Indeed. And she is going along for the ride?'

'Maybe they are coming home via Oudtshoorn.' He thought.

'Oh yes and leaving half the diamonds with Dieter. She will sew up the bag for the boy while Carl has a stroll and then they drive back here with the other half. Very nice – and maybe they get a bit of the mad passionate affair which undoubtedly they richly deserve.' And they both chuckled at the thought, and Alan felt relieved that Carl wasn't driving off into the sunset with Gloria. 'So now we wait to hear from Dieter at the Ostrich Farm, Amit in the kitchen, or the Scot with the Diamonds. But while we wait, I was wondering…' She kissed him, and all of Alan's worries dissipated. He grinned at her.

'Me too.'

Chapter Eighteen

The deliveries begin

In the end, later in the afternoon of the following day, it was the Scot with the diamonds who came through first. Alan was summoned to the High Commission phone and was delighted to exchange a little banter with Roderick, phoning as Mr. James, who was much less official than at their first meeting in Kimberley. The only thing that was confusing to both the Scot and the Englishman was the size of the 'delivery.' There were to be only ten of the smallest 'chips' in this first consignment with the total value being just a nominal sum. De Beers were expecting Carl the next day – a Wednesday – with an appointment for the office booked for 10a.m.

After the call was finished, Alan went and sat in the courtyard to think. The extremely small size of the shipment was exercising his mind. Originally they had discussed a plan to try to intercept this first shipment, but maybe that would not be so clever. If the shipment were small, it seemed likely that the Germans were in fact testing their systems. It would hardly be worth intercepting any shipment if it was a trial run. If they were to intercept such a small shipment, the Germans would be warned and would themselves have hardly lost anything. Surely it would be much better to wait for a large shipment, hopefully worth thousands of pounds before leaping on the diamonds? Also it would be much smarter to make the Germans believe that all was well within their delivery chains. Then they would be lulled into a false sense of security and he and Gloria would have better details of exactly how the chains would work so that if they pounced, they would be properly informed.

Gloria came down to the courtyard as he was finishing his thinking and scheming and he set out the scenario to her. She agreed that watching and waiting was the better option. They discussed who should know about 'the game.' Clearly, London needed to give its blessing. London would also need to know the details so that they could watch the progress through the European end. They discussed whether Sir Robert Lancaster should know and decided that, in the end if they were going to unravel the shipments, the local police would also need to be involved at some point. They decided to agree to wait for the moment, but to involve the High Commissioner when a larger shipment was imminent.

The following morning Dieter phoned, his voice full of excitement and keen to share every detail with Alan, who had to calm him a little, reminding him as discretely as possible about the possibility of a bugged phone call. Fortunately, Dieter managed to keep his language as instructed on their visit, so that the discussion had apparently centred on a shipment of ostrich feathers and the delivery arrangements to the docks for the consignment.

'Dieter expects Carl and his companion on Friday morning.' Alan told Gloria. 'Are we all ready for what is going to happen?'

'Maybe, maybe not. Let's see. We believe that the shipment, small as it is, will be halved, with half going out in silica sachets placed in a consignment of Ostrich feathers for Germany through the docks at Port Elizabeth. The other half is being brought back to the embassy but after that we are none the wiser. Presumably they will try to send it by air but then it will land at Croydon before being flown on to Berlin. The Germans might not like that.'

'Certainly if they land diamonds in England, we would have a great advantage.'

'But you can only fly out of here on Imperial Airways, and Imperial Airways fly to England. Unless...' and she paused in thought. 'Where does the plane stop before it gets to England? Maybe Athens or somewhere?'

He shrugged.

'Well let's ask someone. Whom do you suggest?'

'How about Pretty Useless?' She laughed.

'Yes it's the sort of information that he might indeed have.'

Alan hesitated before reminding Gloria, 'Let's be careful about it though. The less people know about what we're doing, the better. Just in case.'

Gloria agreed and requested that James meet her on a bench outside under the guise of requiring some information about the area for general embassy records. Alan stayed behind in Gloria's office in the hopes that it would arose less suspicion. Gloria and James sat on the bench enjoying the warmth and peace of the courtyard, and Gloria asked a few mundane questions about the Cape before she posed the real question.

'Brindisi and Le Bourget after Athens,' came the immediate response.

'Oh James you always are so useful,' she smiled ingratiatingly. After some more idle chat to ensure James was suitably in the dark about it all, the two departed the sunshine and headed back into the embassy.

Back inside Gloria's office, she and Alan mused over the possibilities.

'Well now that gives them two real opportunities,' Alan said. 'I am sure that the Germans will not want to have the diamonds sitting around in Croydon, so they could disembark them in France or Italy for forwarding to the Reich. Probably more likely France, as undoubtedly there will be regular flights from there to Berlin. I think the French airline is Air Union. Maybe Lufthansa also flies, now that some of the Versailles restrictions have been lifted. I will find out.' 'Obviously London would need to be involved and what else?' He wondered. Little more could be done until some of the contacts gave news of the movements of the German pair. But Alan was still bothered by Louis and felt that there was a danger leaving him as an unknown factor hanging in the background. Louis clearly suspected much and even knew a lot of the game that was being played. If he was to be on side, he could be a valuable asset with his local knowledge and his own string of contacts.

Maybe it was time for Alan to be more assertive, like Gloria had been in acquiring much of the information that had been crucial so far in their mission.

So Alan had called. 'Yes, Louis would be delighted to dine this evening. Yes, Louis would choose the restaurant. Yes, 7.30p.m. would be perfect.' In the end, Alan had asked Gloria to join too. He felt that if Louis had warmed to her, perhaps Gloria's presence would be an asset to gauging where they all stood.

Together Alan and Gloria had walked to the restaurant where they were seated on the terrace with simply stunning views over the bay. The houses around the bay were all lit up along the shore and the lights of the ships glimmered out at sea. Louis was already seated at the table, waiting for them. A warm breeze ruffled the table cloth; the men kept their jackets on and Gloria kept a cardigan wrapped around her shoulders. The diners were all white, the waiters all black. Louis amplified his views of the tragedy that this would lead to.

'I can see a time coming when the whites will legalise the complete separation of the races in everything – housing, sitting on benches, the job market, everything. And eventually there will be violence. You know that we had Mahatma Gandhi here. I remember as a child being taken to meet him by my father. He was a rather dapper young man, an 'English' lawyer at that time, appalled by the British attitude to Indians that he experienced when he arrived. Indeed I recall him telling us how he had been beaten when walking down the street here by a policeman, because he was walking on the 'wrong footpath'. Sadly he has left us now and fights for his rights in his own country.'

'He has been in London recently,' said Alan. 'He chose to stay in a small room in a Hall of residence in the East End. He was mobbed on his arrival by thousands of admirers but he was viciously attacked by Winston Churchill in a speech describing him as 'a half-naked fakir.' Seemed rather unfair to most of us as the man is a qualified London lawyer.'

'Well, we need him and his non-violence movement here to instil sense into the minds of our rulers, both English and Afrikaans.' There was a pause and they ordered – the men having meat while Gloria stuck to a spicy salad mix.

'So perhaps it is time that we sorted out what is going on here,' and Louis sat back and smiled at them both. 'I know exactly what the game is here as perhaps you both realised. And I wish to help you in your endeavour.' And he drank a little wine from his glass. 'The wine here in the Cape is really first class. You must drink a lot. It is so good for your health. I have written a book on the subject, have you heard of it?' Both shook their heads. 'Oh, it's called Common Sense Dietetics. Not much liked by your British Medical Journal, but it has sold well here.' And he laughed. 'My publishers are getting it re-published next year under a new title – 'The Belly Book.' I hate it but they say that it will help sales.'

'You were saying that you wish to help us.' Alan attempted to bring the conversation back to the game.

'Oh yes, I deviated. Good at that.' And he smiled, somewhat sadly.

'Well perhaps you would like to know why I want to help you? It is simple really. When I was a young man we had a family friend named Harry Bolus. He was a botanist and kindled in me an extraordinary love of all things natural. I used to go on walks with him and he would name all the trees. He would show me magical things about nature. We would sit and watch a humming-bird hawkmoth dipping its long proboscis deeply into long-belled flowers to suck up the nectar while hovering quite still.' Louis paused to drink a few sips.

'He was so impressed with my interest and ability to remember everything that he taught me, that he offered to send me to London to study medicine. We had no medical school here at the time and my family were not wealthy people so my parents were delighted at this offer. I passed all the exams here with flying colours and was accepted at Guys Hospital, where I arrived in the summer of 1902. I was looked after by a cousin on my mother's side who lived in Bermondsey. I just loved the medicine. Our teachers were fine men and gave me a great sense of devotion to their subject. And I loved London and your country. I shall be forever in debt to your country which has given me the privilege of joining my noble vocation. So, I will do any-thing that you may wish to help your enterprise.' The story was so heartfelt, and given in such openness of spirit, that Alan felt he needed no further re-assurance. He looked at Gloria and saw that she felt similarly.

'What did you do after qualifying?' Gloria asked him. Louis laughed.

'Well, I had a stroke of luck really. To celebrate the

passing of my final exams, my mother's cousin took me to Simpson's restaurant in the Strand. We went for a celebratory glass of champagne first in the bar upstairs, and there were two other men seated there. One of them had a full head of hair and a commanding presence. Somehow we got into conversation and he discovered our reason for being there. He quizzed me about my exam results and on discovering that I had done very well, offered me a job as his personal physician. His name was Pulitzer. Naturally I knew of Mr. Pulitzer – who didn't? It seemed like manna from the skies, and I accepted on the spot, being also of course young and impetuous.' And indeed Louis' face seemed to Alan to have become younger and more animated as he was telling the story.

'Of course his story ends sadly, as you may know. We were sailing in his yacht, the Liberty, down the west coast of America to Mr. Pulitzer's home in Jekyll Island off the coast of Georgia. He had a whole apartment in the old Club Hotel there, where he saw the winter through, surrounded by other very wealthy personages. Mr Pulitzer felt unwell and told the Captain that he wanted to go on shore, and by chance we were just passing Charleston at the time. Mr. Pulitzer was lying down while his secretary, who was originally from Germany, was reading to him and I was seated close by. We were just entering Charleston harbour when he said 'Leise, ganz leise.' (In English – *softly, quite softly*). And he just closed his eyes, and died. Such a sadness for us all.' Louis stopped, staring into the distance, and neither Alan nor Gloria felt any desire to push him to continue talking. After a moment, Louis continued,

'And of course I was out of a job. After a few weeks in the beautiful old city of Charleston I took a boat back to London where I applied for, and was accepted as, doctor to a large school for orphan boys in the East End. Eventually I left, returned here and became Medical inspector for schools in the Transvaal, before finally returning here.' He laughed; the mood lifted once again. 'My life, spread before you.' And at that moment the food arrived, and Alan decided that the time had come to be open and spelt out to Louis most but not all of the details as he knew it.

'And so you can see that we are at a tense moment. We believe that by tomorrow, one small batch will be delivered to our man with the ostriches, Dieter Furtwangler.' Gloria clearly loved the 'our man with the ostriches' line and squeezed Alan's knee surreptitiously under the table. 'Furtwangler, Furtwangler? Is he by any chance a relative of...?'

'...the conductor.' Alan finished his sentence. 'Yes, the nephew.'

'How did I not know that this man was in our country? Next time that you go to Outdsthoorn, may I come too? I wish to worship like the three wise men at the feet...' and he paused. 'And is his uncle going to come here? Will he visit here? Can we persuade him to conduct the Cape Town Municipal Orchestra? You know that they played in London a few years ago – even played at Buckingham Palace for the King and Queen? I will arrange the concert. I am friends with our conductor here, a man called Svinsky, a wonderful man.' Louis had become uncharacteristically over-excited. He ran out of steam, allowing the others to laugh at his sudden stimulation.

'Of course we will take you to see Dieter. We may well anyway be going there soon. But at the moment there are no plans for his uncle to visit.' Alan told him. The meal slowly wound down, they said their goodbyes, and walked back to their respective homes.

'Well,' she said, 'he told a marvellous story.'

'And so he did,' he said thoughtfully. 'But I was not sure about the 'I shall be forever in debt to your country which has given me the privilege of joining my noble vocation.' It sounded like a prepared speech that he was reciting to me.'

'You are too cynical. Anyway I liked his story.' And she chose not to mention to Alan that he was, in her eyes very handsome with his strong jaw, his large nose and his light brown hair flopping over his forehead.

'And,' asked Alan, 'How did Louis know 'what the game is?''

Chapter Nineteen

How my light shines

Louis

I see them across the table and I, Louis, know them. But they cannot know me and my facility. They are not privy to my world of provenance. I am above their consciousness; their divinity is the lesser. Where they believe that they have their own world of knowledge, they are missing the whole point of the exercise. They will ask themselves about truth in their own trivial world, their microcosm of reality. Perhaps they believe that Conrad's answers were profound. He played with the words without the understanding that the experience of attitude creates its own reality. And they cannot know of the tree of knowledge of the colour which reveals them in the light, exposes their lies – and I suppose their honesty – into the brain of truth. There is no hiding from the truth of the colours.

When I was young I did not know what it was. I thought that everyone else saw it as I did. Don't we all think that our 'normal' is everyone's 'normal?' For the child the family is the normal. And for the child with no family, the orphan? When I realised suddenly around my fifteenth birthday, I all of a sudden understood the utter impoverishment of the orphan. Now I treasure that impoverishment and strive with all my being to improve it. I run this home for these orphans for that reason, to try to overcome the pathetic lack of understanding of loss that is the tragedy of the orphan.

And for ever I return to my colours, to the rainbow of truth that shimmers through the world of man, to the gift that is mine and almost mine alone. The gift that interprets my world. What was it that Pulitzer told me – 'that there is more to the world than the world of literature, to the world of words, there is the world of perception. Without perception, no words have true meaning, just circulate on the periphery.' I loved him, of that there was no doubt in my mind. And when we turned so slowly, so gently into Charleston harbour and James was reading the opening lines of Mignon's song – *Kennst du das Land, wo die Zitronen blühn?*' ('Do you know the land where the lemon trees bloom?') and I felt the wind blowing gently in the leaves of the Italian lemon trees, when I knew that death was with us and I saw the black aura around his beloved head and he turned and it seemed as if death himself had said 'Leise, ganz leise' but of course it was not, and the words came from the mouth of the dread being in the cabin with us. And we could see the roofs of the wondrous old houses of Charleston before us, and the life force left him in a rainbow, slipping through the walkway. James too had loved him but could not see as I could, and was beside himself in utter anguish.

Sometimes the added sensation fails to add to me when I can see the deception of man written across them and I have to discount their words. At first as the realisation came upon me, I was distraught with the perfidy of man and crushed myself down into my own world. I stopped listening as I knew that the lies brought me lower and lower and I contemplated the end of myself. I could not share my facility as I knew that I was alone with it and I would open myself to mockery.

Then, eight long lonely years later, I was at Guy's Hospital soon to qualify and a man from Switzerland came to lecture us on advances in psychiatry. And he used the words, the words that allowed me to open the doors. Afterwards I summoned up the courage and told him just the simplest sentence, 'I see the colours.' And he knew, he knew immediately there standing there in the lecture theatre by the Thames in London, he knew. Immediately he removed everyone from the Theatre and sat down, looking into my eyes.

'Are you very alone and frightened?' he asked. Tears came to my eyes and I was embarrassed before this great man.

'Do not be afraid. You are not alone.' He spoke in the kindness of his heart. It was like Christ on the Road to Emaeus. 'There are others.' I journeyed to Switzerland at his invitation and we spent some hours beside the lake, the beautiful lake at Geneva. He told me everything that he knew and I was comforted and understood that I should feel myself blessed and not alone in the world, and he used the word *Synaesthism*. He told me of the first description by Sachs in the year 1812 and of the work of the famed Englishman Francis Galton.

So they do not know, these English, that I see their colours, their colours of England and St. George, and that their colours are strong and honest so I know that they are righteous and trustworthy and honest people. I see the colours of Amit Jaipur and his colours are the most azure, the closest to Lapis that I have ever experienced. I see the colours of Carl from Alsace and his are the most orange-yellow, sullen, mustard in my experience.

So my colours of synaesthism help me to sort the righteous from the deceivers. They guide me through the paths of life and help me to know of the ways of the good and the ways of the evil, as it was for Adam and Eve before they were banished by God from the Garden of Eden.

Chapter Twenty

The consignments are on the move

Roderick sat behind his desk, trying his utmost to act the part, being both charming but still professional, as he ordered tea to be brought in for the man and woman in front of him. As he poured three cups, keeping his hand on the teapot firm and steady, he couldn't help but smile at the irony of it all. In exactly the same spot that the two Germans now sat had been the two English folk the previous week, and for this meeting Roderick had even ensured the chairs were arranged in the same way, for his own amusement. All the people who had sat in those seats, after all, were sitting in Roderick's own office – not the other way around, no matter how important they might think that they are. Carl was charming, there was no doubt about that, and his travelling companion, Judit, the so-called Cultural secretary was equally gorgeous although she spoke little, letting Carl take charge. There was something measured about his humour, a subtle restraint that made Roderick slightly uneasy.

'So you've come all this way for this?' Roderick took a sip

of tea and nodded to the little sachet in front of him. Carl had already counted out the ten small fragments inside.

'I regard this as simply a start to ensure that my superiors are happy with the products, and I felt that it was my duty to appear in person at your company's offices. Perhaps next time I may be able to purchase a larger consignment from you.' Carl nodded self-assuredly and reclined back into the seat, looking directly into Roderick's eyes as he spoke. Undeterred, Roderick smiled casually back, changing the subject deftly. 'Are you off straight back to the Cape?' he asks.

'Not quite. We're going to visit a friend in Oudtshoorn on the way home.'

'Buying feathers for Judit's hat?' It was a crucial part of sales and negotiation, and one that Roderick thrived at, knowing personal connections in his customer's lives. 'Of course there are other things in Ostrich-ville. But for me the meat is terrible – I refuse to touch it.'

'Perhaps usually it is but we have a new chef at the Embassy, and I've no doubt that he'll make it into a delicious curry. And when you next come to the Cape we'll invite you to dinner so that you can appreciate his magic touch. It's not easy to find someone with that much talent outside of Germany.'

Roderick laughed and not long after the two Germans left almost as swiftly as they had arrived, taking the diamonds with them. After they'd gone, Roderick moved the chairs back to their normal positions in his office and watched out of the window as they drove away.

Carl drove out of Kimberley and took the long road

back to Oudtshoorn, while the beauty of the hills and veldt surrounds them in its warmth and colour. They rested overnight at a small ranch with stunning views over the surrounding hills. In the morning they travelled on past the occasional vineyard until they approach the alfalfa fields on the approaches to Oudtshoorn. They arrived in the town of the ostrich and drove directly to Dieter's house, once more to drink tea and once more to sit in a triangle. Carl rather liked the symmetry of tea and triangle. He produced half of the splints, which Dieter examined with interest.

'So we will make a little mark with black ink on the silica bag that they are to be hidden in, the better to identify them,' and he produces a small silica bag into which he makes a small cut. The diamonds disappear into the bag. Judit produced a piece of cotton and needle and deftly sewed the top. The cut is barely visible. Carl makes a large black ink dot on the bag and Dieter placed it with a dozen others into a consignment of beautiful white feathers, carefully wrapped the package and sealed it into a large solid-looking box for transit.

'Where to, sir?' Dieter asks.

'Peter Shroeder, 14, Lietzenburger Strasse, Berlin.'

'And which boat will it travel in?'

'Well, I was going to send it to Hamburg by the next boat to dock in Algoa Bay. And from Hamburg it will travel by our courier service to the customer – in this case to Mr. Shroeder's house in Berlin.'

'The next boat will be' … and Dieter consults his shipping timetable… 'if I hurry, it could catch the Carnarvon

Castle, which stops at Port Elizabeth next Tuesday en route for the Cape, the Azores, Southampton and Hamburg. It takes about thirteen days. A wonderful ship. Enormous, one of their newest boats. Very luxurious I believe, though I have never been inside myself.'

'Ah now Dieter, we have a couple of specific requirements for our little gift for Mr. Shroeder. The first being that it should travel on a German boat, preferably on the Deutsche Afrika-Linien.'

'That will not be a problem. The ships of the German Africa line pass through regularly. In fact the Adolph Woermann will be here the day after the Carnavon Castle. A great boat too but a little smaller than the Union castle boat.' Carl bristled somewhat.

'And our second requirement is that the boat must not land in England.'

'Not land in England? But I think that all boats stop-over in Southampton, Carl, German, French whatever the Line.' Carl was taken aback.

'Why should that be?'

'I assume that lots of English are travelling. This is after all an English colony.'

'Dominion,' Carl corrected.

'Yes you're right. But the point is that there are a lot of English around. And they and their relatives travel back and forward. Let me look at the time-table and see what I can find. There must be a way…' And he tailed off, searching succeeding pages. A silence filled the room and swirled around it, broken occasionally by vague distant animal-like noises from out-side, presumably the grunting

233

of contented ostriches. Carl wondered why the Lord failed to note that Noah had no ostriches in the ark, and was going to raise the topic with Dieter but then thought better of it as he felt that, as a good German citizen of the Reich, to appear to have a sense of humour might be rather spoiling of the image.

'I have it. The Usambara, a boat of the German Africa Lines calls at Algoa Bay en route to Durban. But this boat, unlike almost all the others then returns to Germany via Suez. Its journey outwards ends at Durban, where all the passengers must leave ship while the ship is cleaned etc. Then it departs homeward, and on its travel home to Hamburg, stops at many places, including Dar-es-Salaam and Mombassa, passing through the Suez canal, and then on to Marseilles and Malaga. From there however it goes to Rotterdam and thence to Hamburg BUT with no stops in England.'

Carl was entranced. 'Well done, Dieter. We will have to give you a good reward for that journey of nautical exploration.' And they all smiled.

'I am totally confused,' she said, 'why all this talk of Algoa Bay. I thought that the town was called Port Elizabeth?'

'It is, my dear.' Dieter noted the patronising manner with which Carl treated her. 'The town is immediately adjacent to the Bay which has deep water very close to shore and so it makes it easy for the big liners to berth.'

'But they need to be a bit careful on the way in and out,' Dieter told them, 'as there are a number of submerged islands and reefs, sometimes only appearing at the lowest tides. A number of ships have gone down over the centuries.'

'So when does the Umbarato arrive?' Carl was bored.

'No, the ship is the Usambara, and it will be in port immediately after the departure of the Adolph Woermann, so you will lose little time. I have never seen the boat myself so I will take the opportunity to drive to Port Elizabeth, see it and make my acquaintance with the Captain. Perhaps that that would be a good move if we are regularly using this ship. We will also have to set up a Customs procedure, as we normally use Union Castle boats for our postages to Europe.'

'That sound's a good plan. And we will of course pay what is required. All invoices to me at the Embassy. Assure the customs officers that we are prompt payers of our bills. Tell them to impound the ship if they are worried – after all it's German,' and Carl could not help smile at his little joke. Dieter was somewhat shocked – there had now been two jokes in five minutes. They stood to say their goodbyes and Carl said

'And how is your uncle Wilhelm? Still annoying the Reichsfurher?' Dieter was horrified. Was this a threat to himself, or to his uncle? Or maybe just a warning shot? He said nothing as Carl waved goodbye with a cheerful farewell gesture. They climbed into the car and drove off along the road back to Cape Town where they arrived that evening.

Carl and the Ambassador dined alone. Amit had conjured up an ostrich-meat curry and the two men were fulsome with their praise for Amit's cooking. Much good

Alsatian wine was drunk. Indeed the ambassador noted the label had the word 'Tokay Pinot Gris' on it. The all-knowing chef was summoned.

'Amit, how can this wine be labelled Tokay and be from Alsace?'

'Ah, my esteemed ambassador, you have noted the conundrum. Forgive my telling of a short but I trust interesting, story. In the town of Colmar, not too far from the home town of the Wasserburg family,' a small nod to Carl here, 'is a statue of a man holding up a vine. This man, most regrettably I forget his name, was a General in the Holy Roman Empire.' 'Aha, so the Indian memory not quite perfect,' muses Carl, somewhat ungraciously.

'Apparently, after one of his raids on behalf of his emperor, one Maximilian 11, he 'liberated' a vine of the famous Tokay wine and planted it in his home soil in Alsace. It flourished, not truly surprisingly, as the original Pinot vines for the wine were stolen from the Alsace in the first place, many years before. With the success of the grapes and its wine, the Baron, as he had become as a result of his successful war-making, applied the name 'Tokay' to his wine in the belief that the citizens of his home land would drink more of it with the famous Hungarian name attached, and of course pay him more. Needless to say, he was right. To his delight, no-one from Hungary objected to the theft of their vinous name, probably because Hungary had other matters of somewhat more importance to contend with.'

'For example?' asked the ambassador.

'Well, a few minor matters, such as invading Turks and

difficult Habsburgs. There were also many different national groups spread across the land, all of whom understandably held allegiance to other rulers.'

'You see, Ambassador, this is why Hitler is right, we Germans must first make Germany a land of purity of race. History tells us so. But I apologise Amit, your story must unfold.'

'So since there are various excellent wine merchants in Cape Town, I have been pestering their owners. One of them found in the back of his store, a crate of half a dozen bottles of this Alsatian Tokay. He told me that the wine would be strong of flavour, and thus ideal to drink where the spices gave the meat great strength. So, having bought some of his bottles, with your Deutschmarks of course Mr Ambassador, I knew that it would ideally accompany an ostrich curry.' He stopped.

'Marvellous, Amit, marvellous. As you can see we are on the second bottle and our palates agree totally with your presumption.' Amit departed, leaving the door open just a fragment and consequently he was able to overhear much of the subsequent discussion about the shipping of the diamonds in the ostrich feathers to Hamburg. Carl filled the ambassador in with the travels of the diamonds and when he came to the detail about the German boat sailing from Port Elizabeth home to Germany, but by-passing the English coast, Herr von Bauer was simply delighted.

'To the great success of this brilliant operation,' and both men emptied their glasses.

'And the other half,' asked the ambassador.

'Oh I am going to cook up a solution to that,' and both

men rolled around at the apparently excellent joke. Amit felt that he had a generic failure to understand what to him felt like a minimalist German joke. At that point Carl apparently had noticed that the door was a little ajar, got up and closed it firmly.

*

The following day Alan found the note from Amit and they arranged a meeting near the quayside in a dingy café, used apparently mainly by sailors and dockers.

Amit sat opposite Alan at a small table near the back of the café where they sipped their lukewarm milky tea. Amit was chatting excitedly, full of his discoveries having over-heard the plans for the shipments of feathers. When Amit looked up at Alan mid-way through talking, he was sur-prised to find that Alan looked bored.

'Alan, you don't seem excited by my news.'

'It is great to get confirmation of all of this, Amit, but I had a phone call this morning.' Amit waited for Alan to continue but he didn't, so Amit brought up something else from his previous day's adventures.

'I do have one other matter to share with you, Alan. Over dinner last night the two Germans shared a joke which I didn't understand.'

Alan looked up at Amit, who was frowning as he spoke. To be honest, Alan couldn't see that a German joke, however unexpected, could be of interest, but he put on an air of expectation. He knew that he hadn't been the most attentive so far and felt that he ought to at least act a little more interested in what Amit had to say. After all, Amit was frequently putting himself in situations considerably more dangerous than Alan and Gloria, to help them.

'Well, they raised their glasses to 'the great success of this brilliant operation and the other half', and once they'd emptied their glasses, Carl said something strange.'

Alan waited expectantly as Amit paused before continuing on.

'He said that he was going to 'cook up a solution to that'.'

Alan felt a haze of déjà vu creeping over him. Surely he had heard that phrase before, and he had rather ignored it. He looked at the puzzled look on Amit's face and it seemed as if the chef was expecting an explanation. But try as he could, Alan could not recall the occasion on which he had been regaled with the cooking joke before.

It was to be presented to Amit almost on a plate, so to speak, the following day.

Chapter Twenty-One

Amit bakes a new recipe

'Amit, Amit, where is that damned man? Usually he's hanging around trying to find out which curry we don't like and then when I need him, he appears to have done some sort of Indian vanishing trick.' Carl talked, apparently to himself, as he searched through the kitchens which appeared deserted. It was, after all, still early morning and unless the man was baking, it did seem not unreasonable that he might be preparing food. Perhaps he had gone to the market, but then Carl was looking through the window into the courtyard and spotted the chef sitting calmly on a bench in the courtyard. Carl watched him for a moment and spotted that Amit was mouthing words, while seemingly concentrating. He approached, Amit noticed him and jumped to his feet.

'No please sit, Amit. I was interrupting you.'

'It is true, Sahib. I was noticing my mind. Perhaps praying would be the correct word for a man of your religion.'

'Have I spoken of my religion?'

'Oh, no. But I assume that you are either of the Catholic or the Protestant persuasion, with possibly the Catholic being more probable since you come from a solid family of Alsace. In any case the rituals seem remarkably similar to me. I once went to observe a service in your magnificent cathedral in Cologne and was unable to tell whether it adhered to the thoughts of Mr. Luther or His Holiness in Rome. I do recall that the smelly smoke hurt my eyes.' And Amit smiled, more at his memory of the beauty of the cathedral than at any part of the service.

'You are right in that my family adhered to Rome. But for myself, my religion has wavered, to the sadness of my parents.'

'So when you arrived I was contemplating one of the proper goals of Hinduism, the dharma, the ethics and duties of my work here in your embassy.'

'And did you come to any conclusion?' Carl was interested, rather to his own surprise.

'Ah, Carl, often it is not like this in my religion, conclusions are often rather low in the priorities. It would be fair to say that the thinking on the matter takes priority over the concluding.' Carl thought about this and decided that he could not cope with either philosophy or religion at that hour of the morning.

'Well, I apologise for the interruption but I wished to talk to you on an important matter of your culinary art. I have a particular commission for you.' Amit's heart skipped. Hopefully this commission would be slightly more interesting than a birthday cake for the ambassador. It would give him something to do aside from the normal monotony of cooking regular meals; even espionage for Alan was becoming a little routine – the meeting at cafes and the spying was nice but Amit missed being able to experiment in the kitchen outside of his usual duties. It made him smile for a moment that with all the things going on in his life he could be excited about a cookery commission but then he remembered that he had yet to discover what it was and focused back on Carl.

'I want you to bake me a cake.' Amit's heart sank. It was times like this that he hated being right.

'When I come to think about it, I want you to bake me two cakes.'

'What sort of cakes?' He dreaded the answer.

'In fact I had in mind Stollen.'

'Hmm. I could certainly do that for you but do we not classify Stollen as bread?'

'Yes, I expect you are right. What I need is a bread with many different fruits and nuts in it. And then when you have cooked them, I want them sealed in a tin for freshness and we are going to send them to my friend in Germany,' and he smiled almost as if it were a joke. Amit was nonplussed.

'You want me here in Africa to send a German bread to Germany. The English have an expression about 'sending coals to Newcastle.' '

'And what does that mean. And where is Newcastle?'

'Well Newcastle is at the centre of the English coal-mining region. So it's an idiom meaning that it is odd to send to a place something that is already plentiful there.

'Indeed.' Carl looked almost stern and Amit realised that

he probably wasn't too interested in sayings used by the English, nor did he particularly care where Newcastle was, and what sort of work was popular in the region.

'And you are not playing a trick on me?' Amit thought out loud. Carl laughed and there was an edge to his voice when he spoke that arose Amit's curiosity.

'Would I do that, Amit?'

'Probably not, Sahib. But the request is somewhat unusual. May I enquire the reason for this unusual culinary episode?'

'It is for my good friend Peter, who of course you met in Livingstone all that time ago, and who loves his Stollen.'

Amit smiled and decided it seemed a reasonable, although strange, request.

'Then of course it will be my pleasure. I will need to go shopping, which I will do now. Are the cakes to go via air?'

'Yes, and the flight leaves Thursday morning. We will need to deliver them to the airport on Wednesday.' Amit nodded and just as he was leaving to prepare for his shopping trip, Carl called out after him,

'And I will have a special ingredient for the mixture. So when you are ready to add the dried fruits, the nuts and the marzipan, just come and bring me down to the kitchen.' Amit opened his mouth to respond but Carl was gone.

'How,' Amit muttered to himself, suddenly less excited about the prospect of retrieving an old Stollen recipe from his student days, 'am I supposed to make something with a special ingredient, without knowing what it is? He doesn't understand that whatever it is will throw all of the proportions out of balance, and baking is all about balance!

No-one here understands the delicacies of cooking, of recipes!'

*

Alan was going over his notes so far about Carl and the diamonds, when he was called to the telephone.

'It is I, Dieter.'

'Good morning, Dieter, and how is the weather in Oudtshoorn?'

'Ah, the English. Always wanting to discuss the weather. Now Alan, two matters. First and most important, have you discussed the arrangements for my uncle with your bosses in London?'

'Naturally, Dieter.' Alan found that his ability to lie smoothly had improved since joining the S.I.S. 'My bosses are discussing it at the highest levels, but I have yet to hear back from them. I will of course let you know when approval has been given.'

'And an escape plan?'

'Of course an escape plan.' Although Alan was not quite certain in his mind that his remit had included assisting in an escape. Hadn't he said something about assisting with his departure? 'And the other matter, Dieter?'

'Ah yes I have been visited by the rather obnoxious Carl. Accompanied as he was by the equally gorgeous Judit, whose sole function seemed to be to put two stitches into a small silica bag.'

Alan frowned, surprised that Dieter had taken such a strong dislike to Carl when so far, Carl had seemed to charm everyone that he met.

'Obnoxious? He seemed mostly charming and smooth to me.'

'As he was leaving he made a rather unsubtle threat to Uncle Wilhelm.'

Alan could hear the distaste in Dieter's tone and felt a flicker of concern for him being a part of this. Although they couldn't do this without Dieter's help, Alan knew that lightly veiled threats could easily put you on edge, and when made by someone like Carl, could probably be carried out if he really wanted.

'Oh dear, I am so sorry. How unpleasant.' The words fell a little flat, but Alan made a note to ensure that he contacted London about the great man, his uncle, with some urgency. It would be a pity if an emergency arose and London was unprepared. Not too good for Alan's own career either, he suspected.

'Anyway the silica bag is in with the ostrich feathers and the specific bag with the diamonds inside has a round black inky dot on it. The diamonds are going in the hold of S.S. Usambara, Deutsche Africa Linien, leaving next Thursday for Hamburg via Durban and the Suez Canal.'

'And stopping at Southampton?'

'Oh no. Carl was insistent that I find a boat that did not stop in England.'

Alan felt a twinge of annoyance. Of course, Carl was smart enough to think of that, but it didn't half make Alan's own job a little more complicated.

'Good gracious. That was rather irritating of him. And rather annoying that there is a boat that doesn't stop in

England. I assumed that all boats to Germany would stop in England.'

'This is the one boat from Algoa Bay that doesn't stop there.'

'Amazing. And how did Carl find that out?'

'Umm well.' Dieter paused and Alan suddenly felt a rising suspicion.

'Umm well what?' Alan asked, unable to help the accusation that crept into his tone.

'I'm afraid that I discovered it.'

'What?' Alan stopped and there was a long pause before he spoke again, his words heavy, 'Whose side are you on, Dieter?'

'I am so sorry Alan. I didn't think really.' Alan was furious and took a few slow breaths to calm down before he continued. Shouting wasn't going to help here, and at least Dieter had told them the information. They didn't have anything else to go on, so Alan would have to trust that Dieter, despite his apparent assistance to the Germans, was still loyal to them.

'Do you have the name and address of the lucky recipient in Germany of these Ostrich feathers?'

'Yes, it's Peter Shroeder, 14, Lietzenburger Strasse, Berlin.' Alan instantly recognised the name. This must be the Peter Shroeder who was in Livingstone. Alan ended the phone call and hurried off to update Gloria on what he had just been told. Alan found her as expected in her office, but when he entered she managed only a weak smile, unable to disguise her furrowed brow.

'You're troubled?'

'Pretty Useless has submitted his expenses for the year. They are in what I can only call 'a state of mild anarchy.' But don't worry about my problems. You look like a man with news.' Alan told her about the silica pack in the feathers.

'So it's off to Berlin via Durban, Suez, Marseilles and Hamburg. Do we have a plan?'

'I think that we need to do two things and the most important is to tell London. We need to recommend to them that the shipment should proceed uninterrupted in the light of its small size. But they might wish to make a plan on how they might intercept a larger consignment. Perhaps Shuttleworth has a man in Marseilles. Probably easier to intercept there than in Hamburg.'

'Yes and maybe easier than in Durban. How about Suez?'

'Well that might be easier still. But we can leave those details up to London for the moment.'

'And Dieter has told me one good thing apart from his idiocy in aiding Carl to find a boat that doesn't stop in England. And that is that he is going to Port Elizabeth to 'get to know' the captain of the Usambara.'

'Now that sounds like a sensible idea and should provide us with useful intelligence.'

'Yes, I encouraged him to try to get to see where they put the feathers in the hold. He said that maybe he could get to see around by making a fuss about the fragile nature of the feathers.' She laughed.

'Good planning. The more details that London have, the easier the theft of the diamonds from the ship will be at a later date. Perhaps London might try to get a man into the boat – either as a passenger or even better as sailor.'

'Now that's a really excellent plan. Suggest it to London. And get Dieter to encourage Carl to use the Usambara again. Then London will have time to infiltrate a man onto the boat before it comes back to Port Elizabeth again. When will it be back?'

'No idea but I will find out.'

Chapter Twenty-Two

Shuttleworth plans the diamond interception

There was something almost magical in the range of products available in the shops in Cape Town. Rare spices that reminded Amit of home, Bavarian Obatzda, a common German cheese reminiscent of his student days, delicacies from the United States, and even next to those, Amit found some Norwegian lutefisk, – although, having tried it, he decided that it was an unpleasantly tasteless way of eating dried fish. For a chef, food-shopping in the brisk trading station was a pleasure. He spent hours strolling around the vast food market, enjoying the banter of the shoppers while searching for the dried fruit and nuts with which to make an authentic Stollen. It wasn't hard work, considering the variety of ingredients which the market stocked. Eventually with his hoard pocketed he returned to the Embassy's kitchens and asked one of the other staff members to let Carl know that he had returned.

'I've just bought all of the ingredients for the Stollen and

I'm ready to start mixing them now. Only the best for your friend.'

'I have my ingredients too.' Carl pulled out five small, slightly muddy-looking pieces of glass and held them out to Amit, who stared at them confused.

'What are they? They might affect the quality of my Stollen, especially if they dissolve in the mix when I bake it. Surely Peter can't want it to have whatever those are inside it?' Carl laughs at him and flexed his fingers, standing a little taller.

'Of course not. They're diamonds.' Amit's eyes widened. Diamonds? But then he paused and frowned.

'They look like no diamonds that I have seen.' Carl grinned at him, nodding his head, not unlike Amit's old tutors at university used to do when they felt they had taught their students an important lesson, a reminder that they were superior, in charge.

'They are uncut diamonds, Amit. Did your father not show you the diamonds that were taken from the ground?'

Amit shrugged, trying to disguise his amazement as it turned to excitement. This was exactly the kind of thing Alan was waiting to discover and Amit would be the one to bring this information across to the British! Not only was he a great chef, but soon to be known as a great spy too. Although, Amit thought, great spies probably wouldn't be known as such. That would, perhaps, defeat their primary purpose. Realising that Carl was still waiting for an answer, Amit cleared his throat.

'Oh no, we only saw them on the rings of the ladies fingers, or around their necks. As a child I remember walking with my father to the office where the men were cutting the stones, but they all sparkled there. So this is the product straight from the ground?'

'Indeed – and I want them well mixed with the other ingredients – and then you will show me the cooked Stollen so that I can make sure that they are not peeping out.'

Amit started preparing the dough for the Stollen, and then suddenly understood about the Germans' joke about cooking up a solution. This was clearly it; everything was falling into place.

The next day Amit explained everything to Alan.

'What a clever solution. And did Carl tell you what Peter is going to do to retrieve the diamonds?'

'Oh yes. Carl was surprising eager to tell me everything – I'd be suspicious, if he hadn't seemed so smug about the whole plan. I'm baking two cakes which will be wrapped in paper; Peter will eat one, and the other will be marked with an ink spot. That one will have the diamonds in and Peter will put that one into a hot oven for a long time until is it burnt and all the cake is powder. Then he'll wash it under the tap into a sieve and the diamonds will emerge.'

Alan smiled, his eyes glittering with excitement.

'Brilliant, very clever indeed. And when is it to go to the airport?'

'He is taking it himself this afternoon. Although, I can't help but feel a bit sad about that wasted Stollen. I choose only the best ingredients, cooking it perfectly, and now it's going to be destroyed!' Alan couldn't help but laugh at the situation; there was that familiar giddiness that came with

251

the knowledge that you were ahead of the enemy.

'Only you would be upset about a cake when you've just provided one of the biggest breakthroughs of the whole mission!'

Cheered by the knowledge that Alan was obviously pleased, Amit grinned. Alan was right, he'd done a good job. Not bad for a chef! And Alan wasn't just excited with the new knowledge of the German's plan, but relieved that his risk in trusting and giving Amit a chance had paid off.

'Now go back to the German Embassy. We can't have them getting suspicious. You've done a great job, Amit.'

As soon as Amit had left, Alan went to find Gloria. Once he'd told her all that Amit had imparted, Alan left her in her office and hurried to let Shuttleworth know about all of the developments. There was a buzz in the air. They were getting close to the end now, the culmination of all of their hard work. Alan spoke to Shuttleworth on the radio-telephone. He was delighted,

'We'll see if we can get a squint at the Stollen at le Bourget. One of our men, possibly Roland, in Paris can pop up there. Or maybe I'll send Sarah over. The flight from the Cape takes four days and so won't be there before Sunday. That means there'll be plenty of time to find a way of following the tin at the airport. Perhaps we can bribe one of the Customs men.'

'And the shipment?'

'Yes we'll also have plenty of time to get ready for the arrival of the Usambara, as she'll take a couple of weeks to dock in Marseilles, better than Suez, I think. When Roland has discovered everything about the transit arrangements at le Bourget, either I will stump up for an Imperial ticket on the following outward flight from Le Bourget to Marseilles or someone can take the train from Paris, and they'll arrive in plenty of time to find a way to get on board the Usambara. And at some point we may indeed get a man on board ship for the next outward journey to the Cape.'

Alan nodded. The plan was forming nicely.

'That sounds good, sir.'

'You are doing a great job, Alan. By the way, any more riots?'

'Not a peep, sir.'

Shuttleworth seemed pleased and Alan couldn't help but feel a bit of déjà vu from his meeting earlier with Amit, except this time, the roles were flipped and Alan was awaiting Shuttleworth's praise and judgement.

'How's that secretary?'

'She is great, sir. Back at work.'

'Excellent. Well done, Alan,' and with that, Shuttleworth was gone.

Despite the excitement of the past few hours, with a plan in place there was now nothing for Alan to do but wait.

As always seemed the case, Alan couldn't just sit still, so he wandered over to the harbour and a little café, which seemed to have become his favourite place for its views of the sea and the ships bustling in at all hours. It was so beautiful here, and with the exception of a few slightly scary moments, he really had grown to love it here. Besides, what was a bit of espionage without a few ups and downs? Being in the field was so much more invigorating than sitting in his office back in London, and the scenery here didn't go amiss either. Was there any part of his life that was better in London? He tried to think of something that he missed now he was over in the Cape, but there wasn't really anything. Especially since he had Gloria here as well. Alan smiled thinking about her working away in her office, behind the scenes, finding things out without him even realising. Shuttleworth was really underestimating her, calling her a secretary. She was so much more than that.

The sky was a clear lapis blue and the sun beamed down out of a lapis sky as the waiter brought Alan a glass of lemonade, cool and glistening, small shards of ice at the surface. The light over the Cape was magical. That was another thing he didn't miss about London; the dreary and grey weather. Now Alan had experienced this sun, he didn't think he could ever willingly leave it behind. How can it be so clear, so transparent and yet so warm?

Once when he was on holiday as a child, they had stayed on a real working farm near Moretonhampstead in Devon There had been days like this, with the twinkling of the sun on the farmyard. He remembered the chicken lying on the cobbles, dying for some reason unknown to his young, medically-uneducated mind. He had poked at it with a piece of straw from the stables. It had lain there looking at him. The farmer had seen and come over, removed the bird from his clutches, and taken him off to pat the horses, tied in to the stable wall. He had been terrified of their size but had wanted to be seen to be brave. It was such an irrelevant memory really, but one that had stuck with him after all these years.

And now, as he watched the waves sweeping towards the

shore, he couldn't help but remember his youth. Endless holidays at the beach – not quite as warm as the Cape, a chill on the British shores, but still, the memories were tainted with a warm glow. On one holiday, Alan must've been about seven, his father had shown him how to make fire-castles on the beach. They piled the sand up to a great height in a cone like the top of Mount Fuji, then broke in to the edifice, first making tunnels at right angles through the base, then with the fingers, scraping out a cavern where the four tunnels met in the middle. The tunnels were to make a good through-draft whichever way the wind was blowing. Then the tricky bit; gently fashioning the chimney downwards from the summit of the volcano down slowly, slowly into the cavern, without collapsing the inside of the wall of the chimney. Afterwards the piling into the cavern of the front page of the Times, crumpled up. (Alan was never quite sure why the front page was so important, but he assumed that there was a good reason in the mysterious world of the adult.) Except now, as an adult, he still found that he wasn't quite sure what his father's reasoning had been. Part of growing up, Alan found, was realising that no-one really knew exactly what they were doing, or why.

When the firecastle was almost complete, they'd post pieces of driftwood down the chimney so that they lay on top of the paper. Then the really exciting moment where, when he had grown bigger, daddy had let him light the match, lie on his stomach in the wet sand, and push it through one of the tunnels until it touched the paper. After a few seconds of agonising waiting, came the moment when the smoke came out of the chimney, and, if they were lucky, flames licked up too. He laughed, remembering his joy at seeing the flames spiral upwards, and the cleverness of creating it on the beach; the sand stopping the flames from catching beyond the castle. He must've laughed out-loud because the waiter was stirred into action and arrived at his table to inquire whether all was well. Alan ordered another lemonade to hide his embarrassment.

He returned from the beach of his youth to the terrace. Shuttleworth would've called this his 'small mental sojourns.' But where had he been before his beach outing? His life, his life. Simply the life here was delightful in every aspect. And of course Gloria. Gloria. At the end of this mission, would he be contented to say something trite such as 'Goodbye, do come and see me when you come to London.'?

So, would he like to stay here in the Cape, with its cosmopolitan atmosphere, its weather, maybe its music? It would be a marvellous option. He had little to keep him in London now. Perhaps he could be assigned to work for S.I.S. here? Maybe he should be planning to appear to be creating extra work here so that Shuttleworth would see that Gloria needed an assistant? If not, perhaps he could get private security work given his background with S.I.S.?

His thoughts were interrupted by a familiar voice. Alan looked up.

'Why is it Louis, that you usually seem to appear when I am distracted by my thoughts?' And he laughed and extended a hand to welcome the Afrikaaner. 'Join me in a lemonade?' The waiter was summoned.

'Deep thoughts?'

'I was considering my future.' And Alan summarised his 'small mental sojourns' without mentioning Gloria. Louis looked at him amusedly.

'You have failed to mention the gorgeous Gloria.' Alan blushed slightly and turned his gaze to the ocean. 'Surely she has a part in your future. She likes you a lot you know.' Louis seemed to enjoy poking gentle fun at him, but Alan had quickly learnt that he was, if anything, sincere.

'Louis, I think that sometimes we men are bad at spotting when someone we like, likes us.'

'So, you admit you like her at least! Stay here, Alan. This is a wonderful land, and it needs men of substance and intelligence like yourself,' and Louis paused, 'and talking of intelligence, have both small packages been despatched?' Alan was instantly wary. Louis had a strange way of interchanging small talk and serious business that was quite disarming, and how on earth did he know about the two packages? Come to think of it, how does he even know that they're small? Louis laughed, obviously enjoying Alan's confusion and attempt to disguise his surprise.

'I know a lot that happens in this town, Alan. Yes a great deal really. People talk to me because they think that I'm a harmless poet and trustworthy medic. I am of course neither.' He finished his lemonade, sighing with satisfaction, and got ready to leave almost as suddenly as he had arrived.

'Stay here, Alan, stay here. And one piece of advice.'

Alan felt his breathing hitch. What else could Louis possibly know or have to say?

'Remove the biggest diamonds from one of those bags, and put it on her finger.' And he was gone.

Chapter Twenty-Three

Action at S.I.S. headquarters

Reluctantly, Captain Morris Shuttleworth decided that completion of the morning's Times crossword had to be postponed, although he had to admit to himself that, since Drayson had been gone, the days when he actually completed the puzzle were few and far between. He stared at the little girl's hair in the print. Maybe if he could just… In fact, he walked out of the door and called Sarah Grandison into his office. She sat quietly, demurely, opposite him with the desk between them. He preferred it this way. Slowly and carefully he filled her in on the situation at the Cape, and, as instructed, she took notes of certain details as he went on.

'Essentially I need someone to travel to Le Bourget to look with care at how we might intercept a future package arriving on an Imperial Airways flight from the Cape. And then travel down to Marseilles to do the same with a box of feathers on the S.S. Usambara, bound for Hamburg and Berlin. Either I could send our Roland, at present idling his lazy life away in the bookshops of the Seine, or you could go. What do you think?' Sarah was surprised but responded quickly

'I would love to do it, sir.'

'Marvellous. Let's get these tickets set up with the office. The Imperial flight arrives on Monday and you will need to be there before that to work out how parcels are transferred between flights. We have a man in the airport there named Michel Udenay. He will help you with the mechanics. And then I will get Roland to accompany you to Marseilles. It's a bit rough at the port there and you will need a spot of male company, even if it is Roland the Rover. You will be in charge of both operations. The boat will take another two weeks to get to the Med. so you have plenty of time to have a day or two sight-seeing in Paris before taking the train to the coast. And hurry back after the Usambara leaves – fly if necessary. Good luck,' and he marched her up to the office where Sheila started to prepare her paperwork.

The next day she flew to Le Bourget. Determined to be ready for anything, Sarah had spent all night imaging various scenarios in which she would, of course, emerge victorious. Finally, she was getting some field work, and she needed to do well, to prove herself. She was shocked that she had been asked in the first place but this was her chance. She wasn't going to let it go to waste.

There was a mid-summer storm blowing up through the English Channel and the Imperial Airways flight rocked around greatly. Almost everyone was airsick with the repeated dips and climbs and she was, unfortunately, not immune. After five hours in the air, Sarah was delighted to be back on land even though rain and strong winds rather spoiled the walk to the Terminal building. She was met in the customs hall by Michel Udenay, who turns out to be short, dark and handsome with floppy mid-brown hair and hazel eyes in a rather classic Gallic manner. He took one look at her pale green face and insisted on taking her straight to the airport bar, placing a large Cognac in her hand and insisting that she drink. Perhaps she had not made the best first impression, but how was she to predict the weather and how she would react to the shaky aircraft?

'It is the best cure for a storm over La Manche,' and three swigs later, she was feeling considerably more human and ready to face whatever was next. While she was regaining her poise, she looked in pleasure at the bar décor with its typical French Twenties wooden surfaces with glitter around the edges. On the far wall of the bar hung a print of a view of Paris by Raoul Dufy, executed in black line with coloured wash on top. The Seine with its bridges extended down the centre and into the distance, exciting her memories of the city, last seen some years ago when her father had taken her with him to an academic conference. He had been rather busy with the other engineers, discussing weight-bearing loads on bridges, so she had had plenty of time to walk the streets and have coffee and a pastry in the little bars of the Latin Quarter. Once she had thought she saw Ernest Hemingway, but had been too scared to approach him.

To be in France had always been her dream at school, when she was not dreaming of being a tennis star. She had thought for a while that she would like to be a chef – and not just an ordinary chef in a restaurant. She had wanted to be a pastry chef. Her mother had been a fine maker of breads and biscuits and ever since helping to stir the flour and butter when her mother was creating food for hungry children at tea-time, this had been her dream. She had known that the best pastry was made in France when she had tasted her first croissant.

Later in her first visit, she had wandered up to the Pantheon and stared in excitement at the tombs of her favourite writers, Victor Hugo, Voltaire, Rousseau and others whom she now failed to recall. It had started her voracious perusal of French literature, and had helped her to enter London University, where she had read French before being recruited to the Service by one of her father's brothers.

And now here she was in a bar with a handsome Frenchman whose English was totally perfect – a spell in London it had transpired, while on a training course in International Goods transport, where he had met Shuttleworth in a bar in Mayfair. 'Not a regular hang-out for the boss,' she had thought. 'Wonder what he was doing there.' She forced herself back to Michel's chatter about the success of France in avoiding the world Depression, their economy being so based on agriculture, and the nation's fears about their neighbour Germany and the Nazis.

'But I am talking too much boring politics. What can I do to help my old friend Morris and his beautiful emissary?' She was annoyed to feel a slight flush crossing her cheeks, and turned away, catching sight of her hair in a small mirror hanging decoratively at the side of the bar.

Whilst Sarah may have recovered from her aviation turmoil, her hair-do apparently had not. She felt herself turn an even deeper shade of red. None of this was going quite the way she had planned or hoped for. Taking a deep breath, she reminded herself that Shuttleworth had asked her – Sarah Grandison – to do this, and that she was perfectly capable. She proceeded to fill him in on the developments in South Africa, and in particular on the details of the Imperial Airways flight.

'How exciting. My life has been so boring recently and I was beginning to think that my friend in London would never have any work for me. Of course we will be able to identify these Stollen en route to Berlin. There are daily flights of Deutsche Luft Hansa from here to Berlin taking post, parcels and packages. The package will be transferred from the Imperial Airways flight into our customs shed, where we will take a look at it, calculate any import tariffs and then deliver it to the German flight. With a small item it will not take long, and we would expect it to catch the transit flight within 24 hours. But it will give me a chance to get a good look at it. I may need even to inspect it in some privacy.' And he grinned.

'But will they allow you in to Customs?'

'Bien sur,' with a classic Gallic shrug of the shoulders. 'This is a small community here. They are all my friends. We all have a glass together here in this bar before we go home. No-one will think anything strange about my coming down for a chat. But for now, I should return to my work. It's Saturday. The plane is not due until Monday afternoon. I'll phone you on Monday morning so that we can arrange to meet here at the bar later that evening,' and he summoned a taxi for her which took her to the hotel near the Luxembourg Gardens, where she slept marvellously well, exhausted by the flight and everything she had encountered so far.

The next morning Sarah woke to blue skies and warm air. She telephoned Roland and arranged to meet him for dinner in a little restaurant in the Rue Gay-Lussac, and then strolled out of the hotel. Paris was even more delightful than she remembered it from her visit as a teenager, and it was clear that Michel had been right about France not having suffered too much from the effects of the worldwide Depression. Everywhere was smart and clean, and the ladies were dressed so beautifully, so much silk and such elegance, such elegance. She felt dowdy, and out of place, and decided that since she had nothing to do during the day, she ought to find something a bit better to wear. If anything, Sarah told herself, a shopping trip might ease her mind, allow her to get to know the city a bit better, and mean that she'll blend in better during her stay, which would be crucial in her mission.

She walked through the Luxembourg Gardens admiring, demurely she hoped, a pair of tall Dragoons in full uniform who were strolling along towards the fountains. She stopped at the Musee, where there was an exhibition of Pablo Picasso, and as a devotee, she bought a ticket and entered. She was shocked. Her devotion was dedicated to his drawings, even his blue period, but she found his modern 'cubism', as it was called, hard to stomach. There was also some art from Georges Braque but again although she appreciated that both could draw so beautifully, she found the unnatural nature of the cubism impossible to admire.

Later she wandered down the Rue du Rivoli, admiring the window displays whilst bemoaning the prices. Apparently being a fashionable Parisian came at a cost. Eventually she bought a long olive green skirt, with a cream blouse and hoped that the two colours, both in a silky material, complemented each other, and would allow her to achieve that casual elegance that the women here seemed to exude. She had a small snack in a bar close to the Seine on the Boulevarde Saint-Germaine and returned to her hotel for a little relaxation before her dinner engagement. Sarah dressed carefully in her new outfit and decided that it had been a good choice. The green complemented her eyes and, if she could say so herself, she didn't look half bad. One might even say, she looked quite beautiful.

Remarkably the boss' description of Roland's enormous eyebrows meant that Roland the Rover was easy to spot. She noticed with some amusement that Shuttleworth's description had failed to include the fact that Roland was enormously, unbelievably tall. When he stood to greet her she had to raise her eyes and relocate her neck to extraordinary angles. But he started so brilliantly that she was able to forgive him everything for the rest of the evening.

'Oh Sarah, such beautiful clothes, the wonderful delicacy of the shades and of course they enhance perfectly the colour of your eyes.' She was conquered by his charm in less than ten seconds.

They talked of many things; their families – his rather aristocratic, with a lovely family home in the Burgundy countryside. He was embarrassed about the servants, but not about the beauty of their garden.

'So English, Sarah, so English. Our roses were the talk of the region. Supplied from a gardener in Sussex, of course. My mother would have no other source.' They talked of everything except, that is, their mission. At his insistence, they started with a glass each of Cremant de Bourgogne. After a wondrous souffle starter, the cheese tickling her palate, she had Sole Meuniere with the capers and lemon so delicately balanced, washed down by a charmingly chilled Pouilly-Fuisse.

'From just below the Rocher du Solutre. You have never been there? When this is all over, we will climb it.' Her alarm – 'oh no, it's a very gentle easy climb. Simple, even in the slight heels you wear tonight.'

She was shocked that he had even noticed her choice of footwear and was briefly pleased, before she remembered why he might notice. Being so observant was a skill that they all needed to do the job, and do it well.

'And the view from the top is magnificent. You can nearly see Papa's chateau, close to Cluny.' Eventually, she managed to consume her dessert; a chocolate mousse with the raspberries and mint patterned delicately around the dark exotic mix. 'The pinch of salt is what is important, mademoiselle,' the well-informed waiter told her.

On the way back to her hotel, they touched on the trip to Marseilles. Shuttleworth had briefed him well but they needed to discuss the details. 'So you'll need a couple more days to sort out the package at Le Bourget, and then we'll take the train from Gare du Lyon. And maybe we'll stop at Macon, and you'll meet my family. I think that there will be time before the Usambara arrives in Marseilles.' She hardly knew what to say, but the words

'Merci, c'est tres gentil,' seemingly slipped of their own accord from her, before her thoughts engaged. At the hotel, he had kissed both cheeks, and was gone. She had slept magnificently and the following morning was summoned to the reception telephone during her croissants and coffee breakfast. 'A M. Udenay,' the receptionist had told her

'They arrive at 3 o'clock. Meet me in the bar at 5.' And he hung up. She was there in the bar sipping a Dubonnet and lemonade when he strode in, laughing, with another man.

'Miss Grandison, meet my friend, Alphonse. He works in Customs.' And he gave her an unsubtle wink. 'We normally meet here most evenings to discuss the stresses of our respective jobs, politics, our idiot Prime Minister and other important matters.' Alphonse shook her hand in a grave manner.

'Mademoiselle, it is of course my pleasure. We all dream of English roses, do we not, Michel?' and he gave a little stiff bow. They chatted about the state of the world while the men drank their glasses of wine. Eventually Alphonse left, and they were alone.

'I have identified the packages. It was easy. There was a large ink blot on one, as Morris and you had told me there would be. I have done nothing, and tomorrow morning the packages will be on the Berlin flight. But I did take a photograph of the Stollen. I thought that it might be useful at a later date. Anyway I photograph everything because photography is my little hobby. I will develop the photograph tonight at home, and will leave it for you at the reception of your hotel tomorrow morning, mademoiselle.'

'Wonderful. And next time you'll know how to identify it?'

'Too easy, mademoiselle.' Sarah thanked him and they parted. Two days passed with enormous pleasure for Sarah. She was surprised to find that field work involved a lot of waiting around, but she wasn't complaining. Paris was a beautiful place to explore in the meantime. She traversed the streets the following afternoon and wandered down the hill of the Rue Mouffetard, passing a galaxy of delicious-looking food shops and ending in an open square full of market stalls. After she had been there a short while, someone had struck up a jig on an accordion, a space had been cleared and the ladies had started to dance to some traditional French country ballads. The scene in the warm sun was entrancing and full of the Gallic abandon which would hardly be repeated amongst the staid British. When she returned to her hotel, the photograph awaited her.

On the Wednesday morning she had been at the Gare du Lyon early in the morning, prepared to journey to Marseilles with Roland. He left it rather late to her slight anxiety, but was his immensely tall charming self when he arrived, full of apologies.

'Desolee to keep you waiting. My taxi was stuck in a terrible jam. There was some parade by the military to

268

celebrate something. Not that, to be frank, our army's recent performance has merited much celebration.' She smiled. The train meandered through the southern suburbs of Paris and built up speed gradually. 'And I have discovered the date of arrival of the Usambara in Marseilles. It will not be there for another seven days.' The news opened a little moment of uncertainty in her mind. But he continued before she could set up her anxiety.

'So, I hoped that you might accept the hospitality of my family for a few days. The train will stop at Macon in a few hours. From there it is only a short drive to our house. I have arranged for the chauffeur to meet us at the station.'

'It sounds wonderful. Thank you.' In fact, it took most of the day for the train to reach Macon. It appeared that French trains did not travel as fast as their English equivalents. He had asked her about how she had ended up in the S.I.S. She had sat back and had not been able to stop herself from telling him a little of her story.

'When I was at school, I made things hard for myself. I was not cut out for my place of education. I hated all work except English and I became disruptive and rather unruly. In the end my parents decided that I should stop formal education and daddy got me a job in the Civil Service at a young age. Before that of course I had run away with a dashing young man. My parents however felt that as I was only sixteen, I was not quite ready for the life of a Bohemian and to be honest, I suppose the fact that the man was twenty-eight did not help. But he was charming and handsome and an early aircraft pilot and it was just after the war had ended. They sent a couple of men to

Chelsea who took me home. My father got me a lowly post in a branch of the English Civil Service. I hated it.'

'About that time, I had started to read Virginia Woolf's essays and I was inspired by her. She gave me the courage and strength to think my own thoughts. And above all to believe that a woman could achieve anything, so I realised that my desire for rebellion and being myself were quite natural.' She paused watching him take it in and was pleased to see that he was sympathetic – and listening carefully.

'I tried to find Miss Woolf and knew that she was living down in Richmond with her husband Harold, but was unable to find the house. So I gave up and went home and read her book called 'To the Lighthouse'. Have you read it, Roland?' But she left no room for his response.

'It's about Godrevy. But it pretends not to be. It pretends to be about a magical lighthouse in the Hebrides. Do you know Godrevy?' He shook his head.

'It's a perfect lighthouse. It rises from a small rock island outcrop off the north Cornwall coast and on a blue sky day there is nothing more lovely than to walk along the coastal path, sit on the beach at Gwithian with a sandwich and look at the sculpted rock covered in the freshest greenest grass with the pinnacle of the lighthouse above. And the rock pools beyond Gwithian are so full of life – the sea anemones and the crabs. And Miss Woolf describes the way in which her women are beaten down into pottering around in their miserable gardens. Do you know Proust, Roland?' Again no let-up for any words that Roland might have wished to utter. Sarah found that now she had started speaking, she couldn't stop, had so much to say.

'Well she writes just like Proust. It's called 'Stream-of-consciousness' writing and it means that the thoughts are all bundled together, just how one thinks them in real life and not edited. And she has written 'A room of One's Own' which is so alive and beautiful in its desire for freedom from you oppressive men. Well, I tried to read Proust but became exhausted with that style of his. So I regret that I gave up.' At last she paused for breath.

'Me too. Not to my taste.'

'And then one day my boss told me that my help was needed in another department of the Civil service. It was the S.I.S. At first I did trivial work. But then one day my new boss told me that I was so smart that he thought I should have more training. And so here I am.' She laughed self-consciously.

They arrived at Macon and the chauffeur awaited them and took them for the short ride to the family home. The next few days were filled with country walks, and visits to the nearby bustling town of Cluny. She was disappointed with the abbey, most of which was in ruin, but the atmosphere of the town was thrilling, so many small shops and full of interesting characters – as if it had emerged from a page on a book.

It was a beautiful day when they made the threatened climb of the Rocher, which from below appeared quite vertical. 'The locals call this Le Sphinx aux griffes plantées dans les ceps.' He realised immediately that her French was not up to it.

'Forgive me – in English, the Sphinx with claws planted

in the vines,' and that had seemed to her viewing it from below, a marvellous description of the enormous rocky outcrop. In fact he had been truthful about the gentleness of the climb, and, taking a slowly winding path, the travelling to the summit was quite un-taxing. On the way to the top, they had been surrounded by small box trees and grassy fields demarcated by little dry stone walls, reminding her of the Yorkshire Dales.

At the summit they had had an entrancing picnic carried, somewhat to her distress, all the way by the chauffeur who had left them with the picnic basket on arrival at the summit. She had eaten bread with local cheese and they drank local Puilly-Fuisse, picked up on the way at a local vineyard just below the overhanging section of the rock. But it was the spectacular view over the surrounding vineyards that was the total delight. He showed her Mont Blanc, just visible in the distance to the south amongst the snow-covered tips of the highest Alps, and the river Saone wriggling through its valley to the East, and finally the vineyards, naming the most famous ones for her. While showing her the sights he had come to be sitting very close to her. At one point, she had looked up into his eyes while he was talking, and he had ground to a halt and kissed her gently on the lips, as she had hoped. When she had been an awkward teenager, very ignorant of the ways of boys, her rather more advanced friend Jane had told her that the way to get a boy to kiss you was to look up into the boy's eyes and not look away. She had not forgotten. She was like a small child wishing the day would never end. To be honest, this didn't feel like field work at all. This was a holiday.

Regrettably, further days passed in his house had not been followed up with further physical contact. The following Monday they caught the train to Marseilles, passing down the endless vineyards of the Rhone valley. The river wound its way around their tracks as the train ploughed a large iron furrow through its length, but always the great Rhone was there, getting gradually wider as they travelled ever southwards. At times the valley was so beautiful that she gasped inwardly with pleasure. They stopped briefly at Montelimar, a town that held no interest for her due to her loathing of the sweet whiteness of its main product. When she told him, he had been amazed that she did not like the nougat.

At Avignon, she could just see the bridge but it was at a distance from the train track. She had asked if they could get off and dance on the bridge but he had refused in his gentle smiling manner. She had sung the song reminding herself of her primary school, and how they had pretended to be there in Avignon. Their French teacher had divided the class so that first the boys sang and then the girls sang at the appropriate verse. Her teacher had shown them how to dance 'tous en rond' and it had been a great hit at the winter term Parents Evening.

And eventually they had arrived exhausted at the St. Charles station in central Marseille. He had booked two rooms at a nice hotel, and for dinner they had eaten at an outside table at an exclusive restaurant beside the old port, where they could watch the bustle of the harbour. But apparently this was not where the Usambara was to dock;

there was a modern port for the big liners.

Frankly the meal had been marginally unsatisfactory. He had made her try oysters, and showed her how to ingest them in one gulp, but she had thought that they were disgusting, although she appreciated the salty, lemony flavour. Then he had told her that the steak here was very fine and although she had loved the crispiness of the chips, and the excellence of the salad, the steak had left her unmoved. He had told her that Cotes-du-Rhone was the only wine to have with Steak-frites but the strength of the wine's taste had meant that she had sipped at it frugally. When they returned to their hotel she had fallen asleep.

The following morning they had wandered down to the port area where the Usambara was due to dock the following afternoon. He had chatted to a docker and had discovered that there was a lot of smuggling and that customs–evasion was widespread. The docker had told Roland that he had a friend who, for a small sum, would be happy to help Roland aboard the ship when it arrived. She was amazed – first the airport now the docks, everything seemed so easy. She had put it to Roland.

'We French are not so good at obeying the rules,' was all he could say with a shrug of the shoulders. As they left the docks and headed back into town, she thought that she noticed two men following them. She had told Roland, who had not been able to spot anyone. But he agreed to try a doubling back technique. But when they had performed the manoeuvre, they had closed the net on... no-one. He had laughed and told her that she needed some lunch. The rest of the day passed without her seeing anyone following, and they had retired to bed after some dancing and cocktail drinking at the hotel's bar.

The Usambara docked at midday, two hours ahead of schedule due to the calmness of the Mediterranean apparently. They strolled down to the docks, where Roland had arranged to meet his newfound friend at the agreed time of 4p.m. There were two men waiting for them and Roland and they had a long conversation. Money changed hands and he disappeared up the gangway with one of the men. Although they were challenged at the top of the gangway by a guard, they disappeared inside and Gloria spent a worrying half-hour pacing up and down. Eventually he reappeared smiling and they left to sit at a café, with a tea for her and a glass of wine for him.

'I found them, just as M. Shuttleworth described. In all those glorious feathers, there were many small packets. And one had a large ink dot on it, so it was all quite simple. I touched nothing and now know exactly where I must look next time.' They stayed looking at the view until the sun set with remarkable rapidity over the sea. They walked back slowly towards their hotel, but this time something felt different and she was certain that they were being followed again.

She whispered to Roland, who glanced back casually and noted the two small characters who pretended to look into shop windows. As Sarah and Roland continued to walk, and were about to discuss what to do, two more men, both tall and blonde, appeared in front of them, approaching rapidly. As they got closer, Sarah noted that the two behind them suddenly seemed to be right on their tails and they were trapped in. Roland held her arm tightly and they tried to find a cut through off the street or a way of doubling back like they had done this morning. In a moment of franticness, they turned down a small alley in an attempt to get away, but as they entered the alley, they realised that that had made a horrible mistake. It was a dead end. They tried to turn around and escape but it was too late. All four men blocked their exit. It dawned on Sarah that as much as so far had felt like a holiday, simply a little trip away, at the end of the day, this was a job, and the job had its risks. Now they faced one of the biggest of them all. Sarah felt her heart drop as she saw the sun glinting off of something metal on their hands. This was it. There was no escape. Roland let go of her arm and moved in front of her, but there were too many of them. It didn't take long for everything to turn to black, and the last thing she saw was Roland on the floor next to her, so beaten that she thought he must be dead.

Chapter Twenty-Four

An Unmasking

S arah heard voices.

'Mais elle est anglaise. Peut-etre elle ne comprend pas la langue francaise. Peut-on parler en anglais? Try speaking in English.'

'Bien sur. Sarah, can you hear me?' Sarah tried to open her eyes but they just wouldn't. Everything was black. She tried to speak instead, and her throat felt dry and scratchy, as if she hadn't spoken in many, many years.

'I can't see,' she croaked.

'Elle parle. Brigitte, demander au médecin de venir toute suite. Sarah, my name is Stephanie. You're in our hospital. You cannot open your eyes because there are bandages over them, but the doctor will come soon and explain everything to you. It's going to be okay. I'm putting a little cup to your lips with water for you to drink.'

Slowly, painfully she came back. Every breath was a challenge. Her world had become staccato, all in tiny snapshots. The doctor told her that she had many broken ribs.

'And Roland?' Sarah managed to ask, quietly, afraid of

the answer. The doctor paused, and she felt it heavy in the room. She couldn't see but she knew, suddenly, deep in her heart, something was appallingly wrong. The image of him on the floor before everything went black flashed across her mind.

'Is he…'

She couldn't bring herself to say the word, but the doctor replied steadily.

'He's here being treated but Sarah, you should know, he hasn't woken up yet. It's not uncommon for someone with extensive injuries, but you should focus on getting yourself better. We're doing everything we can.'

Sarah thought she'd feel relief, knowing Roland was still alive, but instead she felt even worse, because he wasn't alive, not really, not if he wasn't awake. Instead, she found herself feeling on edge at all hours of the day. Scared for him, scared for herself, scared of everything.

After some discussion they took the bandages off her face. On the fourth day, she could just see through the small slits of her eyes and Stephanie gave her a mirror.

'It may come as a shock. You won't look like yourself. Are you sure you want to look now?'

Sarah shook off Stephanie's warning. She wanted to see, she needed to. Her face was swollen, blue, yellow and black. Sarah could hardly recognise herself as the woman who met Roland in that green and cream silk ensemble in Paris. She felt apart from herself. One afternoon a tall middle-aged man came.

'My name is Graham Kingston. I'm the British Consul. My old school chum Morris Shuttleworth called me and suggested that I might pop in. I will arrange your travel home when the hospital is ready to let you go.' Nothing really made sense to Sarah. Time passed in a slow continuum. Sometimes she woke in the night terrified and the nurses would reassure her that no-one was there who would harm her. They would hold her hand until she slept again.

The police came and asked endless questions. And then, one day the doctor told her that Roland had just regained consciousness and would like to see her. She asked to be immediately wheeled down to his bed-side. His mother and father were there, looking distraught. His right leg was raised in the air and attached by a pulley over the end of the bed to weights. Despite all however. he managed a smile when she arrived and finally, she felt something lift in her chest. A step forward, finally. He was awake, at least. Sarah didn't realise how much she had been worrying until now, when she felt a huge wave of relief. She kissed him gently on his cheek and sat holding his hand while they talked, somewhat self-consciously, under the eyes of his parents.

'One of them spoke German. I heard him, just before everything went dark,' he had told her. She did not stay long as he clearly tired quickly and she felt herself ready to cry at any moment, the past few weeks having been under so much emotional strain. It was a relief to see him but it was also hard. He didn't look the same and neither did she. And they weren't the same, not after what had happened. Sarah could feel that everything had shifted.

Eventually the doctors had decided that she was fit to

leave the hospital. Graham Kingston arranged everything and she was flown home in a small private plane. It was a long, exhausting, bumpy journey. She was ill at frequent intervals; even sips of water, administered by a kind flight attendant, failed to stay down for long. Shuttleworth was at Croydon and met her on the tarmac.

'Your mother is waiting for you on the other side. She has a car to take you home. I am so desperately sorry that this has happened. Don't come back to the office until you are completely ready.'

Sarah nodded and then waited for a moment before speaking.

'I need to tell you two things, sir. I have a photograph of the Stollen, and she produced it from her handbag.' He looked at it with interest but gave it back to her. 'Keep it for the moment somewhere safe at home. Who knows what use it might be?' She had no idea why he said that, but everything was very overwhelming. Even returning home felt like a big step, having spent so long away and then at the hospital. Sarah put the photograph back into her bag as Morris spoke again.

'And what was the other thing that you wished to tell me?'

'Roland told me that one of them spoke German.' Shuttleworth was clearly troubled.

'Don't say any more. We'll have a de-briefing when you are ready.' And he escorted her through a side-exit in the terminal building to a small room where her mother was sitting, looking desperately anxious. It was time for Sarah to go home.

Later that day, Morris Shuttleworth sat alone at his desk. Sometimes the loneliness of his responsibility weighed heavily on him and today was one of those days. He knew that Sarah had wanted to get her 'field work' but to be honest with himself, it had never occurred to him that this simple pair of tasks in a friendly country like France would possibly incur any more risk than a trip to a part of England. It was supposed to be a relatively straight-forward job, but he had been wrong, and even Roland had been unable to protect her. He tried to snap himself out of it. It was in the past now, and what was important was focusing on exactly what could have possibly have gone wrong.

His first thought was that this had been a random attack, but her understanding that Roland had heard German spoken radically altered the likely scenario. 'So – no coincidence. The Germans know that we are after them. There must be a leak somewhere.' But where had the leak occurred? It seemed likely to him that the Germans only knew of the consignment by sea. There had been no problems at Le Bourget, or indeed even in Paris.

Was it possible that the leak had come from his office in London? Surely only he had known the details of the meet at Marseilles. Or was it only him? The office administrator, Sheila, must have known. And he thought of Sheila, who had worked for him for so long – must be twenty years, he supposed. 'Could she possibly have been turned?' It seemed totally incredible to him. Plain decent kindly Sheila, a traitor?' His mind whirled at the horror. He summoned her to his office and she came and sat before him with her usual gentle smile, wearing the rather dull

281

woollen suit that appeared to be her office uniform.

He told her about Sarah. She already knew. Of course she did. She had booked all the tickets for the trip, both plane and train ones for the domestic and international travel Sarah was undertaking. She had bought the plane tickets from the Imperial Airways office just down the street in Piccadilly, and bought them herself. No, no-one else had known. Sarah was travelling on an office passport under the name of Jean Miles and the tickets were in that name. Sheila had bought the train tickets at the London headquarters of French Railways in Regent Street herself. The tickets were Paris to Marseilles return, first class and undated, valid for a month. No, no-one else had known. She had kept the tickets in the office safe until she had put them herself into Sarah's hands the day before she left.

Sheila was confident no-one else had known but in her certainty, she also knew what this might mean for her. It was clear that Morris was interrogating Sheila's loyalty and as she left the office, Morris couldn't help but notice that she looked somewhat upset at the need to be questioned. Alas, this was a part of the job. Morris knew that, and at the end of the day, Sheila also knew it.

Shuttleworth's eyes veered to the picture of the girls at the piano, while his mind followed Sarah's trip in France. He thought through the question of why nothing had happened either at Le Bourget or in Paris. Nothing had happened until Marseilles. So the Germans had presumably not known anything about the first part of the trip, or they would have attacked them in Paris. The answer had to be connected to that second part of the trip. So, if they only knew about the boat trip, then the leak must surely have come from the other end, from South Africa. He needed to talk to Alan, and soon.

Alan was nonplussed. One part of him was devastated about the injuries to Sarah, the other troubled as to whether there could really have been a leak at his end. From what Shuttleworth had told him, there seemed little doubt that the flying side of the transportation of the diamonds was unaffected. The problem clearly lay with the maritime venture. So where could this 'problem' possibly lie? Clearly he must think about who knew about the sea trip but didn't know about the other side.

He joined Gloria on his, by now, favourite bench in the courtyard and they sat enjoying the afternoon sun. The bougainvillea on the opposite wall spreads its bracts to greet the warmth.

'I can see that the assumption must be that we should believe that only the sea route is compromised but that may not be the whole truth. They may have chosen simply to attack them in Marseilles, both to warn us and by attacking in only one place, to confuse us. But supposing that you and Morris are correct in the assumption that they only knew of the sea route, then there are only two people down here who knew about the sea route but not the aviation.'

'Two? Surely, it is only Dieter?'

'And Louis.'

'Ah, the omni-present Louis appears like Banquo's ghost.' Gloria looked at Alan as if he had lost his marbles.

'Alan, it is 1933. We are discussing a most serious and

283

important matter. Similes from Shakespeare are hardly appropriate.' He apologised humbly, but deep inside he was rather proud of his lateral thinking. Gloria frowned. Sarah was not unlike herself, and she couldn't help but feel like this could've just as easily happened to her.

'So, which is the most likely?'

'Yes, difficult. Louis is generally suspicious, a man seeking after knowledge and information as he does, is bound to be dangerous. On the other hand, in reality we know little of Dieter.'

'Agreed. Let's examine the problem as we were taught. Most importantly, who stands to benefit from leaking the information? Qui bono? As the lawyers say.' He laughed and Gloria flashed him another look of disapproval before laying out the supposed facts.

'Dieter cannot benefit. He wants us to smooth the passage of his uncle out of Germany.' Alan paused and thought about what he knew of Dieter.

'Does he? That's what he says. Frankly that has always seemed odd to me. I saw an article in the paper a few weeks ago in which the famous conductor was talking proudly of his love of Germany.'

There was a silence then as they considered the possibility that Dieter was simply one very effective foil, and that actually, when they thought they were ahead of the Germans, they were one step behind.

'We shall need to talk to both of them. If we think about Louis, we know that he is an intelligent thoughtful man. He would never have allowed the Abwehr to plan an attack on the two in Marseilles, as it would expose himself to suspicion. He would understand that we would be searching immediately for the leak. Incidentally it does also raise the question as to why the Abwehr planned the whole attack on the two.'

'Yes, good point. Perhaps they were more concerned with getting the diamonds through than with exposing their agent here?'

'If that is so, then the finger would point to their source being Dieter. Louis would be a marvellous agent for anyone. Sacrificing Louis would be madness. If Louis was our agent with all his connections, we would trip over ourselves to protect him. But Dieter stuck in the outback of Oudtshoorn....' And she trailed off.

They set off to Outsdhoorn the following morning. They had decided not to tell Dieter that they were coming, as they had reasoned that a surprise visit would prevent him from concocting a likely story. On the way to Oudtshoorn, Alan had discussed with Gloria the mechanisms for the interrogation of Dieter. They had agreed to play the game of double interrogation – the hard man, soft man scenario. They had talked through how Gloria had recruited Dieter and she had told him that one of the secretaries had met him at a classical music concert in Cape Town. Dieter had apparently 'bumped into' this friend at the bar in the interval and had bought her a couple of drinks at the bar. He had just left Germany and the friend had taken pity on him, partly Gloria had thought at the time because he was quite nice looking. In retrospect Gloria understood that she not been able to do the usual background checks as he had just arrived from Germany. So clearly there was a question as to exactly where his sympathies lay.

'But what about the letter from his uncle asking for our help in the event of his needing to escape from Germany?' Gloria had asked.

'Maybe we were both taken in with the importance of the uncle?' They both thought back to the talk with Dieter.

'But did we see the letter from Uncle Wilhelm?'

'No, we didn't.'

They did some more preparation for the interview. But in the event, little of their careful planning proved necessary.

Chapter Twenty-Five

'What matters most is how well you walk through the fire'

– Charles Bukowski (American poet and distant relation of Vladimir)

Oudtshoorn was at its most charming; the Bougainvillea was flowering everywhere, and lilies and dahlias were blooming by the side of the road. The sun was shining and the citizens seemed to be lazing around, enjoying the weather.

Alan and Gloria arrived in the late afternoon and parked the car in a side-street out of sight. They knocked on Dieter's door, but there was no response so, after a short while, they walked around the side of the house to look for another, more secluded way in. As expected, they found a back door, which Alan forced open with a screwdriver that he had in his pocket, reserved for such scenarios. Then, as the two of them sat in silence in the kitchen waiting for Dieter, Alan smiled to himself. They seemed exactly how

Alan had originally expected when he was in training for his job, sitting and waiting ominously; action but no paperwork. It was satisfying, he thought, when the opportunity arose to do some real fieldwork, although it was definitely more stressful. The stakes now were high.

It was shortly after 5p.m. when they heard the sound of the front door being unlocked, and suddenly Dieter was standing before them in the kitchen. He started, it taking him a moment to realise exactly who it was in his house.

'Alan. Gloria. How did you get in?'

'Please sit down, Dieter we have some questions to ask you.' Alan kept his face neutral which he found from experience was more intimidating than looking angry or stern. No doubt, Dieter was running through all the possible reasons they would be here, unannounced, having broken into his home. Dieter started to bluster but Alan cut in.

'Two of our senior agents have been badly beaten, with both close to death, in the port of Marseilles, shortly after a visit to the Usambara.' 'It's clear that there's been a leak here in South Africa. You are the only person in our organisation who knew that the diamonds would be on the Usambara. You have five minutes to explain what you have done and why.' Dieter's face drained of colour and he looked as if he was going to faint. But Alan was not going to let their advantage slip.

'We want to see now the letter from your uncle requesting assistance with his exit.' No-one moved. Then slowly Dieter's head fell and he clasped his hands together in anguish.

'There is no letter. I was threatened. He said that they would tell my Uncle Wilhelm about my weakness if I didn't help them' There was another long silence as Alan waited to ask his next question, giving Dieter the opportunity to squirm and panic. Sometimes, the best way of interrogating someone, was to let them think of all of the worst possible things that could happen. The imagination is a powerful place.

'Tell him what?'

'I cannot tell you. It is my weakness.' Alan cast a subtle glance at Gloria as Dieter kept his gaze firmly downwards.

'Who threatened you?'

For a moment, Dieter clenched his hands tighter together and Gloria noticed he appeared to go an even paler shade.

'I can't,' Dieter muttered.

Alan went to speak but Gloria threw him a pointed look, before going over to Dieter and placing her hand on his shoulder.

'Look, Dieter, this is serious. We can protect you, but only if you tell us what we need to know so we can protect ourselves too.'

Alan tried to hide his smile. It was a classic routine; Alan going in hard, and now Gloria offering him a lifeline. Dieter looked up at her.

'Carl. He forced me to tell him what you knew. He knew that you had visited me.'

Alan frowned.

'How did he know that?'

'I have no idea, but he knew. I had to tell him everything

that you knew.'

Alan had no doubt that Dieter was telling the truth this time, but how on earth could Carl have known?

'So you told him that we knew about the Usambara?'

'Yes.'

'And where it was stopping en route to Germany?'

Dieter nodded. There they had it; the leak.

After visiting Dieter, and persuading him that they were one hundred percent certain that they had not been followed, Alan and Gloria returned to the Cape. Having decided, on the car journey back, their next course of action, the two of them parked up at the Embassy before walking briskly to Louis' house. To their surprise, Louis had a string of sick children and anxious parents queuing outside his house, but nevertheless welcomed the pair inside where he was seated behind a fine old mahogany desk, piled with notes. Alan noticed that Louis himself was looking rather smart, in what must've been an expensive suit and silk tie. For Alan, it was strange to see him at a time of his own choice, rather than have Louis appearing out of thin air when Alan was least expecting it.

'Good morning to you both. As you can see, I am earning my keep, so I regret that I cannot entertain you on the terrace as I would have hoped to.'

'It's fine, we're grateful that you've taken the time to see us, we can see you're a very busy man. We just have a quick question, and then we'll leave. Where can we find a man who can help us buy fake diamonds?' Louis regarded him with a careful pair of eyes.

'An unusual request. Do you want gems made of glass?'

'We don't actually know exactly what we want but that sounds like what we are looking for.'

Louis nodded slowly.

'You need my friend Vladimir Bukovski. He was born in the Ukraine but has lived here since his young adulthood. He's a wondrous human, and I know him because we both write poetry. His shop is close to here on Dixon Street. Tell him I sent you.' They thanked him, leaving the babble of his waiting room and the queue outside, and walked to the nearby Dixon Street. The street was straight as a die, giving it a direct feeling of honesty; its breadth also spoke of its openness.

It was not hard to find the shop marked Bukovski and Son as it was decorated with the shades of the jewels that it contained. The colours of the painted wood frames were the dark hues of Kashmiri sapphires surrounding the glass of the windows with the glint of diamonds. The red of the front door spoke of the rubies inside. The displays in the windows were discreet, telling of antique rings cast off by the dead or the poor. Interlaced were modern jewels in modern strings, the diamonds arrayed in their modern cuts. The door was locked but their ring was rapidly answered by a young man in traditional Jewish dress; Alan guessed this must be the noted 'And Son.'

'We would to speak with your father, please.' They were admitted into a well-lit space full of glass-topped cabinets containing precious things. The lights were many and very bright. The walls were covered in white paint, seemingly the better to conserve every ray of light.

'Papa,' the son called, 'Britishers – for you.' They laughed.

From the back of the shop emerged a veritable giant of a man. Tall, with a long greying beard and so tall, in fact that his yarmulke was hardly glimpsable. He was wearing a long black coat to his knees in the orthodox Jewish style with a vast table of a belly protruding through its centre.

'My English friends, can I serve you?'

'We come from Louis du Plessis.' A vast smile spread slowly wider and ever wider, like Lewis' Cheshire cat, until Alan began to wonder whether it would stop before it reached his ears.

'The only man in the whole Cape who writes better poetry than myself. Well, a friend of his, is a friend of mine. Come, we will sit in the back and drink tea, as you British do. And I will do my best to warm your hearts before we do business. Solomon, bring tea for us all.'

'Of course, father.' They wandered into a deceptively vast cavern of a room behind the shop. The feature of the room was the safes. Safes; grand dark metallic fortresses of varying hue but enormous size, all set into the wall on the right of the room. Although there were no outside windows, the room was as brightly lit as a hotel lobby with a multitude of lamps, scattered across the ceiling. The other walls, not occupied by the large safes, were covered with rich silk carpets, and bookcases over-packed with books which spewed out of them; with more books stacked high in piles on the floor. There were big comfortable-looking armchairs, covered in dark brown leather, and he gestured at them to sit.

'Don't allow my father to talk too much,' Solomon said, as he entered with a tray of tea. Vladimir laughed.

'Children always seem to know their parents best! My son, I will promise not to read them too many of my poems, if I can be assured that you will care for any customers who arrive.'

Alan caught Gloria grinning as she watched the playful exchange between father and son; their own jobs involved so much movement, and to such unusual places, that opportunities to see their own families were few and far between.

'That seems a fine bargain, father,' Solomon cast a polite smile at Alan and Gloria, 'I'll leave you to your business.'

As he left the room, Vladimir began pouring tea for each of them.

'And my friend Louis, did you leave him in good health?'

'Thriving but busy, tending the sick children of the Cape.'

'Ah yes. Such a good man. I met him first when Solomon was ill when a small babe, with pneumonia. He was recommended. And I saw on the wall of his consulting room at his home, a poem framed and hanging on the wall. I read it while he was listening to my wife talking about the child, and realised that this was a poet of the highest order. I sent him one of my meagre offerings, and next thing I knew, I was invited to the Cape Poetry Society, which of course he had started. Such a man – and you must get invited to dinner. The complexity of the dishes. A man could die contented after dinner at his house.' They all laughed. Gloria took a sip of her tea. The room was surprisingly cool, which for her made the tea taste even better than usual, and it was nice to be out of the heat of the Cape sun. 'But

I chatter, as I promised Solomon that I would not. What business is it that you wish to discuss?'

'We wish to buy some substances that are small, look like diamonds to the untutored eye, but are merely cheap substitutes.' The man kept his eyes fixed carefully on Alan and his open and welcome demeanour quickly turned serious.

'You do not have to tell me why, but it might help if I understood. You will have my assurance of absolute confidentiality.'

Alan looked at Gloria who nodded gently.

'We wish to substitute them for a collection of diamonds, intended for use in machine-tools. We hope that they will look completely like diamonds and that their properties will not become apparent until they are actually used in the machine-tools.'

'And what will the machine-tools be used for?'

'For making rifles and other weapons.' There was a silence. Vladimir looked with care at the English pair.

'Perhaps I made an error in my request for information. This knowledge could be dangerous, not just for me, but for the position it puts my family in, by extension.' He paused. 'Let me see if I have this all correct. From your accents, you are British. I have heard of Gloria from the Embassy, but you Alan, have the pale skin of a new arrival here.' Alan nodded slightly. 'And you come to me with a most unusual request. So, I suspect that maybe you are a man who works for the embassy in, let's say, an unusual capacity. Am I right?'

Alan did not move or speak. 'I will take your silence as

agreement. So I wonder what brings a man all the way from London to my small humble shop wanting glass diamonds? And I wonder to myself whether this has to do with Europe rather than Africa? Am I right?' Alan was silent again, and Gloria decided it was time for her to take the lead.

'That is why we must ensure absolute confidentiality.'

'Yes, I see.' The tea cooled slowly on the table. Without lowering his eyes, he slowly raised his cup to his lips and took a long slurp of the hot liquid into his mouth, before replacing his cup exactly onto the saucer, again without a movement of the eyes. Alan was impressed at the dexterity of such a large man.

'You will need our hardened glass jewels. They look like the real thing and might even cut for a few turns on the lathe before they collapse. And they are cheap and plentiful. I can provide you with hundreds.' Vladimir allowed the two of them a moment to take in what he had said, before he continued.

'But maybe first I need to tell you a story, so that you can trust my assurance of absolute confidentiality. When I was a small boy, I lived in an unassuming village on the vast Steppes of the Ukraine. My parents were good observant people and we children lived a marvellous life. Despite the enormity of the plains, they showed us the world outside the stetl and some of us yearned for that excitement that they encouraged in us when they talked of cities with shops and buses and the theatre. Oh, for myself I yearned for the theatre as you may not be surprised to know that I was a natural show-off. We performed a school play once a year at Hannukah time and to act and show-off on a stage in front of everyone was the highlight of my child's life.'

Vladimir gestured to himself and the room around them, covered in textures and colours.

'And then one day close to my twelfth birthday, on a day with the skies as light blue as a sapphire of the highest purity, even one brought from the scarps of the high Himalayas, the Ukrainian men from the neighbouring village came. They hung all the men of the village from ropes from the tree in the centre of the village, and took all the women away. I was at the village school and escaped out of the back door with my older brother. We hid in a hay barn and when we came out, there was no-one left in the village. No-one, just bodies and blood, blood everywhere, and the animals all slaughtered too. My brother went to our house and brought a bag with food, and a bible. We walked and walked. We slept that night under a hedge.

Vladimir gazed away from them; his expression uncharacteristically melancholy as he continued.

'The next day we reached a road where we were picked up by a business man driving a carriage with four horses. He heard our story in silence and for one moment we thought that he was going to leave us at the roadside. But it was our most fortunate day and he took us home. He lived with his wife and family in a town called Matvivka. They were kind to us and welcomed us into their family. But one day a few weeks later they told us that we could not stay and that they were sending us on a boat to other members of their family in London. He took us to the banks of the Dnieper River and we were taken in a small boat to the town of Cherkasy. We travelled down the great river, disembarked and were shown a much larger enormous boat which carried us through the Mediterranean. Eventually we reached London where we were collected from the docks by these relatives and were enrolled in a school in Hackney.

But by then I had enjoyed my taste for the sea so, after a few years, I ran away and enlisted on a boat of the East India Company. We took manufactured goods to India and brought back tea. I was very happy and made good friends. Usually, we went through the Suez Canal but one trip we had to travel the long route around the Cape, and we stopped for two days at Cape Town. I was entranced by the city, the climate and above all that there was a thriving Jewish community. I felt that this was a moment of destiny for me. I deserted the ship, was taken in by a kind family and immediately tried to found a drama company. In fact, I did, but everyone told me that I had to have a 'proper job' as well, so I joined a small jewellery shop. It was a good time as the country had become wealthy on its diamonds, after the boy had found the first diamond.'

'The boy?' Gloria asked. Vladimir suddenly looked cheerful again and he laughed.

'The first diamond found in South Africa was seen by a 15 year old boy called Erasmus Jacobs in a small tributary of the Orange River. He took it home and showed it to his father saying 'Look, father, for I have found this rock. I can see through it.' I must not digress further or my story will last till night-time, and we will be drinking something stronger than tea.' With that, the mood in the room was lifted once again, although the reveal of Vladimir's past was left lingering in Alan and Gloria's mind. It was almost unfathomable that this man, so joyful, so successful, could have experienced such horrors.

'And now I am here and prosperous and I have my wonderful family. But I remember the days of the killing of the Jews in the far off Ukraine; the pogrom as they call it.'

Alan decided that to not reveal the full story, after all that they had been told, would be to dishonour the frankness and honesty of the man. Although Alan didn't wish to bring the mood back down again, he talked candidly of the attempts to smuggle out diamonds and the German involvement. Vladimir listened intently and nodded along as Alan spoke.

'Thank you for telling me. Now we all know where we stand, let's get to business. What sort of size are you looking for?'

More tea was drunk and a deal was struck. As they waved goodbye, Alan and Gloria walked out with a bag full of glass diamonds, a small book of poetry, and a new friendship to savour.

Chapter Twenty-Six

An English rain is falling

Alan considered himself to be a good sleeper, if that was something you could say about yourself, because he consistently woke between seven and seven-thirty without an alarm. Since he had been in the Cape, he would usually find himself gently roused, in part, by the sunny glow that filtered through the gaps in his bedroom curtains. Today, however, although it was light, there seemed to be none. He looked at his bedside clock; 7.20 a.m. Nothing unusual there. He climbed out of bed and walked over to draw the curtains, and surveyed a most unusual sight. Rain.

Down at breakfast everything was as usual. A number of staff including Gloria were eating bacon and eggs in various forms; conversation was muted and coffee being drunk; newspapers were mainly being hidden behind. It was a totally normal Embassy morning. The only real noise came from Gloria who was having a nice chat with Gladys, whose wound has healed and whose head scar was slowly turning paler by the day. Alan went to get his breakfast and sat down on the other side of Gloria.

'It is raining,' he said.

'Your powers of early observation are improving daily.' Despite waking at a similar time every day, Alan, unlike Gloria, was not a morning person, and often found it hard to cope with witticisms at that hour, even from her.

'But it's just like English rain,' he complained. 'I thought that rain here fell in buckets.' She laughed and took a bite of her toast, before replying.

'Alan, of course we have days of torrential rain, but sometimes it's just gentle like this morning. Remember the Cape is quite a long way from the tropics.' He tried to find his way around the geography of the situation, but his brain was apparently yet to turn properly on, and all he could picture were various shapes swirling around in his mind, refusing to form any sort of image of a world map. To his alarm, a strong smell of a sweet sickly perfume wafted over his right shoulder. Even more alarmingly he knew that the seat on his right was empty. He turned to discover a female receptionist leaning in, rather closely applied to his right cheek.

'Telephone for you from Kimberley, Mr. Simpson. At reception,' she whispered caressingly. Alan pulled a face, although whether at the receptionist or the prospect of a telephone call so early in the morning, it wasn't clear. Regardless, Gloria was clearly not amused by the intervention and Alan found himself feeling quite smug as she gave the back of the retreating receptionist a filthy stare.

On the other end of the line, a strong Scots burr was carried down the wires.

'Good morning. Lovely to see the rain no doubt for you,

Alan. Must remind you of home.' Before Alan could respond, he continued,

'Mr. James here by the way. Our continental colleague will be collecting some presents from here next week on Tuesday. Thought you would like to know. Mostly he is sending them to an old friend for safe-keeping.' Suddenly, Alan was shaken out of his sleepy morning state.

'There are rather a lot of presents. He's a very generous friend. As last time, the presents are to be divided in half. Have a good morning, my English colleague.'

And then there was a click indicating that the connection had been cut. Alan returned to breakfast to find Gloria, but she was nowhere to be seen. He was about to leave immediately to find her, when he noticed his plate of food waiting for him, and his stomach growled. Perhaps he did have time for something to eat. Besides, how could he possibly be expected to concoct a high-stakes plan on an empty stomach? He finished his breakfast first, before wandering off and finding Gloria, as expected, in her office. After he had imparted his information, they quickly decided on a strategy and agreed on the finer details so that Alan could send a telegram to London. The swiftness at which he and Gloria were concoct the plan told Alan everything he needed to know. Firstly, they made a great team, and secondly, eating his breakfast was definitely a good idea.

In the office in Piccadilly, Shuttleworth read the telegram twice and considered his options. He needed to decide whether interception was going to be possible, and it was quickly apparent to him that boarding the ship at

Marseilles was just not on. Roland was by now out of hospital but on crutches and even if his leg should miraculously heal, his face would be known in the port to his assailants. Since the French police had appeared mystified by the attack, none of the men had been arrested and could still be very much at large. The police, of course, were hampered by a lack of understanding of what was going on, since neither Sarah nor Roland had revealed their reasons for being where they were, as it would have blown their cover. It was common knowledge amongst those working in 'special capacities', that in these circumstances, the French authorities would not have been amused to learn that the British had been conducting a covert operation on their territory, without any prior notification.

Sarah was also not back at work and Shuttleworth couldn't possibly ask her to return yet, let alone undertake what would be a decidedly risky operation. And, on top of all of this, he could not rely on Roland's new contact in the docks to act alone, as he had not even been vetted. Morris had no idea who they could trust, and he would have to ensure that Alan and Gloria understood that they were on their own as regards the Usambara and the sea route.

Morris considered the chances for intercepting the air route at Le Bourget, as he paced his office. There was no reason why Michel was compromised, and perhaps if Michel could bring him the Stollen with the diamonds, then they could give Michel an identical Stollen to substitute. Of course, Shuttleworth would need all the details of the Stollen, and their ingredients. He would also need to decide how to get the diamonds back to England without being arrested by French Customs officers. And he would need Alan to send him some of the glass diamonds. Then of course, most concerningly, Shuttleworth would need to bake a Stollen. The exercise had become decidedly complex.

Then he suddenly stopped his pacing. He knew exactly the person to bake a Stollen. Poking his head out of his office, he asked Sheila to bring him the initial vetting papers for Sarah Grandison and read them through carefully. Half way in, there it was, as his memory had informed him. Perfect.

Shuttleworth was sitting with his feet on his desk in his office hoping that the foot elevation will help him to deal with his slight nervousness.

'Hello Sarah. I'm calling to enquire after your health.'

'Thank you, sir. I'm much better. So much better that I'm bored at home, and would like to return to work as soon as possible, if that's OK with you?'

He pretended to be shocked, lifting his feet back down from the desk and leaning forward to rest one elbow as he spoke.

'Much too early in my view. What do the doctors say?'

'They were not very happy,' she admitted.

'Quite,' he said, then prepared to slide the task into the conversation. 'But if you are bored, maybe you might like a little task to relieve your boredom?'

'Anything, sir,' Sarah said readily, but then she paused. 'But perhaps not in Marseilles.'

'Quite. No, the task that I had thought for you involved some pastry cooking. I had recalled that you had wanted at some stage of your life before you joined us, to be a pastry chef?'

Sarah laughed, although he could tell from her tone of voice that she was confused.

'What a wonderful memory you have, sir. What would you like me to cook? Is there to be an office party? Is it a birthday?'

'Not exactly. Sarah, I would like you to cook a Stollen. And, well, let's say I might have a few extra ingredients for you to add to the mixing bowl before you bake it.'

'Alright sir, I don't think that will be a problem.'

Sarah's tone changed again, more business-like this time, and Morris knew immediately that she understood there was more to this then he would be able to tell her over the phone.

'Excellent. Well, I'm glad you're doing well, Sarah. Speak soon.'

'Goodbye, sir.'

He hung up. That had not been too bad, he realised and stretched his arms out, trying to relieve some of the tension that had gathered in his shoulders. Now he had to think about the operational details. *Someone* would need to travel to Le Bourget to exchange Sarah's Stollen and the one from Cape Town, and then bring the other marked Stollen from the Cape back to England. And, after the Marseille incident, and with no other operational agents available, Shuttleworth supposed that that *someone* would have to be him. Although, he had rather assumed that he was getting a bit long in the tooth for field work. Well, he supposed he could get Michel and his friend in Customs to help him.

That would have to work. There really wasn't much other choice. And as Morris Shuttleworth came to the realisation that he was going back into action, he popped his head back around his office door again.

'Sheila, I need to have a wee chat with the boss. This afternoon would be good.'

He returned to his office to compose a telegram. He gazed at the ceiling for a long while. Eventually his gaze returned to the walls. There was a lot to pass on to Alan and Gloria in Cape Town.

Chapter Twenty-Seven

Worrying times at the High Commission

'We have a plan, Gloria.'

Gloria was clearly not paying attention, shuffling papers around absentmindedly.

'Gloria?'

She started and looked up at him, pushing the papers to the side.

'Sorry, sorry. You have my full attention.'

'I have a long telegram from Shuttleworth. You need to read it.'

Alan handed it over to her and watched as she dragged her mind back to reality and focused on the words in front of her. When she had finished he began to speak again,

'So, the plan goes like this. As far as the consignment by air goes, we can let everything through and the boss will arrange the interception. Sarah will bake two new Stollens, and into one he'll mix half of our glass diamonds. We need to send those glass diamonds to Shuttleworth on the next flight to Croydon where he'll pick them up and take them to her home for mixing with the other ingredients.' Alan paused for a moment and then grinned at the thought of Shuttleworth turning up, followed by Sarah frantically baking in her family kitchen.

'I wonder what her parents will think is going on?' Alan added, and Gloria handed the telegram back to him for safekeeping and disposal. 'With the nature of the job, it is likely that they don't even really know what Sarah's job entails. They will certainly be none the wiser after the cooking activity.' Alan imagined Sarah's mother over the fence to her neighbour and suppressed a laugh as he wondered what the two of them would make of it all.

'We need to arrange the substitution of the glass beads for the diamonds in the feather packet for the Usambara. Shuttleworth suggests that the substitution could occur between Dieter's house and the docks at Port Elizabeth, as after that he believes that we won't have an opportunity. He's probably right.'

Alan folded the telegram carefully as Gloria considered the potential pitfalls of the plan. It was a good idea in theory, but there seemed to be plenty of opportunities for it to lurch sideways, and anyway surely the Germans would have extra security in place to ensure everything ran smoothly for them?

'Won't Carl arrange for the diamonds to be watched on their way to the docks? And didn't we discover that Carl had arranged for Cape Connections to transfer the diamonds to the Docks?'

'We did. So assuming that they follow the same procedure, Carl and the woman will take the diamonds to Dieter's house. One or maybe even two, if there are a lot of diamonds, of the bags will be opened, filled with diamonds, re-sewed and placed amongst the feathers. So maybe we will need to rely on Dieter's sleight of hand in the packing of the boxes of feathers. We can get him two bags of the glass beads prepared beforehand and in identical bags, so that all he'll need to do is to swap them over at some point while packing the boxes of feathers. And of course we now have a hold over Dieter which should ensure his compliance. Another trip to Oudtshoorn is imminent, I suspect.'

Gloria nodded and then flashed Alan a grin

'Didn't we promise to take Louis next time?' She joked.

'Maybe this is not quite the occasion for that! We will find him a better trip than this.'

In the end Alan travelled alone to Oudtshoorn, taking with him the glass diamonds. Alan had set off immediately, and arrived later in the afternoon at Dieter's house. A subdued Dieter sat him down and fed them some more Lebkuchen biscuits.

'I shall wear this jacket,' and he pointed to the jacket that he was currently wearing. 'It has deep pockets and so I can put these packets in the right-hand pocket and then, when I am re-packing the feathers, it'll be easy to slip out the packets with the real diamonds and substitute these, before I pack the feathers up ready for transportation to the docks.'

He and Dieter made up two silica bags, and Dieter sewed the bags up to look identical to the stitching used by Carl's assistant. Dieter put an identical marking of black ink on the bags, but was uncertain as to whether he would be able to make the substitution at the point when he was completing the wrapping of the feathers in the box.

Carl had apparently arranged for two couriers from Cape Connections to arrive at Dieter's house. The men were to accompany Carl as a security escort in a separate car from Cape Town to Kimberley and then on to Oudtshoorn from where they would take the feathers from Dieter's house to the docks. So that, short of an armed highway robbery or theft in the docks or on board, once the diamonds left Dieter's house, they would be safe until their collection in Germany.

The journey home was full of doubts for Alan. Would Dieter manage it? What would happen if Carl noticed the sleight of hand? But he and Gloria had agreed that there was no easy other way.

They had to wait three more days for the call from Kimberley. Once again Roderick called at breakfast time but to Gloria's relief, the receptionist summoning Alan to the phone was a man.

'James here,' came the voice. 'A very large consignment will leave in two days in two parcels with our friends, bound for Oudtshoorn and the Cape.'

'What sort of sums are we talking about?'

'Enormous. Each parcel is valued at around two thousand U.S. Dollars,' and he was gone once more.

Chapter Twenty-Eight

Dieter is tested

Dieter

'They came in the early morning as they had said they would. Dawn had just broken over the south of Africa as it always does, like a magnificent apocalypse. How did they get here so early? Maybe they drove through the night thinking that they would catch me unawares. Two cars; two of them in each. Carl and she, I deliberately forget her name to try to insult her, in the first; the Packard of course. They put the guards in the smaller car just to make the point.

The Germans dress like they are some minor gangsters in an American movie. Perhaps they fancy that they are Al Capone and his moll. They put him in prison last year; so even Scarface has gone down. How come they need to play these games? Frightening me, maybe. Treating me like a servant; these Nazis are just bullies at heart. So as long as I keep that in mind, I can't be bullied, can I? But they know my secret so I feel vulnerable. I must remember that the

English treat me like a real man. And even if I am not, they are kind. So I must repay that kindness and perform the magic that they want. I have put on my coat with the deep pockets and now they are at my door. The knocking is loud and prolonged. I walk slowly towards it. I will not be intimidated. I will not be intimidated.

'Hello,' I say. They just barge in, no speech. Just the two then. They leave the Security outside where they loll like a pair of cops against the car. Such big men; One has lit a cigarette. Doubtless they will extinguish it against my drive. No respect. I will clean up after they are gone.

'Would you like a drink?'

'Yawohl, zwei tees.' Not even a please or thank you then. I go to the kitchen to get their teas. I make their teas as strong as I dare. They don't know why, of course. Lebkuchen or not? My mind says 'no' at the same instant as I fail to prevent my hand reaching for the tin. I carry the tray carefully in but I expect that they can see my hand trembling through the waves on the surface of their drinks. But I did have a small rebellion; they didn't get the best china. How brave I was.

'Where is the box of feathers?' I scoot off to get it. I check the packets with the glass chips in my pockets. Both in my right pocket; I must remember that. I bring the box back and open it and there are the beautiful feathers. I have chosen a box of all white plumes; they give me the greatest joy. The exquisite pleasure of their purity. They don't care of course. I take out two packets of the silica.

'How did you know that we needed two?' he asks rudely and suspiciously.

'Just a guess,' I stammer. I can feel myself reddening.

'If I think that you are betraying us, you know what will happen to you.' He threatens me and I know that he is capable of anything. It's the coldness in those staring eyes. 'And when we are done, there will not be much left, but the world will know what you like. And how young as well.'

I shake as I offer him the packets which are still in my outstretched hand. He takes them roughly. She takes out her scissors and I feel that she cuts the packets as if they are my finger-tips. They scatter the silica. He takes out a small bag and tips the real diamonds into each bag until they are quite full. Then she sews the bags up.

'Now into the box with them,' he orders. But before I can act, she interrupts.

'Die toilette.' She has had a long journey, poor thing. And my strong tea has got to her bladder, as indeed I hoped. And at this moment. At this moment, thank the Lord. Oh God I must start church again; you have spoken. She puts the scissors down as I point the way.

'Through the door and on the right.' And she has left the scissors. Those scissors. She leaves.

It must be now. But I am terrified. TERRIFIED. I MUST ACT. And I sweep the scissors so that they travel through the air and fall just behind his chair.

'Ungeschickter Trottel,' he shouts, calling me a clumsy oaf in that offensive manner of his. But he is unable to stop himself in an example of his teutonic need for tidiness, from turning around to pick them up – as I knew that he would. The great orderly German mind strikes again. But I know you, Great Mind. And I knew and had planned this moment of exquisite orgasm.

He bends over and the packets are out of my right hand pocket and into the feather box, as my left hand reaches for their diamonds and slip them into my left hand pocket before he turns back. He looks furious. Did he see? He walks towards me, right hand out. He has seen. The hand goes back, and then comes forward to strike me on the face.

My face is afire. But I don't care. It seems that he didn't see. He didn't see. He just hit me for his pleasure, no other reason.

'You really are a nasty little pervert, aren't you?' He is shaking me and his left hand holds my throat. I can feel my head lightening, my legs trembling. I am falling and I feel myself hit the ground. He kicks me on the legs, and at that moment she returns. He picks up the feather box and hands it to her.

'Tie up this box,' he orders her, 'give it to the half-wits outside, and send them on their way to Port Elizabeth.' And he looks at me on the floor.

'Goodbye you nasty piece of scum.' And he is gone. I hear the cars roaring away and when it is quiet outside, I slowly pull my aching body upright and slump into a chair. But I won. I won. I did it. I did it. And I grin, foolishly.

And now to phone Alan.

Chapter Twenty-Nine

Alan plots diamonds

Alan and Gloria spent two anxious days at the High Commission, where the time passed slowly. Alan discovered that even he was not immune to clock-watching, while Gloria plunged herself back into the S.I.S accounts. Eventually, Alan was called to the phone at lunch-time.

It was Dieter in a state of high excitement.

'Flawlessly, flawlessly, Alan,' were his words. 'It was so easy, Alan, mainly I think because they were unsuspecting. I had it all planned. When they arrived, the escorts stayed outside in their car. Carl and the secretary came in and two bags were opened. There were many more diamonds than last time and they only just fitted into two empty silica bags. After the secretary had sewn up the bags again, she went to the toilet and I was able to make the substitution.'

Alan drove to Outdshoorn and an ebullient Dieter told him all the details of the story and gave him the two bags of diamonds. Alan went back outside and tied the bags securely with a string around their necks, and then lowered the bags into the petrol tank of his car on the string. He was reminded of crab fishing at Blakeney harbour. Next he tied the other end of the string around the petrol tank lid, hiding the end of the string back inside the tank, so that it was not visible from outside. When he had learned that trick on the S.I.S. Introductory course, he had mocked the idea, telling one of his friends that he could never envisage a use for it. In retrospect he felt foolish.

He drove back to Cape Town, slightly nervously, unable to put aside the knowledge that thousands of dollars of diamonds were in his petrol tank, but the drive was uneventful. After he had parked the car back in the garage forecourt, he extracted the diamonds, and reported back to Sir Robert, who seemed rather pleased to have diamonds in his safe despite the stink of the petrol fumes polluting his office. They discussed what to do with the diamonds. Alan had a thought.

'How about we sell them to Vladimir?'

Sir Robert frowned.

'The one who made the glass copies?'

Alan nodded and continued to speak, 'Exactly. He's a jeweller so no doubt would use them, and it wouldn't be at all suspicious if he were to come into possession of such a large quantity. In fact, it seems rather perfect to me.'

'What an excellent idea!'

And so, the following day, Alan, accompanied by two of the High Commission's armed guards, had visited the Bukovsky family business. Vladimir was delighted to help, and paid Alan a vast sum, which he later deposited in Sir Robert's safe. It all seemed to be coming together even better than Alan could've hoped and, in all honesty, there was no one Alan would have trusted more than Vladimir to make good (and appropriate) use of the diamonds. As he was leaving and the High Commission's armed guards were temporarily out of earshot, he hugged Vladimir and whispered something into his ear. The man laughed loudly.

'I'll see you soon, Alan. Thank you again, my good friend. One of these will be put to particularly good use!'

The following day, Alan arranged a meeting with Amit.

'Carl will shortly be asking you to make two more Stollen.'

'You English would say 'More coals to Newcastle', I think.'

'It is so, Amit. In the meantime, I need you to give me your recipe for Stollen.' Amit produces a pen and paper and writes with paragraphs headed Ingredients, Making the dough, cooking instructions etc.

'Of course the Stollen was improved by His Holiness, the pope.'

'Why is it that so many things that you say, Amit, leave me floundering?'

Amit appeared to look perplexed but Alan noticed the twinkle in Amit's eye as he spoke.

'Ah, you're playing with me, Amit.'

'Would I do that?' Amit grinned at Alan before continuing, 'But to be very serious, Alan. It was in the year of your Lord, 1490, when the Pope wrote his Butterbrief, a momentous occasion for us chefs.'

'Go on then. Tell me. What was a Butterbrief?'

'It was a letter written to Prince Erich von Sachen, at the behest of the bakers of Dresden, removing the ban made by one of his predecessors on the use of butter. It came of course shortly before a following papal bull, *Exsurge Domine*, threatening Martin Luther with excommunication.'

'Of course it did, Amit. Please could we stick to the point and not get lost in our Proustian conjunctival clauses about Luther or we will be here all day.' Amit smiles wanly.

'Back to the Stollen, then Alan.'

'Back to the Stollen, Amit.'

'So, here are the instructions to make the Stollen as I do. And then I assume that once again Carl will add his little ingredients as I make the dough?'

'I suspect so, with some teutonic rigour. And then you will be required to mark with an ink blot on the Stollen with the extra ingredient, as before. Then they'll be off to the airport.'

'And will I be required to do anything else?'

'No, that will be all. But I need to know which day the Stollen leave, so that I can tell my boss when they're due.'

Alan returned to the High Commission and telegrammed the long cooking instructions to Morris, who in turn posted them to Sarah. Meanwhile he sent the remaining glass diamonds via the Diplomatic Bag on the next day's flight to Croydon, where they were collected by a S.I.S. courier and taken to Morris at H.Q. in Piccadilly. Once everything was completed on his end, Alan knew that now he had to wait for Amit to tell him when the Stollen was leaving Cape Town, and trust that Sarah's baking skills were a passable match for Amit's. No matter, it was out of his control.

Meanwhile in England, Sarah received the long list of ingredients from Shuttleworth, and had a pleasant afternoon shopping with her mother who, it must be said, found her daughter's suddenly revived taste for pastry-cooking somewhat out of character, as she explained at some length to Mrs. Arbuthnot over the fence later in the day.

'Maybe she has a new young man,' suggested Mrs Arbuthnot somewhat tartly. Mrs Grandison was loathe to admit that that possibility had not occurred to her and so rather poo-pooed the idea. However on her way back to the kitchen, she had to admit that as Sarah had said that the boss would be coming, she had to give some credence to the coincidence of the unusual pastry-enthusiasm with the arrival of the boss. Mrs Grandison spent the afternoon anticipating what he might look like. 'Surely, he must be a lot older than her,' and then she suddenly recalled the age gap that had existed between herself and the late Mr. Grandison. 'Maybe it's in her genes,' she mused indecisively, and returned to the consideration of whether it was better to have the potatoes boiled or mashed with tonight's lamb chops.

Chapter Thirty

Morris and Sarah make Stollen

S arah had spent some time considering the most appropriate dress for a visit from the boss at which she would be cooking. She had decided regretfully that she had better dress practically and put on one of her three home-made floral dresses, all of them sewn by her practically-minded mother. She chose a deep blue pretty one, decorated with marigolds and with ruffle sleeves, but she thought that she could just roll the sleeves up for the kitchen-work. It was fashionable enough, although Sarah wasn't sure he was the sort of man that might notice.

Promptly at eleven o'clock the doorbell had rung and Sarah had run to open it. Morris looked her carefully up and down.

Sarah, you look nice. That blue colour suits you.'

'Thank you, sir. Please, come in.'

Sarah smiled and sat him down at the kitchen table, where she had spread the ingredients out on the table. He looked them over, surprisingly with some care. She thought that in view of his inspection, she had better confess immediately before he taxed her with it.

'We couldn't find any cinnamon.'

Morris nodded.

'I am not surprised. Apparently there has been an appalling shortage since the hurricane struck Sri Lanka earlier this year.'

Sarah was surprised that he knew about the cinnamon shortage, although she supposed that one must pick up all sorts of knowledge when in charge of certain global missions.

'Cup of tea, sir?'

She was already preparing the kettle when Morris replied.

'Thank you. And no 'sir' out of the office, please. Could we be Morris and Sarah?'

'Of course.' At that moment her mother arrived, clearly there to inspect him. Fortunately, in her eyes, he looked rather respectable, dressed as he was in his plaid suit with wide-collared shirt and two-tone shoes. She looked him up and down, before holding her hand out to greet him, clearly approving of her daughter's boss (and he didn't look that old at all!). They had a polite conversation before she left them to get on with it – whatever the job was, because it still seemed a little strange to Mrs Grandison that her daughter was baking again. Especially considering she hadn't baked for a long time before Mr Morris had arrived. She couldn't quite understand why her daughter appeared to be showing him the ingredients so carefully. And come to think of it, what was it that Sarah really did at her work? Mrs Grandison shrugged the thought off. At least he looked like a decent man.

Shuttleworth sat, sipping his tea and watched Sarah at work, apparently genuinely interested in the details, from the quantity of yeast to the volume of apple juice. When the dough was rising, the two of them went out, and she showed him the delights of Weybridge, the village Green where some older schoolboys were apparently playing a match, and the High Street with its shops and cinema where the outside screen advertised that Katherine Hepburn and Douglas Fairbanks were playing in Morning Glory that week.

'She's wonderful, of course,' Sarah told him.

'So my wife says.'

When they returned, the dough had risen beautifully. Sarah mixed it thoroughly in the bowl with the fruits, nuts, spices and marzipan squishing them all into the dough, then turning the dough out and kneading it. She had propped up the photograph that Michel had taken at the airport of the Stollen that Amit had baked on the first run, and was presumably now in Germany. Her Stollen had to look similar both in size and shape. With some care she divided the dough into two halves, allowing them to approximate, she hoped, to Amit's masterpieces.

When Morris brought out the glass diamonds, she watched them in amazement as if they might move or do some other extraordinary trick. They looked quite real to her eye. She mixed them into one of the two doughs and he carefully marked the tray with the diamond-laden dough. After another rising, during which they had lunch, she baked them until they were golden brown on the outside, brushed them in a little molten butter and dusted them lightly with the icing sugar. The result was marvellous. 'They look perfect,' Morris declared.

Sarah agreed, 'Almost exactly like Amit's, if I do say so myself.'

'I have to say, this has all worked out rather well. You're baking skills are a pure stroke of luck for us,' Shuttleworth told her.

'Well, it's nice to have some work to do, if you could even count today as work! It's just good to have something to do, I suppose. Thank you for the company as well, I was getting ever so bored sitting around with my mother all day.'

As she spoke, Mrs Grandison entered the room and caught sight of the Stollen.

'And here I was thinking how nice it was to have you home, Sarah! Oh what is that? May I try some?'

Mrs Grandison moved towards the Stollen, but was quickly blocked by her daughter as Morris began to pack it away into a large air-tight tin.

'No, mother, they're for work. I can't send them off with a piece taken out of them!'

Having persuaded her mother to keep away from the Stollen, Sarah helped Morris to load the tin into the boot of his Ford 2-door Sedan, before waving him goodbye.

The journey to Croydon only took Morris two hours and he arrived in plenty of time for the evening flight to Paris. He walked through Customs breathing a sigh of relief that he went unchallenged, and stayed overnight at the Hotel Barriere Le Westminster, previously booked for him by Gladys. It had only recently opened and the room that she had booked was luxurious, with a view over the beach to the Channel. The next morning, he looked out of his window and noted the trees in the hotel garden bending in the force of the wind. He took a taxi back to the airport just as the Imperial Airways flight was touching down. It bounced twice alarmingly on landing. Michel was there to greet him and had also looked with some distress at the plane's arrival.

'I suspect that your flight home will be somewhat bumpy, Mr. Shuttleworth.' He peeked inside the tin.

'Wonderful. They look perfect,' he said admiringly. Morris made sure that Michel understood that both Stollen were to be exchanged. Michel left with his bread, while Morris sat in the airport terminal, reading his book. An hour later Michel returned smiling.

'All done. Pas de problem. No-one stopped me nor even glanced at me. They will be safely off to the Reich. And he handed Sarah's tin to Morris. Morris peeked inside. Amit's Stollen were slightly smaller but otherwise looked remarkably similar to those baked by Sarah. Perfect.

Although all had gone to plan so far, Morris had an excruciating journey home. The Deutsche Luft Hansa flight to Berlin had left just before their flight to Croydon and lurched from side to side on the runway. They had followed immediately and it was clear that the pilot was battling for control. At one point shortly after they had left the ground, they were down just above the top of the trees, so suddenly had they been forced earthwards by the turbulence of the storm. Eventually they struggled back up but the westerly gale was against them and at one point they hardly seemed to be going forward at all as Morris looked down at the ground.

Eventually he disembarked and then to his horror was singled out by Customs Officers for a search. He tried to tell them that he had Diplomatic Immunity, but regrettably Sheila had given him one of the Department's ordinary British passports. In view of his unsuccessful claims to immunity, the Customs Officers were clearly suspicious and went through his case with great care. They even opened the Stollen tin. Morris held his breath.

'What's this then?'

'Stollen – it's a sort of bread.'

'Why is it here? What's the matter with British bread?'

'It's a gift for my wife.' They looked at him sullenly. It was always when you least wanted it that these things happened. Eventually he was allowed to leave and with a sigh of relief, he returned to Weybridge. Both Sarah and her mother were keen to try Amit's Stollen. They all ate dinner together, including tasting the well-travelled bread, whilst the other was over-baked for an hour in Sarah's oven. After they had finished eating, Sarah's mother left them be, but not before mentioning that it smelt like something was burning quite badly.

'Sarah, did you leave something on the stove?'

Sarah and Morris looked at each other, and Sarah laughed nervously as Morris stood up from the table.

'Don't worry, Mrs Grandison, I'll go and double check the kitchen.'

'And I'll clear the table and do the washing up!' Sarah

chipped in quickly.

Her mother frowned, watching them for a moment, before sighing.

'Alright then. I'll leave you to it.'

The two of them went into the kitchen, Sarah carrying armfuls of plates to keep up the rouse. After placing the dishes into the sink, Sarah put on some oven gloves and removed the cake from the oven. If you could even call it a cake any more.

'It's virtually ashes.'

Morris nodded, 'It's exactly as we need it. I left the sieve for us to use on the side earlier. There it is.'

Sarah poured the cake ashes out into the sieve, which Morris held carefully under the tap. As the water washed away the crumbs, with the exception of a few large almonds, slowly, slowly the sieve began to fill with bright sparkling diamonds.

'I know this is what we wanted,' Sarah began, 'but it really is quite spectacular!'

Morris nodded and couldn't help the huge smile that took a hold of his face.

'You have to give those Germans credit. It's a genius idea. But we're all the more genius to have thwarted them!'

Shaking themselves free of the awe and allure of the diamonds – of which neither had seen such beautiful or clear examples before – Sarah reminded Morris that her mother could return at any moment and they probably ought to start packing them away. It was quite obvious what they were, even to the uninformed, although her mother would be incredibly confused and no doubt ask countless questions which neither would be able to answer. Sarah chuckled to herself thinking of what might happen if her mother came in now, but soon Shuttleworth was heading off, diamonds wrapped and tucked into his suit pocket, waving goodbye once again.

Chapter Thirty-One

An arrest and a trip

On the morning of June 8th 1933 Alan received the cable. When he had finished breakfast, he walked along to Gloria's office.

After their return to the Cape earlier in the week, he and Gloria had told Sir Robert the whole story. When they had finished, Sir Robert had sat silently for a full thirty seconds. For Gloria and Alan they were thirty agonising seconds as they wondered what was about to happen. Then Sir Robert rose abruptly from his desk and called his secretary, Gladys, in a loud voice. She entered, clearly alarmed, and was even more so when he told her to get his friend Peter Dietmuller, the Chief of Police. The Chief arrived rather rapidly and Gloria repeated the story while he made notes. The Chief stood, rather surprisingly saluted Sir Robert and left without saying a word. The three of them looked at each other. Sir Robert almost smiled. Almost.

'He's like that,' was all he could say.

The chief returned to his police station in downtown Cape Town aware that he was about to instigate an important, and politically sensitive operation. He gathered his Inspectors around him for the briefing. They agreed that everyone should be picked up in one simultaneous swoop, and in particular that Carl Hans von Wasserburg would need to be handled with care, given what was presumed to be his diplomatic status. His Officer in charge of Internal Security Affairs arranged a 24-hour tail and two days later, the Chief was informed of a curious fact. According to the tails, Carl was spending time at a secret drinking and gambling den in a small Black township outside the city. And it appeared that he was visiting the rondavel of a woman nearby for short periods. They planned the trap.

On the afternoon of June 11th, three loads of police vehicles sped up the road to the small township of Bellville. Two approached the house from the front and one secured the back. The police, heavily armed, spread out until they were in place, running to secure shady positions. As soon as they were in place, a loudspeaker boomed,

'This is the police. You are surrounded. Come out with your hands up.'

They did. And amongst all the sorry figures was a blond blue-eyed arrogant figure whose words were

'I am Carl Hans von Wasserburg from the German Embassy. I claim diplomatic immunity.' A tall dark haired man in Police Chief uniform strode up to him.

'And I am Peter Villiers Dietmuller, and you are under arrest for diamond smuggling and payment to commit illegal acts under South African Riot Act Number Three. Handcuff him.' The cuffs were applied.

'Oh, and Mr Wasserburg, you have a problem with your

so-called Immunity.' And the diplomat was bundled into the waiting police van.

Earlier in the afternoon, the offices of Cape Connections were stormed by a van-load of riot police, and Cornelius van Der Linde arrested. Some cases of documents and filing cabinets were removed.

Chief Dietmuller returned to the British High Commission where he briefed Sir Robert, Alan and Gloria.

'We have picked up your friend Carl von Wasserburg. And he is languishing in our jail.'

'But surely my opposite number has applied for Diplomatic Immunity and you are about to lose him,' Sir Robert asked in a surprised tone.

'Actually he is going to be with us for a little while yet. When we were considering his arrest, we had a chat with our lawyers about him. They discovered that his Diplomatic Accreditation had been misfiled by the Embassy at the time of his arrival in the country. And so his Diplomatic status is in doubt. We have been advised that there will be a court battle to come,' and he smiled gently. 'But the lawyers tell us that they will win. And that he will come to court.' Sir Robert looked as happy as if he had just won the British chess Championship. He called out to his secretary.

'Gladys, you know that special champagne that the French Ambassador gave me last year. Bring the bottle please and four glasses.'

'And we are going through the documents from Cape Connections,' continued The Chief,' but there are hundreds of documents showing payments of small sums to many people on the payroll, presumably in connection with the riots, so it's all going to take a while.' The four of them were amazed and delighted with the outcome, and later in the day, Alan reported all the good news to Shuttleworth, who informed him that he would be briefing the Foreign Secretary of the excellent ending of the mission.

'This sounds like it is the death-knell of the German attempt to acquire weapon-making capacity, had been Shuttleworth's take on it.' Alan was much more dubious, but nevertheless delighted with his boss' happiness. Alan then made an impassioned plea about his future to Shuttleworth, which his boss heard out with considerably less enthusiasm.

Later that evening, Alan made a totally different request to Sir Robert, who had laughed indulgently.

'Of course you can. Frankly at the moment, Alan Drayson, it would be churlish for me to refuse you anything,' and both men laughed companionably. The next morning the Rolls had been driven into the courtyard and Alan was given the key. Even Louis looked thrilled when he was shown the exotic beast sitting in the courtyard.

'Don't tell me that we are really travelling in that.'

Alan and Gloria laughed at his wide eyes; it wasn't often you were able to catch Louis aghast and it brought out something childish and playful in him that only added to his charm. It was the promised trip, but not as Louis had expected it. The three of them piled into the car with a large hamper provided by the kitchen at the High Commission, and Alan drove, enjoying the smooth feel of the car as he changed gear and cruised along the roads. The

Rolls really was marvellous. On the outskirts of town, Alan turned left onto Highway 7, and Louis peered out of the window, confused.

'You are kidnapping me,' he protested.

'So right,' Alan cast a glance at him and smirked.

They continued to travel relentlessly northwards until the traffic began to thin out to the occasional lorry. They ate their picnic lunch down a side-turning with glorious views over the Cederburg Mountains. After the lunch break, they hit the road again and eventually turned left, reaching the top of the Pakhuis Pass.

'So, Louis we promised you a trip and this is it. It's better than Oudtshoorn.'

Louis looked around astounded.

'How did you know how to find this exquisite place? I have never been here nor heard of it.'

'When I first arrived in South Africa, I was brought here by one of the staff at the High Commission. He showed me the cave,' Gloria told him, and Louis looked at her quizzically. Eventually Alan brought the car to a halt.

'Follow me,' Gloria told them. She led them up a narrow path and there, as it was still winding upwards, was the entrance to a cave. She produced a torch and walked carefully inside. High up on the walls of the cave they could see the outlines of the drawings of animals.

'Bushmen,' she said in response to the unasked question. 'No-one seems to know how old they are.'

Louis looked in amazement at the shapes and figures drawn across the walls, entranced, in part by their history and general intrigue, and in part because he could not

331

believe that he himself had never heard of this place, nor been here himself. When they left the cave and were standing at the entrance, the view far across the mountains left them breathless.

'I will be buried here,' Louis vowed to himself.

They stayed the night at a vast Victorian-style wood-clad house on the lake of the Olifantsriviere, created by the Clanwilliam dam. The woman who let the rooms was busy creating a wonderful wild flower garden in fields looking down to the lake. Reluctantly the next day, they travelled back to the Cape.

'Thank you both,' Louis said as they dropped him back off at his house.

'Better than Oudtshoorn?' Alan asked.

'Much.'

Epilogue

Food for thought

It had been good to get away, and to have a little bit of time off since the arrests of Carl and Cornelius van der Linde, but everything on the work side had gone rather flat and they found themselves with little to do. After all the danger and the stress of the missions, Alan had to admit that the day-to-day life at the High Commission was a little, well, boring. But he knew that there was a more human and personally rewarding evening to come.

The following day, having checked his mail, he strolled around the High Commission and had a conversation with Sir Robert, to whom he had warmed enormously. He remembered the first conversation that they had had and reminded Sir Robert of it. Both men had smiled, one of them somewhat wanly. Sir Robert's secretary Gladys had passed them in the corridor where they were chatting, and a wide smile had transformed the man's face. In her turn, Alan was amazed to notice a small blush creeping over her face. He had wondered.

The afternoon passed and later he had dressed with care

for the evening. He knocked on Gloria's door and found that she had been transformed by a long shimmering silk dress, her hair piled high on her head with curling ringlets dripping down her neck and cheeks. She traipsed along beside him, and down the stairs to the front, with her chattering away but with her progress slightly hampered by appallingly high heels. They waited on the doorstep with a light westerly breeze bringing them the smell of the ocean and the dampness of an impending shower. The taxi took them down towards the sea and they emerged at the destination. It looked splendid and Alan reflected on the transformation of lives that it represented; on how lives can move to higher levels if they are moved purposely onwards, and conversely the depths that lurked on either side of a tricky winding path if poor decisions were made.

The exterior of the chosen house was lit overall by a thousand coloured light bulbs and the simple word

– AMIT'S –

beamed down on them above the entrance. Louis stood on the doorstep to welcome them with an ear-to-ear smile.

'I'm like a small boy again, as on Christmas morning with excitement, and a tiny piece of apprehension awaiting the grand unfurling,' Louis said, as he led them inside and up the stairs to their table which looked through an enormous picture window and over Cape Town's glorious harbour, lights twinkling to welcome them. The table, a large 'Reserved' sign sitting in its midst, was laid with a starched linen cloth, perfectly rolled napkins and glistening silverware. Each setting had three glasses with two flutes and a wide-based champagne glass. They had hardly sat when the others arrived. Roderick Patterson came up the stairs with a guest on his heels. Upon seeing the guest, Gloria and Louis had both risen with shock. Alan did so out of politeness, not knowing who he was.

'I hope you don't mind my joining you, but Roderick wondered, and I told him that I would not miss it for a moment.' He sat himself next to Gloria, who immediately started to discuss the beauty of jewels with him, and although Alan wasn't thrilled at the man's choice of seating, he was immensely proud of Gloria as she spoke animatedly, clearly holding the attention of such an important guest.

'Is it The Highest Level?'

'It is indeed,' came the sotto voce response from Roderick.

Dieter arrived slightly breathless, having driven all the way from Oudtshoorn that day. He had apparently left in plenty of time but had been held up by a farmer choosing to drive a vast herd of oxen down the road from one field to another. He and Louis had met previously and started an animated discussion about the need for a second orchestra in the Cape, possibly centred on Port Elizabeth or Oudtshoorn. Dieter favoured Oudtshoorn in view of the large Jewish population. Apparently the High School was full of musically talented young people, many with parents of ability. Two String Quartets had already been formed in the town and he knew a trombonist of great renown… and they locked into their subject.

While the group were getting settled, the restaurant had filled around them. Alan watched as the business of a full restaurant slid into place with waiters passing seamlessly between tables taking orders, and gesticulating to each other. Their own table's orders were taken and a smooth young man appeared announcing that he was 'Amit's Sommelier' and what would their vinous pleasure be?

And then a great noise was heard on the stairs, as of an approaching herd of elephants, and a vast man appeared, huffing and blowing as if he had just climbed Table Mountain, with a young man behind him.

'Vladimir,' called Louis and rushed to embrace him. 'And this must be Solomon, your poor first born. Welcome Solomon.' Introductions were made, and Vladimir joined the jewellery conversation sitting next to the Highest Level, who welcomed him with open arms to Alan's amazement.

'I know nothing about the relationships in this town. Just nothing,' he whispered to Gloria. She laughed.

'Perhaps some things might've been easier if you had.'

The champagne arrived and at that moment the renowned chef appeared replete with white overalls and an enormous chef's toque perched on his head, giving him the impression of far greater height than his creator had endowed him with. Applause broke out around the room.

'I have come to welcome you, my friends. I shall not stay as my kitchen is full of your orders. Later I will return to be with you all. My thanks for being here,' and he left them to their conversation and food. They were halfway through the main course when there was another heavy tread on the stairs and the head of Sir Robert appeared. Alan and Gloria rose to greet him, and then realised that he was not alone but was followed by his secretary Gladys, dressed unrecognisably in a glamorous outfit. She looked somewhat embarrassed but at one stage slipped her arm into Sir Robert's. They moved off to another table. Gloria giggled in his ear,

'How lovely for them. Isn't it about time…'

'Of course,' and he rose to his feet. Gloria seemed to be fiddling under the table. Silence fell on their table while a cacophony of noise came from all around.

'My new friends, despite my feeling that it has been rather quiet here, remarkably rather a lot has happened this week. For me, two things stand out. The first is that I have been appointed Head of the British Organisation that I represent for the whole of Africa. This is a big promotion and I am delighted to say that my headquarters will be here in Cape Town. I will be wafted up and down the continent by Imperial Airways.' Much applause around the table, causing conversation to stop at other tables, and ensure that people were staring.

'And secondly and far more importantly, to my delight Gloria has agreed to marry me.' And she stood and held out her left hand for the others to see the ring embedded with three diamonds, picking up the glow of the table candles. Cacophonous applause.

'I have many of you to thank. Firstly De Beers for giving us the diamonds. Such generosity.' Roderick and the Highest Level both looked as if they might blush… but managed not to.

'Next Vladimir and Solomon for setting the stones so beautifully – and I believe that Solomon did the extraordinary work.' Much more applause until Vladimir stopped it by struggling to his feet despite the forces of gravity.

'And by chance, on this blessed day, we have heard that my treasured son Solomon has been accepted as apprentice to Eugene and Alexander Faberge. He will travel to join them in their new headquarters in Paris next week. You will have heard of course of the death of their famous father, Carl Peter Faberge, a couple of weeks ago. Eugene and Alexander both escaped the Bolsheviks and have set-up the famous Faberge business again in Paris, where Solomon is to be their first apprentice. We are so proud.'

The boy blushed an almost scarlet hue as his father gave him a clearly unwanted hug.

'And finally, finally I must thank Louis,' continued Alan, 'for matrimonial assistance beyond the call of duty,' and he sat, leaving puzzled looks around the table.

And then the great chef appeared, looking exhausted. Amit slipped into an additional chair at their table, while they all congratulated him on his success.

'Tell us how this all happened?' Dieter asked Amit

'I owe much to you all. It was Gloria's idea in the beginning. I told her that it was always my wish that one day I would have my own restaurant. So then she sneakily went off behind my back and talked to Louis. Then he went and talked to Vladimir and to our friends in De Beers. And suddenly I was told that a house had been bought and that carpenters were hard at work converting it into a restaurant and 'would I advise?' So, I 'advised' for a few days, and then one day I was there, discussing the planning of the kitchen with the architect, when in strolls Louis.

'So when are you starting?' asked Louis.

'Starting what?' I asked in my naivety.

'Well, this is your restaurant. You must have some idea when you are going to open it.'

'I could not understand what he was saying. He had to explain that these wonderful people had bought it as a present for me. Even then I could not believe that it was happening. I had to go around to Gloria as I felt that Louis was fooling with me, but she confirmed it all. And the name is her fault. She got it put up there by the painters and I came in one morning last week and there was this enormous sign.'

Amit waved his hands around as he spoke, gesturing at Gloria, who grinned at him, not looking guilty in the slightest. In fact, she looked incredibly pleased with herself, as all around her, wine glasses were being topped up.

'And then I set to work. All my dreams could come true. I ordered this beautiful table linen from a convent near Leipzig that I had visited in my student days and where I had admired the intricate needle work of the flowers that the nuns had hand-stitched. It reminded me of the flowers on the tapestries of the Unicorn, now of course owned by Mr. Rockefeller in New York.'

'The Unicorn?' asked Gloria.

'The most beautiful tapestries in the world, Miss Gloria. Made in Brussels early in the 17th century. They were made for the wedding of Anne of Brittany to King Louis XII of France. They were stolen in the Revolution and then turned up in a barn of her family, the Rochefoucaulds, in the middle of the 19th century. No one knows what they mean, nor exactly who made them. Some say that they depict the Passion of Christ, but no-one can be certain. Whatever they mean, they show hundreds of small flowers, presumably copied from flowers of the field of that time. The designs have been faithfully copied in the linen, as you can see in the table-cloths and napkins.' The guests looked down and inspected the fine detail on their table-ware. Alan realised that he should have no doubt that this would continue to be a fine establishment for years as Amit was clearly one for detail and perfection; nothing had been left un-thought; no detail too small for care.

'And the glasses come of course from the small island of Murano nearby Venice, where the glass-blowers learn their trade with the skills passed down from father to son.' And the glasses, all in different hues, sparkled in the candle-light, almost eclipsing the beauty of Gloria's diamonds, which sat proudly on display as she kept her left hand rested on top of the white tablecloth. As Alan took her hand in his, and the group continued to eat and drink long into the night, Louis found himself marvelling at the subtle purity of all their haloed colours. No rainbows here, just gentle pastel shades flickering in well-formed hubbubs of crackling auras. And he allowed the colours to merge in his mind forming and re-forming into his deepest pleasures of perception, as he watched Alan and Gloria looking lovingly into each other's eyes.

The End

Requiescant in pace

Alan died in 1942, hit by a stray bullet outside Tobruk when attached as an Intelligence Officer to Montgomery's Eighth Army.

Gloria died in 1964 still working for British intelligence. She lived long enough to see two grandchildren.

Louis never married and died of heart disease in 1947. He is buried in a cave in the Pakhuis Pass. The inscription over his tombstone reads,

> *'Gaan vind vir jou 'n plek in die veld.'*
> *(Go and find yourself a place in the veld.)*

Amit eventually returned to India in the 1940s when apartheid started to bite in South Africa. He died in Delhi of unknown cause, having established a restaurant there, also named Amit's. He also never married.

Sir Robert Lancaster married Gladys in 1934 but sadly had a major stroke a year later and died after a week in hospital.

Morris Shuttleworth became deputy head of M.I.5., was knighted, and died in 1949.

Peter Shroeder became a tank commander in the Wehrmacht and died fighting at Stalingrad in 1943.

Carl von Wasserburg was quietly released from prison in South Africa, returned to Germany, and trained as a pilot. He survived the war despite being twice shot down. He returned to Alsace after the war and became a successful wine merchant. He died suddenly at the age of 63 whilst climbing a hill named Le Petit Ballon just above the village of Wasserburg.

Historical Notes

I t is unclear to me as to exactly why I have ended up writing a story about a land that I have not visited, South Africa, and set in an era, the thirties, when I did not exist. Some authors claim that their characters drive the story – so maybe I can blame Amit, Alan, Gloria and Louis.

The following notes are in no particular order, but incorporate some of the bits of historical background which have enthralled me personally. The story contains no references within the text, because of my belief in the reader wanting to read the story rather than be distracted by pompous author notes. Although this is a work of fiction, with characters mostly created by myself, there is much factual matter embedded within the fictional plot.

- Flying to Africa in the 1930s. In 1926 the legendary Sir Alan Cobham made the first flight for Imperial Airways to survey their proposed route from London to Cape Town, and on that trip made a re-fuelling stop at Livingstone airport. But it was not until 1931 that a regular, mail-only service was commenced. In 1932 this service was opened to passengers. At that time single-engine de Havilland planes took about twenty passengers, stopping many times en route for the Cape. These planes were replaced later in 1933 by the much more substantial Armstrong Atalanta planes with their four engines. There had been fears concerning the safety of the de Havillands with their single engines but despite the anxiety, there were no accidents with the de Havilland planes.

Incidentally all the 'flying' stories in the book are accurate and taken from documented occurrences.

- The origins of the Luftwaffe. My thanks to my friend Seamus Gallagher for the information about the training of German pilots in the 20's and 30's in the Primary gliders.

  By an amazing co-incidence, shortly after my discussion with Seamus, and having written a first draft about the glider in Chapter Eleven, I came across a working Primary Glider in beautiful condition.

  It was a warm summer's day and I was visiting the Swiss Garden, a pasture created in the heart of rural Bedfordshire during Victorian times by a rich man for his Swiss mistress to prevent her feeling homesick! Having finished my tour of the garden, I noticed a sign to The Shuttleworth Collection. Having an hour to spare I wandered over, and there, amongst a fabulous collection of ancient planes, cars, and tractors, all in full working order, was a Primary Glider in immaculate condition. I knew that the great forces of destiny were at work!

- Crosswords in the Times newspaper started unobtrusively on February 1st 1930 and rapidly became an international phenomenon, being copied within a few weeks by the New York Evening Post and many others.

- Sir John Simon was a rather unpopular Foreign Secretary during 1933 in the National Government headed by Prime Minister Ramsay MacDonald.

- Great Britain's relationships with its Dominions, of which South Africa was one in 1933, were regulated through its High Commissions, which were Embassies in all but name. In fact the High Commission in South Africa was sited in those days in Pretoria, with a Consulate in Cape Town. Historians will need to forgive me for placing the High Commission in Cape Town.

- The Secret Intelligence Service was started in 1909, at the behest of Prime Minister Asquith. It moved its centre into Broadway Buildings in 1926, focussing on 'foreign matters.' And changed its name to MI5.

- *Heart of Darkness* by Joseph Conrad, written in 1899 following his journey up the Congo River, spawns a discussion starting here in Chapter Three. It is the precursor to more thoughts in the book concerning the justification of colonialism, and the meaning of the word 'civilisation' in European philosophical and political circles. In particular, the book provides for a discussion of the rights and wrongs of colonialism, of cultural colonisation, and of eugenics in general. Amit discusses these with Von Bauer – I hope, interestingly.

The Heart itself is many things. It is a wondrously written descriptive novella that must be treasured for the power of its use of English, amazingly Conrad's third language after his native Russian and then French.

Some critics have mocked areas of the phraseology as being awkwardly translated from Conrad's French-structured English. They have said that some of these phrases, some of the sub-conjunctival clauses, in a similar manner to Proust's A la recherché du temps perdu, are barely comprehensible in the words translated in his brain from French to English, (and I hope that this last sentence has been constructed in a Proustian style!). For example –

> *'The high stillness confronted those two figures with its ominous patience, waiting for the passing away of a fantastic invasion.'* All I can say to that is – 'What?!'

'The horror; the horror.' Kurtz dying words are rightly revered. Questions are asked – 'Are they the horror of colonialism; of the abuse of ethics; or maybe just words of approaching death?' The interpretation of mysterious phrases in great literature is a magnificent pleasure for the world of academe and these words especially have provided academics with the food for their literary digestion.

For myself, I see the book as an allegory of the life and death of an African Christ-like figure with 'The Intended' as a Mary Magdalene. Maybe Marlow is St. John; the beloved disciple? Maybe this is all my over-simple speculation; an example of the amateur daring to invade the province of the professionals?

Much later, in the 2000s, Conrad's book was attacked as racist by the greatest African writer to date, Chinua Achebe, whose writings in the 1950s portray African village life. For myself, Achebe's biggest fan, and an avid reader in the 1970s of his beautiful stories, I fail to see any deliberate author's racism in *Heart of Darkness*. For me, he is simply describing and commenting on African life at that moment of time as he observed it.

Heart of Darkness was adapted into a towering film, directed by Francis Ford Coppola, set in the heart of Vietnam during their war and entitled *Apocalypse Now*. Surprisingly neither Marlon Brando with a truly remarkable interpretation of Kurtz, nor the film itself, won Oscars.

• C. Louis Leipoldt, twice recipient of the Hertzog Prize, the highest award for Afrikaans literature, is the model for Louis du Plessis. He was important primarily as an Afrikaans poet and a writer of note, who became more revered after his death when his trilogy of tolerance and reconciliation between races was published as The Valley. This collection of three independent, yet closely related novels of historical literary fiction, used characters drawn from people known to him. The novels question Europe's claim to the right to spread its influence of colonialisation and can be seen as a natural adjunct to *Heart of Darkness*.

In life, Louis was an amazing polymath. His South African Cookbook was published in 1933 to much acclaim, complementing the many articles written by him on food and wine over his lifetime. In his spare time he was also a well-known paediatrician, ran a house dedicated to taking in boys needing educative foster care, hosted dinner parties and was an excellent Bridge player.

There is now a large private medical clinic in the northern suburbs of Cape Town named after him.

I have portrayed him as having the condition of synaesthesia, (see below for more detail); the ability to see actual colours when stimulated. Further reading on this subject should include the beautiful story, *The Book Thief*.

- Cocktails in 1933 were of great sophistication. Following the double catastrophes of the Depression and Prohibition, the fashion of cocktail drinking raised the population's morale (certainly in the affluent sector) across the world. *The Savoy Cocktail Book* published in 1930 became the classic book for two thousand of the most fashionable recipes, and the French 75 and the Hanky Panky were two of the most popular.

  The French 75 achieved immortality when drunk by Humphrey Bogart in that great film of 1942, *Casablanca*.

Coley, real name Ada Coleman, for many years bartender at the Savoy, invented the Hanky Panky for Charles Hawtry. He apparently said, after tasting it for the first time 'By Jove! That is the real hanky-panky.' The name stuck.

And Gloria was not quite correct in her description of a 'Sidecar,' which also has Cointreau in it.

- Wilhelm Furtwangler, probably the finest conductor ever produced by Germany, was determined in his opposition to Hitler and the Nazis, although other musicians, such as Toscanini and Horowitz, criticised him for staying in Germany. Toscanini's hostility might well have been affected by Furtwangler walking out of one of his concerts, calling Toscanini 'a mere time-beater.'

In real life, Furtwangler never sought asylum in England or South Africa, preferring to fight the Nazis from within. If you will, read more of the relationship between Furtwangler and the Nazis in the writings of Curt Reiss.

- Synaesthesia is a perceptual phenomenon in which stimulation of one sensory or cognitive pathway leads to involuntary experiences in a second pathway. There are many types, some common, some vanishingly rare.' The most common type involves seeing monochromatic letters, digits and words in unique colors. This is called grapheme-color synesthesia.

Individuals who have this so-called 'condition' are

349

naturally sensitive about it and particularly about being 'labelled'. So in order not to cause distress, I have chosen that Louis should have a type in which he almost has 'magical powers' making him able to 'see' the colours of mood and disingenuousness as a halo around a person's head. In Chapter Nineteen I try to describe Louis' perception of his synaesthetic world that is, of course, 'normal' for him. I have created this halo-form linked to emotion that is partially described in case histories but also partially concocted by myself.

Finally, my thanks go to:

My family and especially my wife, Judy, who provides the love and environment in which I can write.

Tim, my cousin, who has been a constant source of help.

Clio, my wife's niece who encourages me and makes perceptive comments as I go along.

Lily Thwaites, my wondrous editor, without whom this book would be riddled with errors of grammar, tense and other aspects of the language unbeknown to me. This book would be a disaster zone were it not for her attention, care and focus.

The nice people at my publisher, The Conrad Press. And in particular to Nat and Rachael at thebooktypesetters.com for the speedy, thorough, typesetting and especially for the great cover design.